Mother of My Son

Rachel Allord

Mother of My Son

Contact Information: titleadmin@pelicanbookgroup.com

Cover Art by *Nicola Martinez*

Harbourlight Books, a division of Pelican Ventures, LLC
www.pelicanbookgroup.com PO Box 1738 *Aztec, NM * 87410

Harbourlight Books sail and mast logo is a trademark of Pelican Ventures, LLC

Publishing History
First Harbourlight Edition, 2013
Paperback Edition ISBN 978-1-61116-266-0
Electronic Edition ISBN 978-1-61116-265-3
Published in the United States of America

Dedication

To Mom and Dad
for your steady, unquestionable love

Acknowledgements

Thank you to my parents, James and Cheryl Folz, for loving everything I've ever written. Thanks Mom, for all of your adoption expertise. Love and gratitude to my siblings, Sarah Biggs and Nate Folz, and to my Allord family.

Thank you, Ann Brunner, Jane Whitford, Abigail Wallace, and Stephanie Seefeldt, for enduring early drafts and cheering me on. I treasure your friendships. Alicia Bruxvoort, thank you for your unwavering belief in me. Thanks to Sarah Kolling and Angel Faxon for honest feedback, and Erin and Judah Huffman and Laura Menningen for beautifully portraying my imaginary friends.

Many thanks to Jim Rubart, Alison Strobel, and Cecil Murphey for sharing their professional expertise and nudging me forward, and to the staff at Pelican Book Group, particularly Fay Lamb and Nicola Martinez, for skillfully improving the story and turning what was starting to feel like a pipe dream into a reality.

This story required a mother's heart, so thank you Elijah and Maylie. You two can't fathom how much you are loved. And finally, Doug: thank you for reading countless drafts, pushing me creatively, fueling me with coffee, and not letting me quit. Thank you for serving as my sounding board, first editor, and computer guru. I couldn't have done this without your love, encouragement, and belief in me. I'm in your corner, always, and I know you're in mine.

Above all, thanks and glory to the Author of grace.

Part One

1

June 3, 1994

The bundled towel in Amber's arms no longer stirred. Even the soft mewling had stopped. So it couldn't be real, after all.

Amber fixed her gaze on the dumpster across the street and then glanced back at her silent, brick apartment building. Dizzy, she peered at the dumpster once again and took a step forward. The full moon hung above her like a watchful eye, illuminating the metal bin that seemed to waver like water, like the sloshing peppermint Schnapps she'd downed in desperation hours ago.

A sudden gust of wind swept through her hair. She clutched the towel to her chest and stepped off the curb into the street, the blacktop cool and jagged beneath her bare feet. As if powered by something outside of herself, she took a step forward and then another. Somewhere in the distance, a dog barked. The wind picked up. She broke into a run.

Her bare feet slapped against the asphalt, a deafening sound in the otherwise quiet night. A blast of pain shot through her insides as she reached the back lot of On the House, a small shabby bar beneath a neon sign. She glimpsed a cardboard box next to the dumpster, overflowing with broken down cartons and paper. Hastily, she lowered the bundle into the box and straightened. She peered at her empty hands, then at the unmoving towel, her heartbeat rapid firing in her chest

She waited and watched. Nothing. No movement. No sound. No heartbeat anymore, probably.

The headlights from a passing car flashed over the side of the bar, jolting her with panic. She turned and ran, sprinted back to her apartment, breathless and dizzy.

A fleeting sense of horror washed over her. Who was this girl running in the darkness? Something inside of her pleaded for her to stop. Snap out of it. Wake up. Undo. Yet the urgings receded into the fog of her mind. She staggered down the common hall of her apartment, a trickle of blood snaking down her thigh inside her sweat pants. A shower. That's what she needed—a long hot shower to wash away the horror of the night, torrents of water to obliterate the thing that couldn't have happened.

She watched her hand turn the doorknob to her apartment, a hand that seemed disconnected to the rest of her, and stepped over the threshold. The trance shattered.

"Where were you?" Robin was standing in the kitchen with an open jar of peanut butter and a spoon.

Amber gripped the edge of the counter and closed her eyes, willing the figure away. When she opened them, her roommate stood waiting.

"I thought you were at Josh's for the night," Amber said.

Robin excavated a glob of peanut butter. "We had

a fight. I just got home, and I'm too ticked off to sleep." She stuck the spoon in her mouth, pulled it out clean, and gave Amber the once over. "What's wrong with you? You look awful."

The room took off in a spin. Amber turned and made her way to the bathroom, raking her hand against the wall for balance. Either she was going to be sick or pass out.

Robin trailed her. "What were you doing outside? It's three o'clock in the morning."

Her body pricked with sweat, Amber stumbled into the bathroom and knelt before the toilet.

"Oh," Robin said. "You're drunk." She disappeared down the hall.

Depleted, Amber wiped her mouth across the sleeve of her sweatshirt and plunked down on the floor.

Moments later, Robin reappeared. "Whose party?"

Elbows propped on her knees, Amber held her head with her hands. "No party."

Robin leaned in the doorway and crossed her arms over her chest. Her dark eyebrows knit together in scrutiny. "Something's wrong."

"Don't feel good. Just leave me alone."

Amber found a ponytail holder on the floor and bound her hair loosely at the base of her neck. Suddenly, Robin gasped. Amber followed her roommate's gaze to the bathtub and saw the streaks of red.

Robin's eyes grew as wide as a marionette's. "Amber, what's going on? Why is there blood in the bathtub?"

"Just go. Just leave me alone." She hung her head in her hands.

"What happened here tonight?"

"Nothing. It's taken care of."

Robin was silent for so long Amber finally looked up. Her roommate seemed drained of color. "What do you mean it's *taken care of*? *What's* taken care of?"

"Nothing. Never mind." Giving in to exhaustion, Amber laid her cheek against the cold, linoleum floor.

Robin gave a little cry then cursed. "Amber, you're bleeding."

Amber glanced at the insides of her thighs where red stained her gray sweats. "I'll be OK. I just need to sleep."

"You're not OK. You need help. You need a doctor."

"I'll be fine."

"You need *help*!" Robin looked around frantically. "You're scaring me. We need to do something. We need to call someone—"

"No. Don't call anyone. Please. Just let me sleep."

Robin was silent for a minute. "Were you…?"

"Stop asking questions. Just leave."

Robin paced down the hall and came back. "This is wrong. This is all so wrong."

"Robin. Leave. For your own good. I took care of it."

"It. What's this 'it,' Amber? You were, weren't you? And you were trying to hide it." Robin clamped a hand over her mouth. "And now—where is it? What happened to it?"

"It died!" But even as she spoke, she recalled those first weak cries, while she tried to catch her breath in the bathtub, after the impossible happened. She thought she'd have more time. Why didn't she have more time?

At first the signs were easy to push away but as her stomach grew harder and the strange internal thumping more frequent, she had to wonder. Wonder, panic, bury the thought, and get on with life. She couldn't think about that now. She had classes. Exams. It couldn't be happening anyway. And then another sensation would ripple through her abdomen. Another pair of jeans wouldn't button. She'd never been a beanpole, but even Robin mentioned, just last week, she might want to ease up on the take-out.

She looked at Robin's red blotchy face. "I took care of it. It's over."

Robin raked her hands through her pixie cut, her eyes blinking compulsively, a frantic Morse code. "Don't tell me any more. I don't want to know any more. I *can't* know. Just leave. Tomorrow. Get your things and yourself and be out of here by tomorrow, because I can't handle this. I can't know about any of this." She backed away, her hands a shield in front of her as if warding off a dog attack. She let out a whimper and disappeared down the hall.

Pulling her knees to her chest, Amber let her eyelids fall, her mind steadily circling one thought, one statement that might save her if she could manage to believe it:

It never happened.

∂∾∽

She was out of options. The reality of it made her sick, but there was only one person she could turn to now: her mother. Amber gripped the phone, scanned the script she'd jotted in her sketchbook, and rehearsed the words under her breath one last time. Then she exhaled, punched in the number, and waited.

"Hi, Mom. It's Amber."

Her mother sighed into the phone. "Look who's finally calling. My long lost daughter. Your timing's not good though. My program's on."

In the background, Amber heard agitated TV voices and fought to keep her own tone even. "Yeah, sorry about not calling. I've been busy. And I haven't really been feeling that great—"

"*You* haven't been feeling great? You should have seen me last week. Had the nastiest head cold you could ever imagine. I finally went into the doctor and told him he had to give me something. Felt like I was going to die. Course you'd have known this if you ever called."

Amber closed her eyes to steady herself. She couldn't afford to blow this. "Sorry." She glanced at her script. "Hey, there's been a change of plans. My summer job fell through, so I thought maybe I'd come home for awhile, if that's OK with you."

"You want to come home? I thought you wanted to stay close to campus for the summer. I thought you found work."

Amber picked up her pencil and sketched along the edge of the page. "Plans changed. There wasn't anything I could—"

Her mother shushed her. "Hang on a second." The background voices intensified, and a female screamed, "You're not the father. Victor's the father!"

"I knew it," her mother said. "What were you saying?"

"That I'm coming home."

"How long are you staying?"

"I don't know. A couple of months. For the

summer maybe."

"Until you go back to school?'

Amber sketched an oval on her paper and added a wide brow and a small chin. "Until I find a place of my own. I'm not going back to school."

Her mother was silent for a moment. "That's it? One year under your belt and that's it? Well aren't you the little scholar? Quitting already. What about that scholarship? What happened with all of that, Miss Smarty-Pants?"

Amber studied the oval she'd drawn and shaded in wide-set eyes. "College just isn't for me." Her voice almost broke under the lie. She swallowed hard. "It's better that I figure that out now than sometime next year, right? I just don't belong here."

"I thought Mr. What's-His-Name said you had talent? Went through all the trouble to help you fill out that paperwork and get you that scholarship and all. What are you going to tell him?"

The day Amber showed him the letter of award in the high school art room, a lifetime ago, Mr. Morton had beamed with pride. "What's it matter to him? I'll tell him it didn't work out."

"Let go of me!" The soap opera lady sounded hysterical.

"Can't say I'm surprised," her mother said. "I knew this whole college thing would be nothing but a waste of time. You just got too big for your britches."

Amber squeezed her eyes shut. When she opened them, the small face on her sketchbook peered back at her. She added a diminutive mouth. "I'm not planning on staying long. Just until I find a place of my own. So, I'll see you tomorrow?"

Her mom chuckled. "I'll be sure to roll out the red

carpet."

Amber hung up the phone and stared at the small, gray face. She darkened the pupils, erased a speck to add the illusion of light, shaded the lower lip and accentuated the divot between the nose and mouth.

The front door opened and shut. Robin was back.

Holding the pencil like a dagger, Amber scribbled through the drawing, tearing through the paper and leaving pockmarks on the page behind it. She tossed her sketchbook across the bed and started packing for home.

Home. Back where she started. And this time, she'd find no way out.

2

Standing outside her sister's ranch-style house, Beth pressed the doorbell and waited.

Eric grabbed her hand. "Bring on the chaos," he said.

Gretchen opened the door. Her eyes were puffy and she wore no makeup. She offered Beth a quick grimace, an attempt at a smile, tight-lipped and hollow, as she held a whimpering Evan against her ragged t-shirt.

Beth gave her sister and nephew a quick hug before making her way to the living room. She called out a happy birthday to her niece Lily who sat beaming from behind a barricade of presents.

Eric added their gift to the assortment.

As Beth passed her nephew Tyler, she ruffled the top of his head then slid into a chair. Immediately, Gretchen plopped Evan into her arms.

"You don't mind, do you?" Gretchen asked absently.

"Are you kidding?"

Beth tugged off Evan's tiny knit cap and weaved her fingers through his downy hair. He stirred, unfurled his fists, and emitted a breath. She brought him to her shoulder and rubbed his back through his blue terrycloth sleeper, intoxicated by his scent. After a few minutes, she watched as Lily clawed at the present covered in paper ballerinas.

"Card first, Lil," Dave reminded from behind a video camera.

Lily reluctantly opened the card, regarded it with apathy, and glanced around the room. Beth waved and Lily grinned back. Within seconds, the girl uncovered the doll Beth had painstakingly picked out—a doll with the same strawberry-blonde hair as Lily. She hollered out a thank you and attacked the next gift.

Evan whimpered. Beth repositioned him to the cradle hold, and he rooted against her blouse.

Gretchen pulled a kitchen chair into the living room and sat beside Beth. "He's probably hungry," she said, already fiddling with her shirt.

Beth relinquished him, and Gretchen tossed a receiving blanket over her shoulder and swiftly tucked Evan underneath. Tyler climbed into Beth's vacant lap, grinning like a chimpanzee.

Beth gasped. "You lost another one! Tooth fairy stop by last night?"

Tyler nodded. "Yeah, and guess what? I'm rich! Ten whole dollars!"

"*Ten*?" Beth eyed her sister. "My, your tooth fairy is pretty generous."

"Or sleep deprived," Gretchen muttered.

Lily unwrapped Twister, and Tyler jumped from Beth's lap to have a closer look.

"I was tired, and in the darkness I thought it was a single," Gretchen said. "Some precedent I've set, huh?"

Beth chuckled. "I remember when we were happy with a quarter."

Evan made a spluttering sound from underneath the blanket. Gretchen peeked in at him, shifted positions, and then stared vaguely in Lily's direction. After Lily unwrapped the last present, Gretchen handed Evan back to Beth. "I need to frost the cake. Make sure he burps."

Beth grabbed a cloth slung over the arm of the sofa and thumped Evan's back until he accomplished the task. She swaddled him in his receiving blanket and carried him down the hall, burying her nose in the bread-dough suppleness of his neck. He found his fist and nosily sucked. A cool string of drool trickled down the front of her shirt. She kissed his head and scanned the pictures adorning Gretchen's hall.

Most were of the children—Tyler at the beach in a wide-brimmed hat, carrot-topped Lily nestled in Tyler's lap in front of a white tulle background at the JC Penny studio. A slightly faded one of Beth and Gretchen as girls, clad in halter-tops with droopy wildflowers curled over their ears, standing amidst prairie grass on the hill behind their childhood home.

Beth thought of the gift tucked under her chair in the family room and smiled. One more tribute, one more captured memory for Gretchen. Beth's throat constricted, and she burrowed her head in Evan's neck again, drinking in his scent like an antidote.

Eric came to stand beside her.

"Is he sleeping?" she asked, turning sideways so Eric could check.

"Looks like it."

"I'm going to put him down." She heard the false brightness in her voice, and before she could step away, Eric encircled her, his arms a strong rope holding her together. She commanded herself to recognize the gift before her: the husband who didn't blame, who'd seen her at her worst, who bore the brunt of her mood swings and didn't run away. Eric who grieved controllably so she could fall apart. She smiled, finally, and he loosened his grip.

Beth settled Evan in his crib and remembered to leave the door open as Gretchen preferred. In a house like this, her sister had said, the kid needs to be able to handle a little noise.

Beth found Gretchen in the kitchen, rubber spatula in hand, jaw set. "This junk won't spread."

Beth watched her sister's attempt to coax a glob of white frosting across the top of a cake, eroding clumps in the process. "Maybe you didn't mix in enough milk."

Gretchen shot her a look. "What do you mean *mix in*? It's from a can."

"Oh." Beth stepped closer and poked her finger into the canister to sample the store bought butter cream.

"Hey, I'm running out. I need that." Gretchen snatched the canister, scraped out a glob, and smeared it over the cake. A chunk of cake dislodged and fell to the floor. Gretchen huffed and glared at the mess at her feet. With a fierceness that startled Beth, Gretchen hurled the spatula toward the sink. It smacked the counter, bounced off, and hit the floor with a splat. The collar of Gretchen's St. Bernard jangled from under the table, and Murray padded over, sniffed warily, then noisily lapped up the unexpected treat. Gretchen crossed her arms and glowered at the dog.

Beth stood quietly for a moment. "You haven't lost your pitching arm." She picked up the spatula, washed it off, dribbled in a splash of milk, and whipped the frosting into pliability. Rotating the cake plate with one hand, she spread the concoction along the side of the cake in slow, smooth motions and then carefully coaxed the frosting across the top.

Gretchen leaned her backside against the counter. "I should just let you handle this party. I'm not good at this stuff."

"You made your daughter a cake."

"It's from a box."

"You made her a cake. A beautiful cake."

Beth continued to stretch the frosting while Gretchen rummaged through the cupboard until she pulled out a package of pink paper plates. "If I could get one decent night of sleep I'd be a new woman."

Lily sprinted into the kitchen and held out her new doll, still imprisoned in the box. Gretchen closed her eyes and sucked in air through her nose. "Go ask your dad."

"I did. He didn't hear. He's talking to Uncle Eric."

The lines between Gretchen's eyebrows deepened. She yanked open a drawer, pulled out a scissors, and disappeared with Lily and the doll. A minute later she returned, doll-less and muttering. "How hard is it to cut wire *and* talk?"

"There," Beth said, scraping out the last of the frosting. "I hid the holes."

Gretchen handed Beth a package of sugar flowers and candles. "You do the honors. You earned it."

While Gretchen stood by mutely, Beth embellished the cake with the candy and pushed in four candles. Finished, she touched her sister's arm. "Hey. I have something for you."

Gretchen blinked. "It's not *my* birthday."

Beth went to the family room to retrieve the package. She returned and held it out to Gretchen. "It's nothing much."

Gretchen's mouth twisted into the beginnings of a smile. "'Nothing much' she says and hands me a box with a satin bow."

"So I like things to look pretty."

As Gretchen tugged off the ribbon and peeled back the yellow paper, Beth watched her sister's expression shift. Gretchen slid the frame from the box and her face softened. Her lips parted slightly; her shoulders relaxed. She gently caressed the glass covering the photograph. "Oh, Beth."

Beth stood behind her sister and admired the black-and-white image again. To capture the overhead shot, she'd stood on a chair. The result had been worth the effort. Evan's tiny hand encircled Gretchen's finger as Dave huddled beside both of them, his expression proud and protective as he took in his son, only minutes old. The scene had rendered her breathless with desire. "I thought you could hang it in your hall."

"Beautiful," Gretchen murmured.

"I took it minutes after he was born."

"I'm glad you were with us for this one."

"I love your expression, how you're looking at him and how he's straining to look at you. You both look so eager."

Gretchen made a strange tight sound, and Beth felt a shot of alarm. Her sister never cried.

Gretchen propped the photograph on the counter and ran a finger underneath her eyes. She walked over to the sink and stared into the stainless steel pit. "I don't know what's wrong with me. Sometimes I feel like I'm suffocating."

From the family room, Lily's laughter rang out. Gretchen wrung out a washcloth and began wiping down the counter. After a moment, she tossed the cloth in the sink and stared through the kitchen window that overlooked the play set she and Dave had purchased last spring instead of living room carpet. "Why get new flooring with three kids?" Beth remembered Gretchen saying with a laugh.

"I look at you and almost get jealous," Gretchen said, still peering out the window. "You have your blessed *freedom*. You and Eric can go wherever you want, eat out at nice restaurants whenever you want, sleep in as long as you want on Saturdays. You don't deal with tantrums and ear infections and throw-up. Your life is your own." She turned to Beth. "And then I feel horrible. I *am* horrible."

"You're not horrible."

"Yes, I am."

Beth poured two cups of coffee, set one on the counter next to Gretchen and then sat at the breakfast bar and watched the steam whirl from her cup like a dance, her compassion and resentment equally roused. Sure, she and Eric had blazed through London last summer like teenagers. Sure, they often took off for the weekend on a moment's notice and dined out more than they should. But she'd give it all up in a heartbeat, for a tiny heartbeat.

"I love those kids," Gretchen said, bracing herself against the counter with her palms. "I do. But I'm losing myself."

"You'll bounce back to your old self again. Just give yourself time. Evan's only a few weeks old."

Gretchen noticed the cup of coffee and cradled it possessively between her hands. "Dave doesn't know what to do with me. I wasn't like this with the first two."

"Maybe you should talk to your doctor."

Gretchen shrugged. "Maybe."

"Maybe Eric and I could take Tyler and Lily home

with us tonight. You could go to bed early. Get some rest."

Gretchen turned to her. "You'd do that?"

"Sure. It'd be fun."

Gretchen reached for a napkin and blew her nose. "You seriously deserve the Sister of the Year Award or something."

Beth smiled. "I'll take the 'or something.'"

Gretchen looked at Beth, finally really looked at her. "I know you would." She threw away the napkin and sat at the table. "Any news lately?"

Beth sipped her coffee. "No, but we were told from the beginning it could take awhile."

"But it's been a year."

"Yes, I know. There isn't much I can do about it."

"You're more patient than I am."

Beth let out a bleak laugh. "What choice do I have?" If anyone ever caught a glimpse of the raging fire inside her, they might not be so quick to praise.

Gretchen reached for the package of party plates and tore off the plastic. "You're right. You'll get the right child at the right time. It'll all work out."

Beth took a drink of coffee instead of feigning a smile. *And they all lived happily ever after.* She'd lived long enough to know the difference between fairytale clichés and real life. But then, so had Gretchen.

As Gretchen lit the candles on the cake and everyone huddled in the kitchen to serenade Lily, Beth kept watch on her sister, wondering if she truly needed help. Real help. Medical help. Or was this despondency a normal part of motherhood? Yet through the blur of smoke from Lily's blown out candles, Beth glimpsed fragments of the sister she knew. She spied love buried under the exhaustion, a flicker of joy mixed with the frustration. As they sat around the table and mopped up ice cream with cubes of cake, Gretchen brushed back Tyler's hair and then later gently wiped Lily's crumb-spotted face.

Maybe such affection was forced. Maybe Gretchen was merely going through the motions, performing the role for the sake of her children, but at least she had the ability and desire to do that. She hadn't completely thrown in the towel.

After the kids dispersed from the kitchen, Dave claimed the leftover piece of cake for his midnight snack, but Gretchen pulled the cake toward herself. "Only if you can arm wrestle it away from me, mister."

Beth grinned. Gretchen hadn't lost herself completely.

❧

Playing Chutes and Ladders required wearing pajamas. At least that's what Beth told her niece and nephew. She closed herself in her room to undress and waited for her young charges to take the bait. Once they gave up their grandiose plans to stay up all night and put on their PJs, they joined her at the kitchen table where she sat waiting with the game. Lily won the first round, and Tyler triumphed over the second.

"Let's see if Uncle Eric has the blow-up bed ready." Beth hid a yawn. She ushered Tyler and Lily down the hall, monitored their teeth brushing, unrolled their sleeping bags, reminded them not to jump, and read *Blueberries for Sal.*

"What do you think of the yellow walls?" She asked after closing the book.

Lily looked around, seeming to notice for the first

time. "It's pretty. Like a baby chick."

Beth swept aside a fiery tendril from Lily's forehead and replaced it with a kiss. "You are one clever four-year-old, Miss Lily."

Tyler petulantly jutted out his lower lip. "Hey. What about me?"

Beth stood, switched off the light, and crouched on the other side of the mattress. "And you are one unbelievably strong and brave six-year-old."

"Six and a half."

"Right. Six and a half."

"Strong like Superman?"

"Stronger than Superman."

"Aunt Beth, why don't you have any kids?"

His question shattered her contentment. "Well, someday I hope we will."

"'Cuz then we'd have cousins."

"That's right." Her voice sounded tight and trapped. "Would you like that?"

Both heads bobbed enthusiastically.

Lily propped herself on her elbows. "When? *When* will you have a baby?"

"I don't know," Beth said, brightly. "Remember how I told you Uncle Eric and I are praying that God will give us a baby? Maybe you can pray that, too."

"OK." Lily squeezed her eyes shut and folded her hands over her chest, her iridescent purple nail polish shimmering in the darkness. "Dear Jesus, please give Auntie Beth a baby. She'd take good care of it. Amen."

Beth grinned at the four-year-old's sense of urgency and zipped them up in their sleeping bags. "Good night, little treasures."

She paused in the doorway, taking in their small round faces protruding from the makeshift bed in the middle of the gleaming hardwood floor.

Last summer, after completing the paperwork to set the adoption train in motion, she'd torn out the green carpet in this room she hoped would one day be the nursery. After years of trying and failing to get pregnant, the exertion proved to be gratifying. She ripped, and the carpet obeyed, but revealed a layer of dried-up glue that clung to the old wooden floor like hardened tar. After experimenting with various chemicals, she found that a simple razor blade worked best. Driven by some unseen force within her—a dogged belief that one day, she'd get through it—day after day, she'd knelt on a rolled up towel and scraped until her back ached and her palms blistered.

The tedious work, the quiet house, her subservient posture, led to reflection that morphed into prayer. Raw and uncensored. She was Jacob, demanding her blessing. She wept, fought, repented, and accepted.

After a week, her knees were numb and her back sore, but her heart mended. And one day she'd straightened and realized she'd conquered. Eric rented a sander, stripped the floor naked, and bathed it in a honey-colored stain. Now the floor gleamed in anticipation.

And right now, her charming nursery held two of her favorite children. Her insides stretched in love, and she wondered how her ribcage would contain her heart if the room ever embraced a child of her own.

3

Amber's homecoming mirrored the scene of the day she'd left for college ten months earlier: her mother sitting on the stoop in front of her doublewide, taking a pull on a cigarette while Amber made trip after trip from the trailer to her Geo Metro.

"The prodigal returns," her mother called out. "I banged my toe on the coffee table this morning. Had to ice it with a bag of peas. I think the little one's broken. Won't be able to help much."

Amber rolled her eyes and popped open the trunk of her car. After grabbing an armload of clothes, she made her way up the gravel driveway.

Her mother exhaled a curl of smoke. "School's out for summer, huh? Or I guess school's out forever." She chortled, coughed, and managed to scoot over an inch to allow Amber to mount the cement steps.

Amber unlatched the screen door and pushed it open with her hip, feeling like a convict returning to prison after a taste of liberation. The thin, grubby carpet seemed to sneer at her in triumph, and the brown-paneled walls felt as oppressive as iron bars. Here she was, back where she started.

She trudged through the hall to her bedroom and noticed a stack of boxes in the far corner. But other than that, the room looked the same as when she left. Had her mother anticipated her failure? She dumped the armload of clothes on her bed and went out for another load.

"So?" her mom called from her perch. "What happened?"

Arms full, Amber climbed the steps again. "Nothing happened. It just didn't work out."

When the car was empty, her mother roused herself and followed Amber to the bedroom. Amber didn't notice a limp.

"You just missed me, right? Decided you had things pretty good at home."

Amber parted the closet doors and discovered an assortment of her mother's sweaters. She pushed the throng to one side and turned to the accumulation of clothes on the bed.

Her mother leaned in the doorway. "Come on, Amber. Spill the beans."

"What do you want me to say? That you were right? That I'm not cut out for school? *Fine.* You were *right.* I'm not cut out for school. Happy?"

Her mom cleared a space on the bed and plopped down, a ribbon of smoke curling up to the blades of the ceiling fan. "I tried to tell you this was all just a big waste of time. If you hadn't lost your head and wandered off to where you didn't belong, you could've taken that opening at the factory."

"If you want to spend your life working at that factory that's fine, but I'm going someplace with mine."

Margaret looked amused. "Oh really? Looks like you're right back where you started."

"Lay off, Mom."

"Don't cop an attitude with me. You always did seem to think you were better than everyone else, above all of this. Hate to disappoint you, but that job at the factory is gone. Got to grab them when they come. I don't know where you're going to find work, but you better find something, and soon."

Amber scooped up a few of her hanging clothes and dropped them over the closet's metal pole. "I've been home all of ten minutes." She turned and caught a hint of triumph in her mother's eyes.

"It's a man, isn't it? You dropped out of school because some guy broke your heart, didn't you?"

Heat crept into Amber's cheeks. She faced the closet again and rescued a sweater from slipping off its hanger.

"Oh, Amber. Let me tell you something for your own good. Men are all alike. They will use you and spit you out faster than you can see it coming. I thought you had men figured out by now. Do we need to have a heart-to-heart about the birds and the bees?" Her mom leaned back into the matching pair of camouflage throw pillows leftover from seventh grade Home Economics class.

"Little late for that, don't you think?" Of course she'd had men figured out. She'd had them figured out ever since junior high. There was never a shortage of boys to hold her and whisper in the darkness as long as she gave them something in return. Nothing was free.

"Then why'd you let some guy chase you out of school? I thought you were smarter than that."

"Can you just drop it?"

"Look, you're the one who came home. If you wanted me to leave you alone, you should have stayed at college. Rick's coming back any day now. So the sooner you find work and a place of your own, the better."

Amber turned away. Rick always might be coming

back. Or leaving. Creepy Rick with his yellowed teeth and flannel shirts and restless eyes.

The closet full, Amber unzipped her suitcase, grabbed a rumpled t-shirt, and snapped it in the air before folding it and tucking it into a drawer. Her still life, *Monday Morning*, stared accusingly at her from the top of the dresser.

The piece showcased a host of everyday objects—a pack of gum, an expiring flower, a hand-addressed envelope, a tube of lip gloss—all tediously familiar until she arranged them just so, constructing a tiny city that transformed the mundane into something interesting, into art. The composition won an award her senior year and hung prominently behind the checkout desk at the public library for three months. Of course, three months wasn't enough time for her mother to view it.

As Amber stashed another shirt, a canary-yellow envelope on the dresser caught her attention. She picked it up, the slanted cursive giving away its sender. She wedged a fingernail underneath the adhesion and pulled out a glitter speckled birthday card.

Her mother made a soft grunting sound. "That came for you awhile ago."

Amber skimmed the inside inscription and scowled at the handwritten *praying for you* hovering above *Grandma Ginny*.

"Crazy old woman," her mom said. "Still trying to win us over."

Amber added the card to the contents in her top dresser drawer, odds and ends she hadn't bothered taking to college: socks without mates, nail polish bottles, and a few other Hallmark greetings from the grandmother she hadn't seen in fourteen years. The steady stream of birthday and Christmas wishes made no sense. Certainly didn't align with her mother's accusations. If Grandma was the heartless witch Margaret alleged, why bother sending cards? Sometimes with money.

Amber wiggled the drawer shut and returned to her heap of clothes. What did she know about Grandma Ginny anyway? The woman was little more than a shadow of a memory, a character that seemed to stem more from a dream than real life.

Amber had more pressing things to think about. Like where to get a job. And when to start looking for an apartment. And how to get on with life as if last Wednesday had never happened.

4

The maple tree in Virginia Swansen's yard stood as a beacon of beauty and strength, flaunting its splendor season after season. Decades ago, when Margaret brought the baby tree home from school on Arbor Day, she'd insisted they plant it right away, or else it might die. From her kitchen window, Ginny gazed at the tree and recalled Margaret's pudgy hands next to her own as they dug out a home for the plant and covered it with earth. Ginny envisioned the tangle of roots under the lush greenness, an unseen labyrinth that expanded year after year, nourishing the tree so it grew and flourished while the family inside the house, not twenty feet away, crumbled.

Ginny took a deep breath and exhaled. This was not a day for gloom. This was a day for celebration. She went to the curio cabinet and selected two teacups, one with a pedestal foot, splattered with hand-painted butterflies, the other a sturdy mother-of-pearl cup and saucer. At the sink, she washed off the layer of dust clinging to the insides of the mismatched pair and placed them on the tray. She glanced at the clock. Lizzie, as always, was late.

Typical Lizzie. Loved to make an entrance.

Ginny arranged a few of the still warm buttermilk biscuits on a plate and set them on the tray beside a jar of her strawberry-rhubarb jam. She carried the tray to the door and attempted the latch with her pinky. The tray wobbled. With her knee raised to steady the tray, she tried the latch again. Through the screened door she spied her Harold attacking a patch of crab grass with a bottle of weed killer.

"Harold! Need some help here."

He didn't hear. Or pretended not to.

Story of her life.

She slid the tray on the kitchen counter, propped open the porch door with a chair, transported the tray to the table on the porch, closed the door, and settled herself into her rocking chair.

Harold climbed the porch steps, breathing heavily. He yanked out a bandana from his front pocket and mopped his brow. "She ain't here yet?"

"Not yet."

"Probably forgot. She always was a scatterbrain."

He was right, to some extent. Lizzie did lose track of anything that wasn't attached to her. Keys. Money. The time. But she hadn't lost track of their friendship. Not even with hundreds of miles separating them. "She'll come."

Harold tucked the cloth back into his pocket. "Think I might go into town and pick up some lawn seed."

"Whatever for? The lawn looks fine."

"I want to get rid of those bald patches."

Ginny's gaze followed her husband's pointed finger and barely made out the specks of earth among the lush greenness. He bestowed whatever hidden passion still lurked in him on the lawn, like a mistress. And yet today, she considered, that might work to her advantage. Best to have him out from underfoot. "Pick up some more birdseed while you're at it. That blue jay was scouting around the feeder this morning."

Minutes after Harold's Buick disappeared down the road, as if waiting for her cue, Lizzie pulled up in her sky-blue Caddy and burst out of the car like a jack-in-the-box.

Ginny skittered down the porch steps to embrace her.

When they finally untangled, Lizzie pushed her oversized sunglasses onto her mop of brunette hair revealing her dark, deep-set, eyes. "Virginia, dear. So sorry I'm late. I got lost."

Ginny chuckled. "In Spring Valley? That's impossible. Even for you."

"Nothing's impossible, love. You know that little cafe that used to sit on the corner of Second and Pine? Well apparently it's been torn down, so I missed my turn and ended up over the river. I stopped to fill up and ended up chatting with the store attendant who just happens to be the world's biggest Boston Red Sox fan. Isn't that ironic? I mean heavens, what are the odds?"

"How did you find that out?"

"Oh, we got to it somehow. Anyway, I told him if he ever makes his way to Boston to actually see a game, in person, he should give me a jingle, and John and I could put him up for a night..."

"Lizzie, you don't even know him."

"I do now. Besides his manners were impeccable, even if he did look like a walking comic strip with all of those tattoos splattered up and down his arms, but that is the style these days. He was so tickled by the invitation he offered me a complimentary cappuccino. Wasn't that thoughtful? Of course I told him no thank you, that I was on my way to see a dear, dear friend and didn't want to spoil my appetite, and here I am!"

She took a breath. "Oh, and don't you look lovely."

Ginny patted her newly dyed red hair. She told Shelia at the salon yesterday that she was ready for a change, and change it was. "What do you think?"

"Bold. Daring. I love it."

Ginny absently wondered if she should have changed out of her worn-in jeans and Mt. Rushmore T-shirt. "You look stunning, as always."

Lizzie curtsied in her red-and-white floral dress that could have been a costume piece for the *I Love Lucy* show, but the look suited her. *Retro* was what the kids called it nowadays. Lizzie winked. "Too stunning to be a pastor's wife, right?"

Ginny grinned. Years ago, when one of the church ladies criticized Lizzie for dressing too fashionably for a pastor's wife, Lizzie laughed and said, "Pastor or not, the man still has to *look* at me!"

They linked arms and meandered up the front walk. "So how is Boston suiting you?" Ginny asked.

Lizzie's eyes ignited. "Perfectly. The Freedom Trail, the colonial style churches, driving along the Massachusetts coastline in the fall. John and I try out a new bed-and-breakfast every few months. It's such an enchanting part of the country. And of course I love being closer to the grandkids. Oh, you'll have to come out and visit us sometime. We'll take you to all of our favorite spots. I miss sweet little Spring Valley, but I'm a city girl, through and through."

Ginny nodded, her insides aching. "I knew you would be. And what about John? How has he transitioned from preaching at United Methodist to teaching seminary?"

"His students refer to him as The Zealot, so that should give you some idea. No one falls asleep in his class."

They climbed the porch steps, and Lizzie gasped as she took in the spread assembled on the small table next to the porch swing. She pressed her hands together. "Simply beautiful!"

Ginny swelled with joy. Pulling out the fussy lace tablecloth and good china had been worth the effort. "The tea is in your honor, my friend."

Lizzie fanned out her skirt and fell into the porch swing. "I did throw some charming tea parties when John and I occupied the parsonage, didn't I?"

"Oh, they were more than charming. Even though I did wonder if you were off your rocker that day I saw how you'd transformed your backyard into the likes of the lawn of Buckingham Palace with all of those flowers and finger sandwiches."

"And?"

Ginny smirked. "The jury's still out."

Laughing melodically, Lizzie flicked through the basket of assorted teas. She tore open a ginger spice and plopped it in the pedestal cup. "You do realize now there was a method to my madness, don't you? All that loveliness enticed you to come. Beauty has a way of captivating us."

Ginny doused Lizzie's teabag with hot water and rummaged through the basket for her trusty Earl Grey. "I suppose so. But it wasn't your pretty decorations that got to me. It was you, silly."

Lizzie raised her teacup. "The beginning of our beautiful friendship." She took a sip and set the cup, now marked with lipstick, in its saucer. She glanced around the yard. "Where is Harold? That old grizzly bear is going to get a hug from me whether he likes it or not."

"At the hardware store."

"How are things with him these days?"

Ginny dumped a spoonful of sugar into her tea and clicked her spoon around. "Same as always. He's takes care of the lawn. Changes the oil. Balances the checkbook. And I can be thankful for that, right?"

Lizzie held her gaze. "Yes, but you can be honest, too."

Ginny took a sip of tea. "It's nothing I haven't told you before. We're adequate roommates."

Lizzie slipped out of her red pumps and nudged them under the swing. "How about Margaret? Have you talked with her recently?"

"I called on her birthday. She hung up about thirty seconds into the conversation."

Lizzie sighed and studied the house across the street. "Bitterness is a heavy weight to carry. You'd think she'd be tired of lugging that around for so long. She doesn't know what she's missing. And Amber, too." Lizzie turned to Ginny. "How old is she now?"

A little round face flanked by two blonde braids flashed to Ginny's mind. "She just turned nineteen."

"Nineteen. Well, now." Lizzie fell silent, her eyes penetrating something in the horizon, something Ginny couldn't quite see yet.

"What?"

Lizzie sipped her tea. "Hmm?"

"Your mind is spinning faster than a hamster's wheel. I can see it."

"I'm just thinking. Amber's no longer a child. Certainly old enough to make her own decisions. She may love nothing better than to reconnect with the grandma who helped raise her."

"Oh, we haven't seen each other in years. She

probably doesn't even remember me."

Lizzie leaned forward. "Of course she remembers you! She lived right here in this house the first five years of her life. How could she not remember you?"

Ginny took a sip of tea and set the cup on the saucer. "Margaret would have a fit."

Lizzie sighed, obviously exasperated. "For mercy's sake. So Margaret would have a fit. Let her have a fit. What about Amber? If Margaret refuses to see you, that's one thing. But she can't make that decision for Amber. Not anymore. Give your granddaughter the chance to decide if she wants you in her life or not." Lizzie gave her arm a little shake, her eyes ablaze. "Oh, dear heart, can you imagine? Reuniting with Amber after all this time?"

Ginny pulled away and slathered a biscuit with jam, a shoot of hope stretching straight up inside of her, like her tulips that boldly poked through winter's ground. Of course she could imagine it; she'd imagined a reunion hundreds of times. But fourteen years? Too much time had passed. Amber probably wanted nothing to do with her. Who knew what Margaret had told her? The girl probably thought Ginny snacked on neighborhood children. And attempting a reunion would only exacerbate Margaret's anger. But then, how could things get any worse? Margaret had already shut her out of her life and taken Amber with her. What else could her daughter do to hurt her?

Ginny took a bite of biscuit, aware of Lizzie's scrutiny. She swallowed and said, "I don't deserve to see Amber."

Lizzie set her plate on the table. "Who deserves anything? My dear Virginia, when are you going to stop punishing yourself? Don't let guilt rob you of having a relationship with your granddaughter. This has been going on far too long. Call her."

Ginny smiled at her friend, her heart racing at the possibility. Such a thing seemed too wonderful even to hope for. Then again, sometimes those cheeky tulips bloomed despite the ice surrounding them.

❧

Amber awakened with a start, a part of her still trapped in the nightmare. Her skin pricked with sweat, she sat up and pulled her knees to her chest and tried to regain control of her breathing. Had she screamed? Or was that only in the dream? Maybe light would drive away the demons.

She swung her legs over the side of the bed and sprang for the light switch across the room, barreling into the dresser. The Mason jar topped over with a clank, sending the spare change trickling to the floor. She flicked on the light and knelt to rake her fingers through the carpet. A bang on the door made her jump.

"Amber? What's going on?"

"Nothing."

Margaret opened the door and scowled. "You rearranging furniture at three in the morning?"

"Couldn't sleep. I was going to read or something and ran into the dresser."

Her mother's upper lip curled. "That was dumb."

Amber caught a whiff of the yeasty stench of whiskey. She hadn't been the only one awake in these wee hours. She poured a handful of nickels and dimes back into the jar.

"You should be quieter," her mother slurred, her head resting on the inside of the doorframe. "People are trying to sleep, you know. Do you wanna wake up the whole neighborhood?" Her voice rose in admonition.

"Sorry." Amber had enough nightmares to deal with right now; she didn't need to suffer her mother's temper as well.

Margaret staggered in and sat on the edge of the bed, clutching the opaque bottle. "You know what, Amber? Sometimes you just have to tell people where to go."

Amber stood. She swiped her hand across the top of the dresser, sliding the stray coins into the jar.

"You don't think so? You don't think I'm right? You think you know better?"

"No, you're right, Mom. You're right." She pushed the jar to the back of her dresser, willing her mother to leave. She was tired. Her shift started in a few hours.

Margaret tapped the side of her head with her index finger. "I know about some things. You're not the only smart one around here."

Amber stood motionless, waiting for her mother to philosophize her way out the door, but Margaret swung her legs onto the bed. "There's nothing you can learn in college that I don't already know. And the best part is that you don't even need a scholarship. I'll teach you everything I know for free." Margaret roared with laughter, which deteriorated into coughing, the remaining whiskey sloshing up the inside of the bottle with each spasm. When she quieted, she tucked the bottle against her chest as if it were a doll, shifted to her side, and dropped her head on Amber's pillow.

Amber waited for the rhythmic snoring. Then she

dislodged the bottle from her mother's grip and gently set it on the dresser. She dragged a sleeping bag from the closet and headed to the couch, the sound of a distant cry still echoing in her mind.

5

Beth tried her best to love Vicki Sanders, but the woman sometimes acted like the moon hung for her sole approval. When Vicki caught Beth's eye across the foyer of Elkin Community Church, Beth had no choice but to smile and wait for Vicki to click her way over.

"Welcome back," Beth said after accepting a quick hug. "How was your year in France?"

Vicki gave a little gasp and shook her head at the ceiling. "Oh, *très magnifique*! If Roger is ever offered a teaching stint overseas again, I'd pack my bags in a heartbeat. Of course the travel to and from Pairs was horrendous, and the accommodations were anything but five star, but, oh, the cheese. The bread!"

Beth smiled. "Sounds wonderful."

"I must say, I am glad to be home. Say, I was just asking Ruth Martin if she was planning on organizing another women's group this summer. Remember when we met in her house for study? Was it two summers ago?"

"Yes, I think it has been two years."

"What a fun group." Suddenly, Vicki frowned. "So. How *are* you?"

"Glad it's summer. I love my kindergarteners but by June I'm ready for a break. I'm doing well, thanks."

Vicki raised her overly plucked eyebrows. "*Are* you?"

"Yes," Beth said, puzzled. "We're fine."

Vicki drew in air through her nostrils and gave her head a little shake. "I still pray that the Lord might open your womb and allow you and Eric to conceive," she said ceremoniously, a benediction for her and everyone around them.

Beth froze, struck dumb.

"I'm sure it must be *so* difficult for you to have to walk through this dreadful infertility for *so* long."

Behind Vicki, Beth noticed Allen Davidson. Face scarlet, his eyes flickered over her before he ducked around the corner.

Vicki placed her shiny red nails on Beth's forearm and patted. "Don't lose faith. The Lord is a miracle worker. He can open the womb of the barren if He so desires. He can open up yours."

Beth felt feverish and trapped. She scanned the area, hoping Vicki might do the same and notice the crowd swarming the foyer. "Yes. I know," she mumbled.

"You know, just last week I read an article about how sometimes overcoming infertility is as simple as the husband switching to boxers. Guess it has to do with sperm production. Couldn't hurt, right? Do the doctors know anything more about your specific disorder? Has there been any progress?"

The question slapped Beth across the face. Progress? Was her tummy protruding? Was she cradling a baby? She fought for her voice, and it emerged from her throat like gravel. "We're trusting in God's plan and timing to start a family."

"Well, yes, of course you are, but—"

Shock receded and anger swelled. "Actually, we're in process to adopt and we're thrilled." She didn't sound thrilled. She didn't sound thrilled at all.

Vicki pursed her lips and nodded. "Oh. Well, you never know. I've heard of lots of stories about couples who start the adoption process and then get pregnant. Isn't that just like the Lord? So don't give up hope. Keep praying. God just may reward you for your diligence. We can move mountains, you know, if we have enough faith. If we just keep on praying."

Beth struggled to breathe. Was that what people thought? That her malfunctioning ovaries were a consequence of lacking faith? That if she merely prayed hard enough, God would reward her with a baby? That she was too *unspiritual* for God to grant her a child?

Eric appeared and Beth gripped his hand. He offered an amiable good morning to Vicki as Beth pulled him toward the sanctuary doors. Someone handed her a bulletin, and her lips mechanically pinched into a smile. She found a seat toward the back and pretended to study the announcements. Eric leaned over and whispered something about an upcoming picnic. She nodded and wondered why he hadn't noticed the gaping hole in her back.

The worship leader strummed his guitar and invited the congregation to stand. Like a robot, she obeyed. She always obeyed. Minutes later, the offering plate passed before her, and she dutifully dropped in her check. She could play along. Join the production. Play church like she and Gretchen had done as kids when they lined up all their dolls on the couch and preached to them, when she never imagined she might not become a mother for real. When she assumed she knew exactly how life would turn out.

Eric belted out the words next to her. Bitter over his brightness, Beth mouthed lyrics to hymns she knew too well, the phrases jabbing like thorns. A toddler gawked at her from the row in front of her, eager for engagement. The child was breathtaking, yet Beth offered no smile. Her gaze darted around the room at the sanctuary peppered with infants and children perched in fathers' arms, cradled by mothers swaying in time with the music. She clutched the back of the chair in front of her and shut her eyes, Vicki's words churning inside of her like a storm. How *dare* she?

And yet she'd wrestled with those very thoughts.

Shouldn't her presence here count for something? For as long as she could remember, she'd been in church every Sunday, most Wednesdays, and not merely as a spectator but as a Sunday school teacher and cook and member on the serving team. Didn't that afford her enough chips for God to grant her a child? And wasn't it God himself who had planted the desire within her to mother in the first place? Of course He hadn't denied other parents, even undeserving parents who abused or neglected their kids, who didn't care if they came into her classroom sockless in January.

A slew of comebacks for Vicki flooded Beth's mind. She mulled them over throughout the service like sour candy in her mouth. She imagined putting Vicki in her place with brilliantly executed one-liners. She envisioned Vicki humbled. Ashamed. Breaking the heel to one of her ridiculous stilettos as she slinked out the door.

When the service ended, Beth beelined to the main doors. Eric followed at his own lackadaisical pace, pausing now and then to small talk. "Not feeling well?" he asked once he caught up to her in the parking lot.

She clipped to the car and shut herself inside. "I

cannot believe the nerve of that woman!" she said once he joined her.

Eric started the engine. "Who?"

"*Who?* Vicki."

"What do you mean? What happened?"

Somehow, irrationally, absurdly, she thought he should already know. "She said she was still praying that I'd get pregnant."

Eric pulled out of the parking lot. "Isn't that a good thing?"

"No. Not in the way she said it."

"But you *asked* her to pray."

"Two years ago! I asked her to pray for me *two years ago*. When I was in that Bible study with her. Remember?" Of course he remembered. He'd been the one to push her into it in the first place, telling her she couldn't spend the whole summer sulking in bed, dysfunctional ovaries or not.

"So she's supposed to know when to *stop* praying for us?"

"Eric, you're not *listening*. I shared a confidential prayer request with a group of women two years ago with the understanding that this request was personal, not something to fling in my face on any given Sunday. Does she have no propriety, no sense at all to consider I might not want to talk about it in a room full of people? Poor Allen Davidson looked like he was going to pass out."

Eric glanced at her. "Allen?"

"He was standing behind her and heard every word. If she had any tact at all she might have realized that."

Eric sighed. "Settle down, Beth. Her heart may have been in the right place. You're overreacting."

"Eric, you weren't *there*. You didn't hear her. She acted as if I was her little pet project failing to follow her agenda. She seemed disappointed that we were adopting. *Disappointed*! Like it was second best or something."

He was quiet for a moment. "Well, that was something we had to work through."

"I know, but she doesn't get it. She feels sorry for us. She thinks I'm still the basket case I was two years ago."

"You don't know that. You don't know what people are thinking about you, or if they're thinking about you at all. Don't jump to conclusions and—"

"Stop trying to fix me and just listen."

Eric maneuvered the series of turns that led them to their neighborhood while Beth glared out the window. Before the car stopped moving, her feet hit the garage floor. She stomped inside and kicked off her pumps, slammed herself into her bedroom, the force of the motion causing the serenity prayer plaque to thud to the floor.

After a while, Eric came in and grabbed his workout clothes. "I'm going for a run."

She heard him change in the bathroom and exit through the front door. Leave it to Eric do something constructive with his anger.

His calmness fueled her fury. Secretly, she'd hoped he'd lash out in some unpredictable benign way like clear off all of her knick-knacks from the top of her dresser in one enraged swipe or stomp around the house like a toddler. Like she did. Then at least her anger might be justified. But Eric was unflappable. It exasperated her, made her look worse. Rendered her the crazy one. The spiritually stunted one limping behind.

Beth studied her face in the vanity mirror above her dresser.

Maybe Eric was right; maybe she should give Vicki the benefit of the doubt. Even if Vicki was only after a morsel of gossip, couldn't she let the woman's comments slide over her? Eric deserved that. He deserved a wife who assumed the best about people, who could brush off insensitivities without turning into a willful child.

He deserved a wife who could give him children.

"*Stop*," Beth told herself. Or the devil. Or the both of them.

She needed to occupy her hands, to bake something and then eat it. Wiping her eyes, she shuffled to the kitchen and pulled out her tin recipe box. The comforting familiarity of a piecrust beckoned, as did the rhubarb ripening in the backyard. She went outside and yanked out ten crimson stalks, washed them, chopped them into one inch chunks, then set about to make the crust. The dough, pliable and supple under her angry hands, proved to be therapy, and her shoulders loosened as she transferred her weight and worries into her work. This certainly wasn't the first time she and Eric had fought over this.

Two summers ago, when she finally gave up on the hormone drugs that left her weepy and crazy but not pregnant, she retreated to her room, clutching the fragments of her broken dream like a security blanket. Eric seemed like an intruder. She hadn't wanted to share her pain and loathed any attempts at comfort, even from him. She wanted to wallow in her misery all by herself, fester in her grief like algae in a cesspool.

Joining the summer Bible study group, as much as

she hated to admit it right now, provided the first rung on which to set her foot on to begin to climb her way out of the well of depression. Slowly, she came out of it, out of the all-consuming pity. Little by little, food began to regain its taste. Sunshine on her face felt good again. She came out of herself and back to Eric. Back to God.

And then, a few months later, Eric voiced the possibility of adoption.

In theory, they'd always supported adoption. At a distance, adoption was a wonderful thing. For other people. At first, she was lukewarm to the idea. Out of all the prescriptions she'd tried to open her womb, as Vicki would say, no pill existed to flip the switch on her heart, to suddenly turn off the yearning to become pregnant and turn on the desire to adopt. How did one do that? Could she release the dream? Let it go completely? Not bury it and give it a chance to sprout into a thistle of resentment but unclench her fist and let the desire fly away so she could chase a new one? Could she love a child not of her flesh and blood?

Prayer became sustenance. God didn't perform the miraculous, he didn't fix her malfunctioning, broken body, but he did replace her heart of stone with one of flesh, one softened to adoption. As the pain and disappointment dimmed and faded into the background, hope mounted and soared.

Why couldn't Vicki Sanders understand that? Beth and Eric had crawled out of the well of despair, and she had no desire to return. They'd licked their wounds and let go of the dream, and now they stood eagerly, wholeheartedly ready to adopt. Why couldn't Vicki simply be happy for them?

When Eric returned from his run, the rhubarb pie

was browning in the oven. He poured himself a glass of water and didn't meet her eyes. "Smells good."

Beth leaned against the counter and looked at him. "Sorry I yelled."

He finished his water and wiped his mouth with the back of his hand. "Sorry I didn't listen."

She stepped closer and caught a whiff of perspiration. "I don't want to keep fighting, especially about *this*."

"Look, maybe Vicki was out of line—"

Beth placed her palms on his sweat-damp t-shirt in protest. "Let's not talk about Vicki anymore."

"Good idea." He encircled her around the waist. "I'm in your corner."

"I'm in yours. What do you want for lunch?"

Eric glanced at the oven. "What are you making?"

"Rhubarb pie."

"We have ice cream."

She shook her head. "You're impossible."

Eric set the ice cream on the counter to soften as Beth got out two plates and forks and waited for the timer to ring.

❧

Gretchen stopped by later that evening, looking fresh in a denim skirt and sleeveless blouse and a hint of eye makeup. Grinning, she held out a book. "Guess what I found?"

Beth took the book and scanned the title. *Choosing the Right Name for Your Baby.*

"I was sorting through clothes and found it in the basement." Gretchen's eyes danced. "Come on. Let's pick one."

"This is sweet, but we don't really need it. We've had our names picked out for a while now."

Gretchen deflated. "You have? You haven't told me."

"I can't tell you everything. I've got to have some secrets, you know."

"Oh." Gretchen crossed her arms. "So, what are they?"

"You'll find out when you're supposed to."

"Oh, come on. You know you want to tell me. Tell me, or else I'll start calling your baby Gunther."

Beth sighed. "Promise you won't tell anyone?"

"What are you, twelve? Yes, yes. I won't tell."

The names had grown so precious to Beth that when she practiced them out loud in an empty house, they sounded like music. "For a girl, Grace. And for a boy, Michael."

Gretchen cocked her head to one side. "Grace and Michael. OK."

"What? You have a look."

"No they're fine. Nice. Not very original, but fine. I know a ton of Michaels."

The silent music fizzled. "Well, who asked you anyway? I love Michael. It's strong and beautiful. Like the angel."

"Michael," Gretchen said, practicing. "Mike Dilinger."

"No. Not Mike. *Michael*."

"Sorry. *Michael*," Gretchen said again, her tone softer. "Yeah, it's growing on me. Just as long as little Michael, or Grace, realizes that Auntie Gretchen is going to spoil him or her rotten."

Beth grinned. "I'm counting on it."

6

Ginny opened the pink envelope right there at the mailbox and pulled out a homemade card dripping with sequins and lace and character. She read the profusions of appreciation and smiled. Lizzie didn't believe in leaving anything unsaid. Below her celebrity styled signature she'd admonished, "Show me your spunk, Ginny, and call your granddaughter!"

Spunk. Maybe she used to live on spunk, but it had been long depleted.

Fanning herself with Lizzie's card in the August heat, Ginny strolled up the front path and observed Harold yanking weeds sprouting through the cracks in the cement. He straightened and stretched, kneading his shoulders with his fingers. For a brief moment she considered going to him and rubbing his back but gave into their settled, separate rhythm of life.

From her rocking chair she sorted through the rest of the mail and deemed Lizzie's card the only thing worth the price of the stamp. She set the stack of junk mail on the lower tier of the small wooden table beside her, reached for her Bible, and tucked Lizzie's card into the cover pocket.

Some time later, Harold ascended the steps. Ginny poured and handed him a glass of lemonade. She set the scarlet ribbon in its place and shut the book. "Look at what Lizzie made," she said, sliding out the card. "Isn't it something else?"

45

Harold offered a vague glance.

A breeze rustled a cluster of leaves that had collected on the porch. "You'll never guess what she thinks I should do?" Ginny waited for a hint of response. "Call Amber."

He scowled at her. "Amber?"

"Yes, Amber. Our granddaughter."

"I know who she is. You think I'd forgotten?"

"Sometimes I wonder if you have." She sniffed and studied the front of the card again. "So, what do you think?"

Harold took a swig of lemonade. "Needs more sugar."

"About calling Amber."

He sighed and fixed his attention on the house across the street. "Margaret will be up in arms."

Ginny fingered a peacock feather glued to the homemade card. "Margaret's been up in arms for twenty years. I don't know what else I can do for her. Amber's all grown up now, although who knows what kind of upbringing she's had. I may try and track her down." She turned to Harold. "Well?"

"What are you asking me for? You'll do whatever you darn well please anyway."

"Lizzie thinks it's time to reach out to her."

Harold cursed and shook his head. "This is all Lizzie's doing, isn't it? She's always planting crazy ideas in your head." He tipped his head toward the Bible in her lap. "She's the reason you sit out here and bury your nose in that old book. She's the reason you waste half your time at that church."

Ginny took a breath, ready to retaliate, but exhaled without a word. Mustering all the sweetness she could, she said, "Lizzie was sorry to have missed you. Said she wanted to give the old grizzly bear a hug. I'm assuming she meant you."

Harold shook his head. "That woman has a few screws loose."

Ginny chuckled, desperate for the banter to continue, even at Lizzie's expense. "She is a character, I'll give you that."

Harold set his lemonade on the table and worked a thread of dirt out from under his thumbnail. "That church went off the deep end when she and John moved in. Used to be a person could go to church on Sunday and live the rest of his week in peace. Until those two took over."

Ginny couldn't deny it. Half of the congregation had stormed out when John and Lizzie shook up the little Methodist church on the corner. Yet the irony was lost on her husband for it was Lizzie who'd told her more than a decade ago to stop preaching at him and *just love the man*. If it wasn't for Lizzie, she might still be screaming on Sunday mornings for him to put on decent pants and come to church with her to hear about the love of God. The devil's foothold indeed.

Ginny chuckled. "Yes, that Bible study Lizzie roped me into all those years ago was quite a group."

Harold's eyes flashed over her, no doubt surprised by her placidity. He downed the last of his lemonade, stood, and shoved the bandana in his back pocket. "Well, I suppose one good thing came from you going to that church and reading that Bible."

Her heart skipped a beat. "What's that?"

He walked to the edge of the porch and leaned a palm against it. "You stopped reading those trashy romance novels."

She gasped, indignant, then laughed.

"Better get started on that oil change. She's as dry as a bone."

He strolled to the Buick and disappeared under the hood.

Ginny's spirits boosted, she opened the card again and pondered Lizzie's call to action. Maybe, just maybe, she could scrape together a little leftover spunk after all.

⌘

Rent swallowed almost all of Amber's earnings from The Kettle, but she'd live on peanut butter and tomato soup for the rest of her life if it meant evading Rick. A month ago, when he wormed his way back into Margaret's trailer, he grinned too eagerly when he saw her and when she retreated to her bedroom, she felt his eyes follow her every step, like a wolf. That very day she signed a lease to a one bedroom across town.

Explaining any of this to her mother would be pointless. She'd tried years ago, after Rick leaned into her, looked her up and down, and asked if she'd ever been with an older man.

Her mother had been instantly enraged, although not at Rick. "Well, whose fault is that?"

Rick's, Amber had assumed.

"Quit your teasing and strutting your stuff. Don't mess this one up for me, you hear? If he's noticed you it's because you *wanted* him to notice you."

Some time after that, when Rick grazed her breast and acted as if it were purely accidental, Amber never said a word. From then on, whenever Rick slithered in, Amber crept out.

Although now, as she played games with her male

customers to fill up her tip jar faster, she wondered if her mother was right. A little flirting, a coy smile, and bingo—a nice fat five appeared on the table after they left. Sometimes more. Age didn't matter; men were men.

She tucked a wisp of hair behind her ear and hoisted the tray of coffee over her shoulder. Why anyone would order the scorching liquid in this August heat was beyond her, but the group of elderly men who'd occupied the corner booth every Tuesday morning always requested the same thing: a pot of strong coffee and four giant sticky rolls. Securing her grin, she approached their table. "Looking good with those suspenders, Herbert. Got a hot date tonight?"

"That depends. You busy?" His fellow comrades chuckled good-naturedly.

"Sure she's busy, good looking gal like that," Walt chimed.

Amber flashed them a smile and set down the coffee and rolls. "You do flatter me, gentlemen. Marvin, are you going to treat yourself to eggs this morning, sunny side up, wheat toast on the side?" The bigger the order, the better the tip.

"You talked me into it, sugar." He winked at her as if they were old friends.

After pouring their coffee, Amber headed for the kitchen, her smile vanishing with the swing of the door.

Pete, her manager, eyed her. "You know those men by name."

She shrugged and clipped her orders to the metal swivel for the fry cook

Pete nodded approvingly. "Good for you. Customers like that. Adds to the homey ambience of the place."

Amber smothered a smile. With the outdated vinyl booths, frequent truckers, and greasy food, The Kettle possessed about as much ambiance as an outhouse. One of the last restaurants in the world that boasted liver and onions as a weekly special.

Pete glanced at the dining area. "It's slowed down. Take your ten. I'll get these orders out."

The oppressive August air hit her like a virus as she stepped out the back door. She undid another button on her blouse and tugged the fabric back and forth in hopes of creating a breeze. She lit a cigarette and sat down on the lone bench, her feet throbbing inside her sneakers. The play yard of Bright Future Day Care faced her with oodles of vibrantly colored plastic toys splayed out behind a chain-link fence. Two small boys bobbed on a teeter-totter. She inhaled and exhaled, losing herself in the rhythm of the apparatus, spellbound by the boys' laughter.

Suddenly her leg was on fire. She jumped to her feet and cursed, sending the ember that had dropped from her cigarette onto her knee to the ground. The cigarette between her fingers was a mere stub yet she only remembered taking a couple of drags. She snuffed the stub and lit another, inhaled, and paced away from the sound of the children.

Not soon enough.

The scene floated to the surface of her mind like driftwood on water, and the tiny image she told herself didn't exist flashed before her eyes. All at once, the air around her disappeared. She was in a vacuum. She couldn't breathe.

She made her way back to the table, lowered herself to the bench, pressed her hand over her heart that slammed against her chest like a bird. *Breathe.* She fought to fill her lungs, to keep her head above the rising tide of emotions. This was her body, and she would master it. This was her life, and she was in charge.

Something inside her thudded like an anchor. This was her life.

She concentrated on breathing, the laughter of the daycare children seeming to mock her. Her heart slowed, and she glanced at her watch and realized she'd expired her break time. Herbert and his gang would be waiting for their checks and a playful farewell. She allowed herself a couple more drags, pushed herself to her feet, flicked the cigarette to the ground and twisted it under her toe.

᠗᠖

Hours later, shoulders aching, Amber slipped out of her sneakers and crashed into the one piece of furniture that came with the place, a plaid, battered armchair. She fantasized about owning an air conditioner or the sky breaking open and exploding in rain, washing away the grating heat of these final summer days. Robin and everyone else would be gearing up for fall semester, buying books, checking class schedules, hanging out at the coffee shop that overlooked the lake...

The phone rang, rupturing her musings. Her mother had been nagging for days to come by and pick up the rest of her things. Sighing, she squeezed her temples, preparing for a headache. She answered.

"Amber?"

"Yes? Who is this?"

The woman took a quick intake of breath. "This is Grandma Ginny. It's been such a long time. Do you remember me?"

Amber glanced at the birthday card she'd propped on the TV. The cards hadn't mailed themselves all of these years. "Sort of."

"It's wonderful to hear your voice."

Amber could hear the smile in the woman's voice. "How did you get my number?"

"Your mother. I've been badgering her for some time now. I guess I finally wore her down."

Amber dropped into her chair. "Oh."

"I know it's been years since we've seen each other, but I was hoping we could meet, do a little catching up. I'm wondering, would you like to come here for supper? On Thursday night?"

The question, the whole conversation, left her mind reeling. "Thursday? OK," she heard herself say even as her mind screamed *no*.

"I'm still on Hillman Street in Spring Valley. Do you remember where that is?"

She couldn't tie her shoe the last time she'd been on Hillman Street. "No, not really."

"I'll give you directions, then. Got a pen?"

As if entranced, Amber got up and found a pen and jotted on the back of the birthday card while the woman spouted off directions.

"I'm looking forward to Thursday."

"Me, too," Amber answered mechanically.

She hung up the phone and stood in the tiny kitchen, trying to make sense of what just happened. After a minute, she went to her bedroom, stripped off her work clothes, and put on a clean tank top and shorts. Back in the kitchen, she grabbed the card and stared at the directions sprawled across the pink cardstock, in her own handwriting— proof that she hadn't dreamed up the conversation. Grandma had called to invite her to the little house she used to know so well and she had agreed. She opened the card and stared at the tidy, slanted signature of the woman she thought she remembered loving, a long time ago.

7

Beth hadn't voiced it to Eric or anyone else, but in her heart of hearts, she hadn't expected to return to school this fall. Dashed hopes again. She stood glowering at the calendar.

Only a few more weeks remained of her time being her own. In a short while, a new batch of kindergarteners would scamper into her classroom, all needing to rise to state requirements, all the responsibility squarely on her shoulders. She loved her students, and they loved her. But only for a season. In spite of the hours she'd invest settling disputes, gasping over lost teeth, speaking in exaggerated phonetics, unjamming zippers, pressing their chubby little hands in tempura paint and then onto cardstock for Mother's Day, they would not remember her. Not vividly, anyway. Every spring, if she did her job right, her students would walk out of her classroom, equipped with skills for a lifetime, but she, their teacher, would fade in their memories until she was nothing but a smiling face in a classroom photograph that might make it into a box marked "school stuff."

This August she felt particularly gray. She had hoped this was her summer to be chosen, for a birth mother to connect with her and Eric's photos and words and select them from the lot of other wannabe parents whose greatest hope was tethered to a scrapbook. It felt like playing the lottery. Her optimism last spring ran so high she even told her principal that she hoped to take a yearlong leave of absence once they got a baby. Maybe longer. Maybe she'd quit for good, she thought, giddy with the prospect that, come fall, she may not be teaching. She may be a mother.

Beth turned from the calendar and washed the breakfast dishes. The dishwasher was on the fritz and no amount of scraping or rinsing mattered anymore since everything came out coated in some unnamable residue. She'd called for repair days ago, and they were supposed to send someone this morning. It was now past noon.

And she was tired of waiting.

Restless, she made a quick inventory of the refrigerator and jotted out a list, grabbed her purse, and drove two miles where she sulked up and down the aisles. She picked up meat to grill, potato salad, and ingredients to make a medicinal batch of chocolate chip cookies, then headed home.

Arms full of groceries, she was fiddling her key into the door when she heard the phone ring. With her luck, the repairman probably stopped while she was out and was now calling to berate her. Let him call. She was cocked and loaded to fire off a piece of her mind. The phone trilled again. She pushed open the door, dumped the bags on the table, and grabbed the receiver before the machine picked up.

"This an OK time to call?" Her social worker's greeting took her by surprise since she'd already checked in this month.

"Yes," Beth said, her tone brightening. "I just got in. What can I do for you?" One of the brown sacks on the table toppled over, and the carton of eggs plunged to the floor.

"Is Eric home as well?" Cheryl asked.

Beth gaped at the mess on the floor. "Ah, no. But I'm here." She reached for the paper towels, crouched, and turned over the carton. Four were broken. "I mean, I'm listening."

"I have some news. I believe we have a baby for you and Eric."

Beth stood up. Egg white from the broken shell in her hand oozed between her fingers and seeped back onto the floor. "Pardon?"

"Are you sitting down?"

"You mean, you have a *birth mother* for us."

"No. I have a *baby* for you."

The eggshell dropped to the floor with a crack. Mindlessly, Beth wiped her hand down the front of her Capri's and dropped into a kitchen chair.

"I need to tell you right off the bat, this isn't the open adoption we were planning on," Cheryl said. "In fact, this is a unique case."

Beth forced herself to exhale and focus. She could fall apart later. She could clean up later. "Yes, go on. I'm listening."

He was two months old, Cheryl told her. *He*. A boy. A *boy*.

Beth grasped on to the nugget of gold and turned it over and over in her mind until she reminded herself to keep listening. He was born in Madison, but they didn't know the birth mother or birth father and had no background or medical information.

Cheryl paused. "He was abandoned, Beth." Her tone took on a strange quality.

The world screeched to a halt. "Abandoned? You mean at a hospital?"

"No."

She waited, sensing more.

"A young man heard crying as he was walking past a bar close to campus. He found the baby in a box, next to a dumpster, and called the police right away."

Beth pressed a hand to her heart. Lord, have mercy.

"I know this is a lot to take in—"

"Is he all right? Is he hurt?"

"From what the doctors can tell, he's perfectly healthy. He was small when they found him, not even six pounds, so his mother might have been a smoker, or he could've been born premature. At any rate, he's been gaining weight like a champ."

An image of a naked, shivering baby flashed to Beth's mind, accompanied by a wave of nausea. She propped an elbow on the table and rested her forehead on her free hand, suddenly remembering the tacky residue of egg coating her fingers.

This phone call, this moment, was supposed to be one of pure joy, not flashing scenes from a horror movie. Not this mess before her feet. Not this mess Cheryl described. She needed to do what had to be done. Isn't that what mothers did? She reached for a notepad and pencil and wrote down the details she remembered. Boy. Two months. Madison. Abandoned.

"Beth? Are you still with me?"

"Yes. Just trying to take it all in."

"It's tragic, but these cases are more frequent than you'd think."

Beth's thoughts circled a question, a question she didn't want to empower by speaking it into existence, but one that she couldn't push aside. "What if—what if she wants him back?"

"In cases of abandonment, the state has to run a

termination of parental rights so that's why I had to wait a couple of months to contact you. I can explain more of the details after you and Eric have a chance to talk it over. What I *can* tell you is that the biological parents of this baby no longer possess any legal rights to him."

"So she couldn't have him back?"

"No. Even if on the rare chance she was able to track him down and tried to reclaim him, the courts would invariably rule in your favor. He would legally belong to you and Eric."

Belong to you…

"What you do need to consider if you decide to proceed with the adoption, is the lack of any medical information, that and his difficult personal history. I must say, though, I think you and Eric are a great match for little Michael."

The tip of Beth's pencil broke. "*Michael*?"

"That's what his foster parents have been calling him. They say the angels must have been watching over him. The name suits him, too. He *is* a beautiful baby, Beth."

"His name is Michael…"

"Well, yes…" Cheryl faltered. "For now. But you know you'll get to decide his legal name of course."

Beth laughed. "No, it's perfect. Just perfect." She promised to call Cheryl back tomorrow after she had a chance to talk with Eric, and replaced the phone and returned to the table. She sat motionless, afraid any hint of movement might interrupt the dream. Her eyes scanned the pencil scribbles she'd made, the proof they had found Michael. *Her* Michael. The barren winter was over and glorious spring was sweeping in.

Her gaze shifted to the disaster on the floor and

she laughed. Then all at once she found herself crying, and she was grateful for the solitude, for this beautiful messy moment, as she sat covered in raw egg and tears.

She finished cleaning the floor, washed her hands, put away the perishables, and then made her way to the bathroom to clean up the rest of herself, her thoughts bouncing like a ping-pong ball, from pure elation to horror. She had a son! How could someone do such a thing? A baby boy. Did darkness have no bounds? What a wretched place to live. And yet the whole world seemed to be spinning for joy.

She hunched over the sink and rinsed the tacky substance from her forehead, struck with a new thought. Eric. He didn't know. She got to be the one to tell him. This was her news to share.

For years, she'd fantasized about how she'd tell Eric he was to be a daddy. She'd pictured sharing the news over a candlelight dinner or handing him a white box with a blue or pink satin bow containing baby booties or tucking a little note beneath his coffee cup. Or making love and whispering it afterwards as she lay in his arms.

She rubbed her head with a towel, a fresh idea sprouting. She scrunched up her hair, powdered her face, and found her purse. If she left now she'd have enough time to set her plan into motion.

She burst out the front door and nearly barreled into a man clad in a gray shirt with *Tony* inscribed on the lapel. She took a step backward and he apologized. "I'm here for the dishwasher," he said.

She looked past him and stared vaguely at the Sears truck parked beside her Camry.

"Mrs. Dilinger? I'm here to fix your dishwasher."

She turned to lock the door behind her. "Ah, no. Not now."

He consulted his clipboard. "Didn't you call somebody—"

"Yes, but I don't need you now." She brushed past him and hollered over her shoulder, "You're late, but that's OK."

"So… it's working, then?"

"No. Everything comes out caked in grime."

"Do you want to reschedule?"

She opened the car door. "Yeah. Sure. Whatever."

"For when?"

Time was ticking. *Whenever.*

"Monday?"

"Fine. Wait. No. Not Monday. Monday's no good." She climbed into the car, turned the engine, and hollered at him from her rolled down window. "I may have a baby by Monday!"

∂∽⬥

Hours later, the sound of Eric's car rolling into the garage cued Beth to hit the lights and race to the living room. She plopped onto the couch and held her breath. The back door squeaked open and shut.

"I'm home," he called.

She heard two identical thuds of his shoes hitting the floor and then the whispered swish of his stocking feet as he maneuvered around the kitchen. The fluorescent lights flashed on. Moments later, a can of pop hissed open.

"Beth? Are you home?"

The floor creaked as he approached, and she felt a rush of nervousness. He stood in the threshold of the living room, flipped on a switch, flooding the area with light. She watched his face, watched how his eyebrows knit together in bewilderment.

As if in slow motion, he set his Diet Coke on the end table and stared at the ceiling, mouth open. His hand reached up, like a child grasping for falling snow, and his fingers brushed across the ribbons dangling from the multitude of baby blue balloons that clung to the ceiling like bubbles.

"Beth?"

Maybe she'd gone too far. Even she could see that this whole scene veered into the ridiculous. But the years of waiting begged for this moment of absurdity because this was how she felt inside: light as air and bursting at the seams and liable to float away. She stood and retrieved the one silver balloon amidst the blue spheres.

"It's a boy," he read the balloon. His eyes flashed to hers. "Beth?"

She placed her hands on his chest and looked up at him. "It's a boy."

He stared at her, and she saw the struggle in his eyes, of wanting to believe, but wanting to be sure.

"They found our Michael," she said.

Eric released the balloon and it drifted back to its flock as he grabbed her hands. They sank to the floor, beneath the canopy of blue, as she spoke the words she'd imagined saying a thousand times. "You're going to be a daddy."

They celebrated by ordering in Pad Thai and opening a bottle of Zinfandel, then clambered down to the basement and hauled up the crib Beth had bought on clearance a year ago. She'd passed the thing countless times on her way to do laundry, wistfully running her hand across the white railing each time. Today, finally, they were setting it up. It took nearly an hour to assemble it, but after she secured the fitted sheet—also on clearance—and fluffed the classic *Beatrix Potter* bedding, she stood back to admire their accomplishment. Picture perfect.

She sank onto the circular area rug in the center of the room, wanting to linger in the glow of the pale, yellow walls. The hard wood floor shimmered around her like glass. "I wonder what he'll look like," she said again.

Eric joined her on the wooly island. "He might be bald."

"So cute."

"His ears might stick out."

"Mmm. I love that."

"He probably doesn't have any teeth."

"Hopefully not."

"Bald, protruding ears, and missing teeth. I'll remind you that you like these traits in about thirty years."

She pulled out a crocheted afghan from the bottom shelf of the changing table and curled up on her side. Eric lay beside her, and she tucked herself into the nook of his body and they murmured and dozed like kittens.

☙❧

The following night, Beth feared her family would see right through her before she had a chance to utter a word. The simple gesture of inviting Gretchen and her parents over for an impromptu supper might have already given her away. Yet she relaxed when

Gretchen, Dave and the kids burst into the house. Their chaos buried any possible suspicion.

Gretchen carried Evan into the kitchen at arm's length, announced that he was stinky, handed him off to their mother, and rustled through the cabinet under Beth's sink for a plastic bag.

"Must have been the peas," she declared after changing him in the other room and disposing his soiled diaper in the garage trashcan. She handed him back to her mother and disappeared to the family room, no doubt to search the diaper bag for a clean romper.

Beth pulled out a package of strawberries from the refrigerator as her mother danced Evan around the room and sang that *he* was the little sweet pea. Beth smiled to herself as she rinsed off the strawberries, vaguely wondering if her mother was making up the song on the spot or if it stemmed from her repertoire of childhood favorites.

Soon there would be two little sweet peas. Two peas in a pod, she hoped. Her family surrounded her, unaware that she held the most delicious secret, cupped in her hands like a butterfly, and soon the moment would come to release it, to let it unfurl and flutter around the room to everyone's wonder.

Beth retrieved a cutting board and began decapitating the berries' green tops. Eric sidled up to her and stole a strawberry. She swatted his hand. "Go away. I've got work to do."

He lifted his eyebrows conspiratorially and planted a kiss on the back of her neck before strolling out of the kitchen. The singing stopped. Beth glanced over her shoulder at her mother, now motionless, and spied a glimmer of suspicion and joy in her eyes. Beth controlled a smile and turned back to the strawberries.

She *knew*. Meek and mild on the outside, her mother could sniff out truth like a bloodhound on a fox.

From the family room, Lily shrieked. Beth heard her sister beg Grandpa to stop tickling since she hadn't packed an extra change of clothes for Lily. Gretchen came in to the kitchen, oblivious to the shift in the room, the electric charge that hung between Beth and her mother. Gretchen thumped her foiled covered casserole dish. "Are we going to eat soon, or should I put this in the oven?"

Beth regarded the dish absently, still conscious of her mother's scrutiny. Last night as she lay in bed not sleeping, she'd envisioned revealing the news while they ate, like a dinner course. Gretchen huffed. Maybe that was asking too much.

"Hello, Beth? Should I stick this in the oven or what?"

Beth glanced at her mother, already beaming, and then at her sister who wasn't nursing at the moment. Her eyes sought Eric's. From across the room she caught his gaze and silently asked the question. He shrugged, indicating it was up to her. Evan wailed. Lily screamed in delight. Gretchen gave the casserole dish a little shove and muttered something about cold food. Beth wiped her hands on a towel, the serenity of the yellow nursery calling to her. "Before we eat, Eric and I wanted to show you all something."

Gretchen crossed her arms. "So *show* us already."

Beth started for the hall and everyone followed. Her father asked if they'd finally re-caulked the tub.

"No," Beth said. She led the way down the hall to the closed nursery door, her family's footsteps behind her like an army of unruly soldiers. She paused, her hand on the doorknob. "It's in here."

She nudged open the door and stepped aside and watched as her family entered the room as if it were a sanctuary. Gretchen tentatively slid her hand along the crib rail. Her mother fingered the plush lamb perched on the changing table. Her father stood gaping.

"It's all ready," Lily broke in matter-of-factly. "So where's the baby?"

Gretchen turned to her, her eyes bright green circles. "Beth?" she whispered, as if a baby already lay sleeping in the crib.

From behind Gretchen, the flock of balloons tethered behind the rocking chair quivered with excitement, a congregation of baby blue heads wordlessly nodding *yes, yes.*

Beth grinned at her niece and then regarded the rest of her family. "It's finally happening."

The silence swelled, as expectant as the hushed moment between the end of a symphony and the outburst of applause. And then the room erupted. Gretchen screamed, passed an equally shrieking Evan to Dave, and swooped in on Beth like a giant, crazed bird. Their mother's arms encircled both of them, and as Beth inhaled the sweet apple scent of her mother, she felt as if her feet were lifting off the ground, as if she were hovering someplace between heaven and earth, held up by her family's love.

By the time they sat down to eat, the chicken was overcooked and the potato casserole tepid, but no one seemed to notice. Beth hardly ate two bites during dinner as she unfolded the details of getting *the call* and relayed how, technically, the checkout girl at the Dollar Store ended up being the first to know since she asked what in the world Beth was going to do with all of those balloons and Beth couldn't hold herself back.

When Lily and Tyler had finished eating and escaped to the nursery to play, she quietly divulged the other details concerning Michael. They sat in stunned silence for a moment, absorbing. Grieving. Her mother wiped her eyes and reached out to clutch Beth's hand over the oak tabletop and prayed, her quiet, earnest words like gentle drops of rain. Then Eric made a pot of coffee and Gretchen sliced the pie.

"I'm taking you *shopping*," Gretchen promised when everyone was settled with a plate of apple pie and ice cream. "Penney's is having a sale right now, and we'll stock you up. You know I'd let you borrow our boy clothes if Evan wasn't using them, but I'll throw you a shower in a month. Michael will get lots of clothes then."

Beth's grin felt as if it couldn't be stretched any further. Her shower. Finally.

8

The house was small, smaller than Amber remembered. A porch with white pillars protruded from the front of the bungalow, the sloped roof covering it like the brim of a hat. A swing hung down one side of the porch and a lilac bush, although not in bloom, sprawled on the other side. Amber instantly smelled the floral perfume as if it were May.

She sat in her car and stared at the house, her memory coming into focus. It was like seeing a picture from a storybook she hadn't read in ages but used to know by heart. Maybe she should leave this scene where it belonged—in her memory. She felt the urge to floor it and squeal away, but curiosity gnawed almost as much as hunger. It was only a dinner, she told herself. Even if her mother's accusations were right, and Grandma's buddying up to her was only an attempt to twist the knife and irritate Margaret, so be it. Grandma Ginny had tried to reconnect with Margaret plenty of times over the years, and Amber couldn't count the times her mother slammed down the phone or tore up birthday cards. When was the last time the two women had seen each other, anyway? Maybe not since her seventh birthday, when Ginny showed up, unannounced, gift in hand.

Amber remembered the flood of relief she'd felt upon seeing her grandma's face. Finally, she'd thought, finally Grandma could tell her what she had done wrong to make her mother so angry, to make her mother pack up their things and leave late one night. She recalled how she raced toward the door, only to be intercepted by Margaret.

"Just let me talk to her, Margaret," Grandma had said. "That's all I want. I just want to explain things. This isn't fair to her. She's too little to understand."

But her mother's grip on Amber's wrist tightened. She'd tried to sneak through her mother's legs to hug Grandma, but Margaret swung her around, smacked her backside, and ordered her to her room.

And that was the last time she saw Grandma.

Until today.

She flipped down her visor mirror and finger-combed her wind-tossed blonde hair. Then, looping the straps of her canvas bag over her shoulder, she stepped out of the car. A canopy of branches rustled overhead in the breeze, the shiny green leaves waving her in like a choir of children's hands. She started up the short, winding cement path to the porch as if stepping into a dream.

As she reached the top of the porch, the door opened and a woman stepped out. She wore navy cropped pants and a white polo shirt. The screen door banged shut. A hand flew to the woman's mouth. "Amber?"

Amber stood, paralyzed.

The woman took a tentative step closer. "Can that really be you?"

Amber nodded. Had the woman really expected her to show up in knee-highs and pigtails?

The woman crossed the porch and stood before her, her hands clutching her chest. "I know I shouldn't be surprised to see that you're all grown up, but I can't believe...it's hard to believe..." And then all of a sudden the woman's arms enfolded her. Amber's nose rested in a nest of hair that smelled of Aqua Net, her arms awkwardly trapped at her sides. After a moment, the woman released her but held her by the shoulders. "Let me look at you."

Amber took a step backward, freeing herself, and studied this woman as well. She'd expected her to look older, with gray Orphan Annie curls and orthopedic shoes. But this woman didn't look beyond her fifties, with stylish hair and Nikes.

"Amber. You're beautiful."

Heat crept into Amber's face. She glanced at the maple tree towering from the center of the meticulous front lawn. "Thanks," she said finally.

"Well, come on inside. Your grandpa will want to see you."

The floorboards creaked a hauntingly familiar tune as they crossed the porch and entered a tidy, yellow kitchen. The scents of citrus and dish soap and some kind of roasted meat greeted Amber, rousing the depths of her memory, instantly confirming what she'd begun to doubt in recent years: her childhood was rooted to this place. She belonged to this house somehow. She remembered now.

Ginny led her through the kitchen into the living room and addressed a figure hidden behind a newspaper. "Harold, look at your granddaughter. Hasn't she grown?"

The paper rumpled down, and the man behind it offered a thin smile. "Hello, Amber. Nice to see you again."

Amber echoed the greeting and then glimpsed his brown suede slippers. She'd paraded around this house in those slippers, or ones just like them, a lifetime ago. The front pocket on the man's shirt bulged slightly and she instantly knew a handkerchief lay tucked inside, a sturdy, stained bandana.

"Glad you could come for supper," Harold said and snapped the paper back in place.

Ginny scowled. "Well, *he* hasn't changed much over the years. Come on, Amber. Let me give you the grand tour; see if anything looks familiar to you."

Amber followed Ginny through the living room to a short hallway. Ginny stopped at an open door. "Our bedroom," she said, fanning out her arm.

Amber peeked in at the tightly made bed, the simple oak furniture, the gleaming windows, and nodded mutely. Ginny pointed out the bathroom in the middle of the hall and then stopped at a doorway on the opposite end of the hall. "And the spare room, of course. Yours and your mother's, if you remember."

Amber stepped over the threshold, and a vault sprang open in her mind. Fragmented memories spilled out and floated around the room like dandelion whispers, teasing her one after another. She walked to one of the walls and touched the gold brocade velvety wallpaper, recalling how she'd pet this wall, like a kitten, as she fell asleep.

"You remember this funny wallpaper?" Ginny asked. "It's been up forever. Your mother picked it out when she was a little girl. I really should have replaced it years ago."

"I'm glad you didn't," Amber said instinctively.

Ginny's eyes brightened. "So you do remember this room."

"I slept on a mat. Right here. Next to Mom's bed." She stood in the spot where she was certain it used to lay. "We kept it under the bed during the day and pulled it out at night."

"Yes, that's right. And this little desk was here," Ginny said and drummed her fingers over the top of it. "You used to arrange your toys on it—"

"Some kind of circus set, with plastic animals and clowns and people." She had loved that thing. Up until this second she'd forgotten all about it.

Ginny let out a laugh. "Yes. I gave that to you for one of your birthdays. Or maybe it was Christmas."

Amber could almost see the assortment sitting there: the big top, the colorful clowns, the man with the ice cream cart, the perfect plastic families. What had happened to all of those smiling figurines? Where were they now? Stashed in the attic? She ran her hand across the desk, yearning to linger in this room, wanting to capture and ponder all the bits of memories floating around this house. She glanced at the closet. Spellbound, she walked over and opened the door.

Exactly how she remembered it, only smaller. Oak floor and blue walls. Men's clothing hung down from a wooden pole, trousers draped neatly over wooden hangers, a collection of cotton shirts beside them. She tugged the string and the bare bulb filled the space with light, illuminating the sky blue walls. Her haven. Her secret place. Her shelter in the midst of the madness. One time she'd even taped white paper clouds along the walls, here in her perpetual spring. She'd been hiding in this closet the day they left, the day Margaret yanked her out by the arm and told her to empty her dresser drawers into a suitcase so they could move into a trailer with ugly, panel-lined closets.

"It's just a closet," her grandmother chuckled from behind.

Amber spun around and felt her face flush.

Ginny eyed her quizzically.

"Everything looks smaller than I remember," Amber said. She meandered to the window and ran her finger across the sill.

"Well," Ginny said after a moment, "I hope you're hungry." She led the way back to the kitchen, slid on mitts, and pulled out a roast from the oven.

Amber watched, hit with the image of herself standing on a stepstool, her grandmother's arms around her like a shawl, stirring the contents of a black pot. She took in the room. A fussy wallpaper border encased the room. A small shelf of cookbooks sat below a wooden cuckoo clock with white hands and Roman numerals. She couldn't see it, but she'd bet her last dollar a red bird waited behind the tiny door.

With the tip of her knife, Ginny pointed to the silverware drawer. "Would you mind setting the table?"

Amber relaxed as she busied herself with the task. She loosened three napkins from the wire rack on the table, folded them into triangles, and set forks on top of them.

"Your mother mentioned that you were in college this past year," Ginny said, not looking up from her slicing.

Amber's stomach knotted as she dealt spoons around the table. "Yeah. University of Madison."

"Good for you. What are you studying?"

She returned to the drawer for knives. "Art education."

Ginny looked up from her task. "So you're an artist?"

Amber shrugged. "Sort of. I try to be anyway."

"What's your favorite medium?"

"I like painting." She loved it actually, relished the endless possibilities her oil paints promised, the first soft sound of a brushstroke on a white, waiting canvas, the way the colors mingled and bled and layered upon each other. Made little difference now.

"You'll have to show me your work sometime. I'm no artist, but I certainly do appreciate it. A few summers ago my friend Lizzie and I met up in D.C. and spent hours wandering around the National Art Gallery. Do you remember Lizzie? Probably not. How was your first year of school? Good, I hope?"

Amber stiffened. Had she really thought this visit would be question free? "It was all right."

Ginny directed her to the cabinet holding the plates. "When do classes start up again?"

Amber opened the cupboard and wanted to crawl inside. Apparently, her mother had failed to brag about her dropout of a daughter. She carried three plates to the table. "I'm not going back."

Ginny stopped slicing. "You're not? Why not?"

"It just didn't work out."

The tick of the clock sliced through the silence. "I'm sorry to hear that," Ginny said at last. "You seem like you'd do real well in college."

She *had* done well. Once she gave up the party scene. She could have graduated; she knew she could have.

"You know you're the first one in our family to make it to college. That's an accomplishment in itself. You're young. You can always go back."

Amber straightened one of the butter knives alongside a plate. College was nothing more than a pipedream. Like Grandma said, no one in her family had ever gone. Why should she be any different? "I'm working at a restaurant now," she said too brightly.

Ginny placed the platter of meat on the table. "Is that so?"

"Yeah, it's a great place to work," she lied.

Ginny called in Harold and motioned Amber to take a seat. Harold shuffled in, coughed thickly, and propped his elbows on the table. Amber reached for her water, her fingers just touching the cool glass when her grandmother's voice startled her. Amber glanced up.

Her grandmother's eyes were closed. "Thank You, Lord, for the food and the weather and the blessing of having Amber with us."

Amber stiffened, her hand not moving from its spot by the glass. Her mother was right about one thing. Grandma had turned into a holy roller.

Ginny said amen, Harold grunted, and Amber took a drink. Then Ginny passed dish after dish— mashed potatoes, dilled carrots, roast beef, garden salad—and Amber in turn passed to Harold. The food was worth the trip, worth the questions even, and Amber contently let her grandmother chatter on about the neighborhood and her church and her garden. Amber ate, nodded, helped herself to seconds, nodded, and ate some more.

Harold ate silently and efficiently. He wiped his mouth across his napkin and scraped back his chair. "Good meal." Three long strides and he was gone.

Ginny sighed. "As you can see, I just can't get your grandpa to shut up." When they finished, she began to scrap and stack the dishes. Then she clicked on a radio, filled the sink, and tossed Amber a clean flour-sack towel. "I'll wash. You dry."

As Amber wiped down silverware, the radio droned in the corner. An oscillating fan patiently swept across the room, ruffling their hair and the curtains at the window.

Amber stacked the clean silverware in the drawer, surreptitiously studying the woman at the sink and wondering if her mother's horror stories were fabricated. The small, white scar that ran across her mother's arm flashed to her mind. No, she knew they were true, at least some of them. She remembered trembling under the kitchen table in this room, a lifetime ago, as a plate shattered against the wall. Whether her mother or grandmother had thrown it, she couldn't recall, but in spite of the warmth and light the kitchen emitted right now, fifteen years ago, hostility reigned in this house.

A red bird popped out from the clock on the wall. Amber dried the last dish, taking the cuckoo as her cue to leave. She draped the towel over the oven handle and reached for her bag next to the table. "Thanks for dinner. I should get going…"

Ginny spun around from where she was wiping down the counter, her eyes filled with alarm. "No! Not yet. You can't go yet. I have peach crisp in the oven." Her eyes flashed to the window then back at Amber. "And there are things I need to say."

Amber set down her bag.

Ginny squeezed out the dishcloth, hung it over the faucet, and drained the sink. "Why don't you go on out and have a swing, and I'll be there in just a minute. *Family Feud* is on so Harold won't be budging."

Amber went out to the porch and looked over the row of modest houses that lined the street like loaves in a bakery. She turned to the green swing suspended by thick chains, sat, and pushed off. The chains creaked a familiar melody and all at once, she was five-years-old. Closing her eyes, she leaned her head against the back of the swing and felt a strange rush of... what was it? Contentment? Her mother had warned her about Ginny, not only last night on the phone but for as long as Amber could remember. And for what? In case the woman might feed her to death? Hug her too hard?

Ginny appeared with a wooden tray and slid it onto a small table beside the rocking chair. Amber reached for a glass of what she presumed to be lemonade, took a sip, and blinked. Ginny broke into a smile. "The real stuff."

Amber held the glass up to the sun. "You mean from real lemons?"

"Real lemons. I can't stand the powdered stuff and don't even care for the concentrate anymore. Once you've had the real thing you can never go back."

Amber indulged in another sip, the citrus bursting in her mouth like sunlight. "I could drink this all day, every day."

"Then you'll have to come back."

Amber shifted her gaze. Ginny handed her a plate of peach crisp then took up her own and leaned back in her rocker. Amber pierced the golden crust with her fork and took a bite of the warm cinnamon-speckled dessert.

"I'm not too proud to try to win you over with my cooking. How do you think I snagged Harold? I swear that man married me for my chicken and dumplings."

"I remember your chicken and dumplings."

"You do? I'll have to make that for you next time. Your mother must have made it at some point. I know

I taught her how."

"Mom doesn't cook. She does drive-thrus."

Ginny chuckled. They ate their desserts in silence for a moment. Ginny set her plate on the tray, her gaze shifting. She focused on something across the street. "I want you to know I tried. I tried to see you, many times."

Amber fiddled with her bracelet. "I got all of your cards."

Ginny looked at her, gave a little nod then returned her focus to the street. "I can't really blame your mother. I certainly didn't make things easy for her. Not that she ever made things easy for me. But I should never have kicked her out. I was just so angry I couldn't see straight. Sixteen is so young—too young—and when she told us she was pregnant, I was so shocked. I...I shouldn't have forced her out." Ginny sniffed and squeezed her hands together. "After you were born, when she came back home, she had no idea how to care for a baby. I took over, too much, but what else was I supposed to do? She needed to graduate high school."

Ginny turned to her and smiled. "And, oh, how I loved taking care of you. Every minute of it. After all the fighting with Margaret, all of a sudden, there you were. This beautiful newborn for me to love, to cuddle, and dress up. A brand new perfect little person who needed me." Her features darkened, her smile fell. "But Margaret needed me, too. Maybe more so. And I failed her."

Amber watched a boy across the street wheel a lawn mower out of his garage.

"You need to know that you're not responsible for our mess," Ginny said after a moment. "I don't know what she's told you, but none of this tension between me and your mother is your fault. You didn't do anything to cause all of this."

Except for being born. Amber watched the boy yank the start cord, and the machine rumbled to life.

"I would love nothing more than to reconnect with both of you," Ginny went on, "but she wants nothing to do with me."

The earnestness in Ginny's clear blue eyes struck Amber as sincere. She dropped her gaze and studied her toes peeking out over the top of her sandals. The power had shifted. No longer was she a pawn in her mother's grasp, a desired object of the enemy to be dangled and snatched away at her mother's whim. This visit proved it. Now she could make up her own mind about Grandma, about everything. "Don't hold your breath for Mom to come around."

"Heaven knows I've tried."

Amber shrugged. "Her loss."

Ginny studied her a moment, the look in her eyes pained. She took a drink of lemonade, set the glass back on the table, and continued rocking.

By the time Amber headed to her car, a Tupperware of leftover peach crisp in hand, the blue sky bled into the rosy hues of twilight. Ginny embraced her before she climbed into her car and for a fleeting moment Amber felt her body relax and surrender. Then she said good-bye and drove away from the house that seemed to glow like a candle in the darkening street. At the stop sign she glanced in her rearview mirror and spotted Ginny, still on the sidewalk, arms folded over her chest, watching.

Did Grandma know she'd merely embraced a memory tonight? And did she mean what she said in her antiquated table prayer?

Thank you for the blessing of having Amber with us tonight...

Blessing. Maybe she used to be a blessing, when her hair trailed behind her in ribbons, when she helped Ginny cook in the kitchen and spent her days creating make-believe lands in painted blue closets, but Ginny had no idea what, who, she'd become. If she knew, her name certainly wouldn't have tainted the prayer. If Grandma knew the truth, there wouldn't have been any welcome embraces at all.

Amber turned on to the highway, her mind wandering to Jeremy. She hadn't allowed herself to dwell on him, but now she did. She remembered his arms around her. Had he been the last person to truly embrace her before tonight? Before Grandma? And that happened nearly a year ago.

She recalled that night with Jeremy in a string of hazy snapshots: his sandy blond hair, his disarming, impish smile. Amidst the mayhem of the house party, he'd wrapped a lock of her hair around his finger as they talked. He claimed there would never be a band as visionary as U2. They both agreed Rancheros on State Street beat Fiesta Fiesta for tacos, hands down. And then...was it minutes later? Hours? He took her by the hand and led her upstairs. She'd followed, willingly. Eagerly. The encounter was quick, but he was charming and sweet, and she was drunk.

The next morning, when she woke in her room, a million jackhammers needling her head, something clicked. She'd worked like a dog to get here, had clawed her way out of her go-nowhere life, had fought for the scholarship, and what was she doing? Did she really want to mess it up now? Like this? The day she left for college she'd vowed not to follow in her mother's footsteps. She was better than her past, and the art scholarship proved it. After Jeremy, after the epiphany, she frequented only a few parties. And she never saw Jeremy again. Or if she had, she hadn't recognized him. She threw herself into her studies and loved it.

Maybe her drive was what blinded her to reality. Maybe that overwhelming desire to alter her destiny, to break free from the trappings of her past, overshadowed any sign her body presented. At first, rationales came effortlessly. Her weight gain? Too much fast food. She'd always been voluptuously plump and didn't most freshmen gain fifteen pounds anyway? Her irregular cycles? Not enough sleep. Too much stress. She'd never cycled like clockwork anyway. Say it and say it and say it until it drowns out any hints of reality. But eventually even she couldn't submerge the truth.

The highway stretched before her like an infinite black line, and she bolstered her defense with thoughts from last semester's biology class: existence, in its most primal state, was nothing more than random chance, cells and tissue haphazardly joining together that resulted in life. Cells to fish to ape to man. So if life was a fluke brought about by happenstance, humans were little more than walking mistakes. After wrapping him in the towel, he went so still and quiet he didn't seem alive anymore. Didn't seem real. And even if he was, unwanted life called for termination. In a clinic or elsewhere. It shouldn't matter. Survival of the fittest.

But even so, her mind roamed to places she'd trained it not to tread. She saw herself in the bathtub, the bottle of peppermint Schnapps on the edge of the tub. She recalled how the pressure in her abdomen intensified, pushed lower, until finally, to her horror and relief, she felt a great release of weight and fluid escape between her legs. A pair of scissors lay inside the top drawer. A green towel hung next to her on the towel bar.

Amber gave her head a shake. Would she fight this image every day for the rest of her life? The weeks hadn't erased the scene burned in her mind. In fact the details seemed to rise to the surface more frequently, more vividly, even as she fought to push them down. She saw him in her mind's eye. A tiny pink body with scrunched up legs and arms. A quivering mouth that made pitiful, mournful sounds, as if he'd been pleading for her to stop. Stop and see him. Call for help. But what could she do? She could hardly grasp what was happening. He shouldn't even exist.

It was as if someone else's hands had wrapped him in the towel, until he was only a silent, limp mass. Someone else ran into the night. Dropped him by the dumpster.

She thought of Grandma's words, how her face sparked to life when she spoke about caring for her as a newborn. *A perfect little person to love on.* His perfect face flashed to her mind again.

What had she done?

She pulled over and shut off the car, tumbled into the ditch, and heaved into the untamed grass. The highway lay empty and dark behind and before her, not a soul around to see her or to hear the wails that suddenly filled the night.

9

By five in the morning, Beth admitted defeat and threw back the covers. Although it was still dark, she convinced herself five was a respectable hour to rise. Farmers did, and since she remembered having at least one dream, she figured she'd captured a couple hours of deep sleep, if not more. She crept to the kitchen, started the coffee, and while it percolated, stood in the doorway of the nursery, her stomach fluttering in anticipation.

Today was the day.

She sipped coffee and rocked in the silent nursery, dawn blazing through the window. Then she refolded blankets and straightened the stack of diapers, petted the plush toys and swept the floor, even though it didn't need it. By the time Eric woke, the coffeepot stood empty.

When she stepped out of the shower and into a sleeveless dress, she noticed Eric tightening the laces on his Nikes.

"Going for a run," he said, making for the door.

"What? You mean now?"

"Just a short one. We won't be late."

"We're leaving at nine. Not nine oh-five. *Nine.*"

"Roger that," he said and left.

She dried her hair, put on makeup, and watched the clock. At eight forty, he returned, smelly and damp. He had the audacity to whistle in the shower while she asked him why he even *owned* a watch. When he didn't answer, she went to her room to change earrings, anger clawing up her throat. Today was supposed to be perfect. Today she was going to be a mother.

Minutes later, she found Eric in the kitchen, inhaling a piece of toast, his hair still damp. Still wearing Nikes. "Aren't you going to change your shoes?"

He shrugged. "No. Why?"

He downed a tumbler of orange juice and grabbed his keys.

As they backed out of the garage Beth thought she might explode. An involuntarily sound slipped out of her, a grunt of sorts, and Eric looked at her, his eyebrows wrinkling in examination. He shifted into park, grabbed her hand, and prayed. Time ceased, her stomach unknotted, and the frost of anger began to thaw. This was the day. This was the day.

On the heels of the amen, he planted a kiss on the ridge of her knuckles. "Let's go get our baby, baby."

Cheryl had arranged for all of them to meet at her office instead of the foster family's home since they were hosting out-of-town guests. Beth and Eric arrived first, ten minutes early.

Cheryl greeted them with a smile and directed them to the overstuffed loveseat they knew so well. Could she get them a cup of coffee? No, she'd had her fill, Beth said. A glass of water maybe? Beth could only shake her head as she kept vigil on the doorway, Eric's hand sheltering her own. She considered apologizing to Cheryl for their curtness, but she couldn't assemble the words to do even that. Besides, Cheryl seemed unruffled. Amused even.

When they heard the main door jingle from down the hall, Cheryl stood. "I'll go see if that's them."

A pool of moisture was growing between her and Eric's palms, but she tightened her grip anyway. She glanced at him, his pale face dotted with perspiration alarming her. "Eric, are you OK?"

He licked his lips. "I don't know. I'm dizzy."

What would she do if he fainted on her? She sprang to the water pitcher sitting on a bookshelf and filled a Dixie cup. "Here. Drink."

He obeyed. She sat next to him and rubbed his back. He handed her the cup and propped his elbows on his knees, dropping his head into his hands.

"Breathe, hon. Just breathe."

"What are we doing?" he murmured.

"What do you mean what are we doing? We're fulfilling our dream. We're becoming *parents*."

"Are we ready?"

"Of course we're ready." She fought the urge to shake him or slap him like they did in movies. What happened to her rock? "Eric. Look at me."

He turned to her, his forehead now marked red from the pressure of his hands.

"You are going to be an amazing daddy. There's no doubt in my mind." She brushed back the hair hanging across his forehead. "You know how I know? Because you're an amazing man. Whatever happens, we're in this together. I'm in your corner, right?"

He gave a slight nod. "I'm in yours," he mumbled.

She squeezed his knee, leaning in until he looked at her, and emphasized each word. "I'm in your corner. No matter what happens, I'll *always* be in your corner." She held his gaze and saw something, a realization, return to his eyes. He straightened and exhaled, his face gaining color.

The voices down the hall grew louder. Like a musician paces herself against a metronome, Beth tried to synchronize her heartbeat to the steady tempo of Cheryl's wall clock. She ran her moist palms down the front of her dress as a quick, strange laugh escaped. Unexpectedly, she thought of her wedding day, of when her sister grasped her elbow just before she glided down the aisle and urged her to drink in the moment. Take her time, be present, and drink in the moment. That's what she wanted to do right now. She didn't want to miss a second.

The voices drew closer, burying the sound of the clock that ticked down the final seconds in a lifetime of waiting.

And then it was as if all her prayers, her struggles, her desires, condensed into one second: She saw him.

Fair skinned and dressed in white, he lay nestled in the arms of a gray-haired woman.

Beth stood and steadied herself against Eric who stood as well. Her knees trembled under the tent of her dress. Eric pressed his hand into hers.

Cheryl said something.

Eric said something back.

Beth didn't speak. Couldn't speak. She only wanted to move toward this creature, inch her way closer to touch him and see if he were real. But like many of her dreams, she couldn't unglue her feet from the floor. He came to her instead, floating in the arms of the gray-haired woman.

"You must be the lucky parents," the woman said.

Beth nodded, not daring to take her eyes off this little cherub before her, lest she wake up and he disappear.

"This is Michael."

Beth looked up into the woman's eyes for the first time. Kind eyes. Loving eyes. Was she really going to hand her this beautiful baby?

As if sensing her question, the woman nodded, smiled, and placed him in the crook of Beth's arm. She stared down at the baby—*her* baby—the sorrow of the last few years melting like snow as his tiny hand encircled her finger, as if to say he'd been expecting her.

Part Two

10

May 2007

Amber opened her eyes, registered that it was morning, and nestled into the single wrought-iron bed, the chocolate-colored walls around her as warm and soothing as a cup of cocoa. Over a decade ago, when Grandma encouraged her to redecorate the spare room and make it her own, she'd chosen warm sepia. It proved to be a good choice. As timeless and versatile as chocolate itself.

For months after she and Grandma peeled off the textured wallpaper, scrubbed and painted these walls, each time she visited, Amber discovered some new little trinket. A braided rug beside the bed. A pewter candleholder on the windowsill. A second-hand nightstand for her to refinish. She hadn't remained in the same apartment or duplex for more than two years in a row, but this room remained her fixed sanctuary. Her home.

Amber propped herself up on her elbows, straining to hear the voices in the kitchen where Grandma and Lizzie apparently sat talking. Thank God for Lizzie. As much as Amber wanted to comfort Grandma while she grieved the death of her husband, she felt like a floundering fish. Lizzie understood better, having lost her John two years ago. The day before Grandpa's funeral, Lizzie had flown in from Boston and planned to stay a couple of weeks.

Harold's death, a week ago, was neither sudden nor utterly tragic, but the house felt altered by his absence. And although the man had spoken only a handful of words to Amber since she'd reunited with Grandma thirteen years ago, not counting the times he'd read bits of the paper out loud, she'd miss him. Miss seeing him putter in the yard. Miss his crooked smile and how he'd pat her back in greeting or good-bye, the closest gesture he knew to a hug. At the funeral last week, Amber sat between her mother and grandma, the tension between them palpable. Afterwards, when Ginny tentatively approached a tearful Margaret, obviously intending to extend comfort, Margaret only turned away and blew her nose.

Amber got out of bed, pulled on a clean pair of jeans and t-shirt, snagged a fleece hanging in the still blue closet, and headed down the hall. As she passed through the living room, she spotted Harold's slippers peeking out from beneath his chair and wondered if she should discreetly move them. How long would Grandma leave them untouched?

"I keep thinking he's just run to the hardware store," Ginny was saying to Lizzie when Amber padded into the kitchen. "Or that he's in the yard and will stomp in at any moment asking what's for dinner. I miss him, I truly do. But I can't deny feeling a sense of freedom."

Lizzie reached across the table and clutched Ginny's hand. "The Lord giveth and the Lord taketh away. Blessed be the name of the Lord."

Amber put the kettle on and rolled her eyes. If Grandma was a religious fanatic, Lizzie was a full-blown cuckoo clock. Albeit a lovable one.

Amber set the basket of tea on the table, admiring the ruby ring protruding from Lizzie's hand that covered Ginny's. Once Grandma had mentioned that Lizzie had money. Old money, from parents born and bred in the Deep South. If she got talking fast enough, Lizzie slipped into an entertaining Southern belle accent.

Lizzie smiled up at Amber and blinked a good morning. Neither she nor Ginny were dressed. Grandma wore her flannel nightshirt and pants, Lizzie a velour leopard print robe. "You know what I'm thinking," Lizzie said, looking at Amber. "I'm thinking we all could use a change in scenery. Let's get out of here. Let's spend the day in Elkin."

Amber flipped thru the selection of teabags and pulled out an Earl Grey. "I just got here late last night."

"You're staying the night though, right, dearie?" Lizzie said. "Elkin's not even an hour's drive. Just think of it. Fresh air, darling shops, and I'll treat you to gelato. What could better?"

Amber looked to her grandma who was staring out the window at the budding maple tree.

"Maybe Margaret would want to join us," Ginny said. "I think I'll give her a call."

The teakettle whistled. Amber tore open the Earl Grey and dropped the tea pouch into a cup and saturated it with boiling water. She set it before Ginny and gave her shoulder a little squeeze.

Ginny looked up at her, offered a weak smile, and then pushed back her chair and went to the phone. A half-minute later she returned to the table, clutched her mug, and vacantly watched two squirrels terrorizing the yard.

Lizzie exchanged a glance with Amber. "Who wants pancakes?" she said, tightening the sash on her robe.

Amber set the table as Lizzie clicked on the radio and whisked batter, now and then singing the lyrics to whatever song played. Within minutes, Lizzie set a plate-sized pancake in front of Ginny and then one before Amber. She hacked off a chunk of butter for each of them, and doused both with syrup. "Bon appétit."

The pancake melted in Amber's mouth, yet Ginny took only a few kid-sized bites before pushing her plate away. "I don't know what's to become of her. She may never step foot in this house again now that Harold's gone..." Her voice caught, and she buried her face in her hands.

"Come on," Lizzie said, rubbing Ginny's shoulders. "Let's get you out of here for the day."

Amber sensed the wisdom in Lizzie's appeal. "Yeah, Grandma, it'll be fun."

They arrived in Elkin in Lizzie's rented red convertible—just in case they needed a joyride—wind-tossed and awake. They strolled up and down the quaint streets, popped in and out of boutique shops, and lingered in art galleries with a handful of other weekend tourists. Amber watched the gallery owners—the brave lucky people who were living out her dream— with alternating shots of jealously and admiration. She fell in love with a small watercolor of the marina in Elkin, and Lizzie insisted on buying it for her. "To always remember our day together," she said and whisked it up to the cashier before Amber could argue.

They feasted on chicken salads for dinner, and then Lizzie led the way to a green-and-white awning-covered storefront. Heaps of gelato sat like whipped clouds behind a glass counter. Amber took one bite and deemed the trip worth it. With gelato cups in hand, they found an empty park bench next to a fountain that Lizzie said sprang to life in summer.

"Wouldn't it be fun to rent one of those little cabins by the lake?" Lizzie said, peering toward the harbor. "Such a pretty little town. John and I once spent an anniversary here at a lovely bed-and-breakfast at the top of the hill..." She fell quiet and took a bite of gelato.

Ginny commiserated with a smile.

After a while Lizzie turned to Amber. "So, tell me about this Vince of yours."

"What do you want to know?"

"Well, from what I saw of him at the funeral I know he's rather dashing. Does he treat you like a queen?"

Amber shook her head at Lizzie's hyperbole. "He makes me laugh. And he can make a mean pot of chili." She instinctively tugged down the sleeve of her sweatshirt, even though the bruise had faded weeks ago.

Lizzie leaned in close. "How long have you two been dating?"

"About six months. He moved in with me at the beginning of September."

Lizzie nodded but something in her eyes receded. Amber heard Ginny sniff through her nose, a quick intake of breath, a soft sound that spoke volumes.

Amber stood and tossed her empty gelato container toward the trashcan. She missed. "Grandma doesn't like him."

Ginny gaped at her. "I didn't say a word."

"You didn't have to."

"I just don't want you to get hurt. Sometimes I wonder if Vince takes *anything* seriously, the way he seems to bounce from job to job. Call me old-fashioned, but I wonder what his intentions are toward you."

Amber snagged her gelato cup from the sidewalk and pitched it into the trash. "Yes, you are old-fashioned. People don't get married like they used to. We're not living in the 1950s anymore. Having a ring around your finger doesn't mean everything, you know."

Ginny stared at the lake. "That's half of our society's problems."

"And the other half is judgmental attitudes. As if marriage is so wonderful. So I'm living with the guy to see how things turn out before I commit to anything. What's so wrong about that?"

"I'm not sure your generation knows the first thing about commitment," Ginny said quietly.

"Well, marriage isn't always what it's cracked up to be either. Marriage can end up being nothing but a lifetime of regret, right, Grandma?"

Ginny stared at her. Clearly, Amber had struck a nerve. Struck it hard.

"I'm sorry," Amber said. "I didn't mean... I'm sorry." Words didn't exist to undo the wound. She needed a cigarette. She turned and headed for the beach.

She plopped down in the sand and let the particles trickle through her open fingers. She watched a man with bare feet and cuffed jeans launch a kite while two little girls bounced and squealed. The kite took a sudden dive, but the man tugged the string until the diamond looped and soared again. The girls clapped their hands and jumped up and down. Amber's throat tightened, as dry as the sand. She couldn't remember if she'd ever flown a kite herself. She didn't think so.

Her cigarette was down to a stub when Ginny's shadow fell over her like a cool cloth. The sun was sinking lower and lower into the lake, a great round creature submerging itself into a shimmer of glass.

"It's been a good day, don't you think?" Grandma said.

Amber squinted up and nodded. It had been a good day, a perfect day until she'd opened her big mouth and ruined it. "Lizzie's crazy ideas pay off sometimes."

Grandma extended her hand. Amber took it and stood, then brushed the sand from her backside.

"She bought a carton of gelato to take home," Ginny said as they walked across the beach.

"Think it'll make it?"

The older woman smiled. "I don't know. I told her to grab a couple of spoons in case it starts to melt. We won't let it go to waste."

Amber linked arms with her grandma as they ascended the steps to Lizzie, her rented red convertible, and a quart of pistachio delight.

๑๛๕

A few days later, when Vince left purple finger marks around her neck, Amber retaliated by kneeing him in the groin. She said she was sorry and begged him to stay, but he packed his things and left that night anyway. She wouldn't mention anything to Grandma. Not for a few weeks anyway.

11

June 2007

Beth stood in the middle of Michael's room, wondering if her latest idea topped the crazy list. Eric seemed to think so. Last night, when she told him her plan, he laughed and accused her of being an over-indulgent parent. She was only being supportive, she'd said. Unless she didn't know her son at all, Michael was going to love this one last birthday present. And if he didn't, too late now. She'd already bought the paint.

She bought enough to cover the three walls of the alcove encasing Michael's desk. The girl at the store insisted she only needed one coat. Beth hoped so. She wanted to be finished by the time Michael came home from Evan's, before supper.

She shimmied the desk away from the wall, stretched out a drop cloth, and starting in the top corner, carefully edged along the ceiling, blotting out the bright green. Posters of Reggie White and Brett Favre covered much of the room, on the walls she'd leave untouched. Before Michael's Packers craze, dinosaurs ruled. As a toddler Michael spent hours sprawled under the dining room table surrounded by crayons and markers, turning out sheet after sheet of triceratops and brontosauruses. Drawing calmed him and served as a conduit to his inner, mostly wordless world.

In fact, he could draw a dinosaur before he could pronounce it, and by the time he turned three, clearly behind Evan's speech progression, Beth took him in to have his hearing tested. The pediatrician reassured her Michael was fine, that some kids preferred to have all the sounds mastered before speaking in sentences. Her son might be one of those kids. A couple weeks later, when she'd hung one of Michael's drawings on the refrigerator and praised him for his rendering of a Dalmatian, he glowered at her. "No, Mama. He's a cow," he'd said as clear as day.

Beth stared, astonished, and then folded him into her arms. From then on, he spoke in complete sentences.

Beth dipped her brush and outlined the window and then the baseboard, recalling how this alcove once housed her rocking chair, eons ago, before the dinosaurs. When the nursery glowed yellow. This was the spot she'd spent hours rocking Michael. Sometimes she'd prop her feet and doze, Michael a sweet, warm loaf on her chest. Her little lump of sweetness who didn't like to sleep. Gretchen was quick to offer her expertise. Michael would sleep through the night if Beth would simply let him cry it out, but Beth didn't want to let him cry it out. She'd waited too long to hold him. And she wasn't about to let her sister or some expert whose name appeared on the cover of a book tell her otherwise.

Infancy was but a blink of an eye, over before she knew it, and while she marveled in Michael's growth, she cried when he took his first independent steps away from her. Eric mistook her tears for happiness. She was happy in part. Happy, but mourning the steady march of time. As he grew from infant to toddler to child to, most recently, teenager, each birthday certainly called for celebration, but also moved her to mourn privately.

Michael's birthdays felt lacking. There was no way around it. No matter how many streamers she hung or how painstakingly she decorated his cake, the day felt wanting because she could not give him what other parents gave their children without conscious thought: the retelling of his birth story.

For Michael's sake, she granted his birth mother the benefit of the doubt. She told him his birth mother desired him to be a part of a family who'd love and take care of him forever. But other than that, what else could she say?

Each year on her son's birthday, Beth woke up with a piercing sadness, pondering the nameless, faceless girl who'd simultaneously committed the unthinkable and given Beth the greatest gift. Each year her thoughts vacillated between compassion and judgment. Did the girl think about him? Did she regret it? Where was she now? How did she live with herself knowing what she'd done? And the most disparaging question of all: How? *How could she?* If Beth lingered too long on these unanswerable questions, she felt herself spiral downward into some dark unreachable place.

Beth finished edging the alcove and switched to a roller brush. She dredged it in the paint tray and swiped it across the wall, recalling Michael's fifth birthday. Since Michael and Evan were only weeks apart, she and Gretchen often took turns hosting joint parties. Messing and cleaning up one house proved to be easier, and the boys loved it. One big cake and a gaggle of friends.

After the guests had gone home and the kitchen lay in ruins on this particular birthday, Evan snuggled into Gretchen's lap, begging her to tell him the story about the day he *got born*. Gretchen detailed the great event, described when her water broke while she was cooking spaghetti. How she had to call Daddy out of an important business meeting to take her to the hospital. How Aunt Beth watched and took pictures.

Evan giggled, clearly pleased that he'd been the center of the hullabaloo, and then Beth felt Michael's warm hand on her knee. He looked at her with those earnest, blue eyes and said, "Tell me about when I got born, Mama."

Gretchen looked at her and froze, her eyes wide with guilt. Beth set Michael in her lap, weaved her fingers through his hair that was softer than anything, and reminded him how he grew in his birth mom's tummy and God saw that he was to be a Dilinger, so he put them together as a family on the day they adopted him.

Michael's eyes narrowed in contemplation. After a moment he turned to her. "So I wasn't borned?"

Her heart snapped in two. Of course he was born, she reassured. Everyone was born. She just wasn't there to see it. But his birth mom was. And God. And the angels. God and the angels and baby Michael and his birth mom, who not only gave him life, but gave him his beautiful eyes and his strong, fast legs.

He seemed to absorb this until Evan pulled him off her lap and recruited him to help dig out worms from Gretchen's flowerbeds.

Gretchen apologized profusely, but for what? For giving Evan what all children should have in a perfect world? The wonderful story of their birth? Michael's adoption day rivaled his birthday in festivities, a day brimming with happy memories and sharp details, details they shared enthusiastically with him, year after year.

Beth moved on to the second wall, thankful for Evan, her trouble-seeking nephew, thankful Michael had a cousin-brother. The boys stuck together and complemented each other like peanut butter and jelly, as she and Gretchen affectionately dubbed them. Michael's thoughtful contemplativeness balanced out Evan's reckless playfulness, and vice versa. Sometimes Michael plus Evan equaled disaster. Like the time they decided Murray needed a haircut.

Gretchen nearly burst a blood vessel when the St. Bernard trotted into the kitchen one warm summer evening as they chatted around the table, wrongly assuming the boys were running through the sprinkler in the backyard. Gretchen had gasped. Beth turned and looked at the creature. Someone had cleared a path clear down the middle of his white and brown fur, nose to tail. Two someones, more likely.

Gretchen demanded Evan's appearance. Evan sauntered in, smiling in a satisfied way. Michael stood behind him, peering over his shoulder, the truth of the matter already setting into his eyes: they were in for it.

Gretchen demanded to know what had happened to this poor dog, even though it was plain as day that the creature had been accosted by a pair of electric clippers. They still dangled from Evan's grip. She lectured while Beth tipped her head down and swallowed her laughter.

"He was hot," Evan countered when Gretchen ran out of words. "So I gave him a haircut. He feels better now. But don't worry, Mom. We cleaned up. We did it in the bathroom, and Michael held him real still."

The dog stared at Gretchen woefully. When Gretchen paced away, no doubt in search of patience, Beth asked the boys what they thought their punishment should be. They both knew better than this.

Evan gave an exaggerated *how should I know* shrug. Michael wrinkled his brow and looked at her with the solemnity of a soldier. "You can shave our heads, too."

Beth chuckled at the memory. Oh, to have such short-lived problems now. When parenting could be whittled down to quick punishments and cure-all hugs, when she could bank on the wisdom she'd acquired from years of teaching. When Michael rested fully in her and Eric's love and his identity as their son. When simple answers sufficed. That season had faded as surely as the knees in his worn blue jeans and while she loved Michael just as much as ever, even in his reticence, even though he didn't smell as sweet as he used to, she often longed for those little boy days.

"Who has stolen my sweet little boy and replaced him with this ogre?" she'd lamented to Gretchen only days ago.

"Puberty, who do you think?" Gretchen answered immediately.

But she could barely hug the kid anymore, Beth went on to say. He recoiled at the slightest sign of affection from her, and his eyes forever rolled in his head, and she'd suddenly turned into the village idiot.

Her sister looked at her and sighed. "He's thirteen. What do you expect? This is all normal. Welcome to the club. No matter what you do, you are officially and irrevocably stupid. Congratulations."

But with Michael, it wasn't all normal teen stuff.

Like when he came home one day last year from seventh grade and announced he wasn't going back. After careful prodding, Beth finally put together that some idiot kid somehow found out Michael was adopted and taunted him about not having a "real" family. Evan, standing nearby, jumped between them, fists raised. "And this isn't a real punch in the nose." He earned himself a week of suspension. Gretchen tried to hide it of course, but her eyes shined with pride for weeks afterward.

Thank God for Evan. Beth started in on the third wall. Sometimes the world called for a little recklessness. In spite of Evan's quick defense, the words stung Michael, but nothing like this recent blow, a blow she should have seen coming.

She hadn't thought twice about directing Michael to the file cabinet in the basement last month when he mentioned needing a copy of their family tree for a social studies project. She was folding laundry on the couch when he came and stood before her, minutes later, holding out a piece of paper. She glanced up at him, saw the hardness of his eyes, and all at once knew. She knew what he'd found before her fingers brushed the sheet of paper.

Their family trees weren't the only documents lurking in the file marked *Family History*. Like a child, she shut her eyes for a moment, wishing away the moment. She opened them to her son, who stood waiting for an answer.

"It's true, then." He spoke an accusation, not a question.

She prayed for some providential escape. For the phone to ring. For the smoke detector to go off. For the floor to give way. She knew any disruption would only delay the inevitable. Maybe that's what she'd been doing all of these years, but what else was she *to* do? How did you prepare to pierce your child's heart?

She pushed the laundry aside and patted the spot on the couch next to her.

"No," he barked. "I want to know if this is true. I want to know if my birth mother *threw me away.*"

Something like nausea swept over her. "Your birth mother was probably very young and confused and scared…"

"Why didn't you tell me? When I asked about her, why didn't you tell me this? You should have *told* me!"

Eric was more equipped to handle this. Michael would listen to him. But he wouldn't be home for hours. She glanced at the driveway in vain. "Honey, we weren't trying to keep anything from you. We just thought it'd be best tell you when you were older."

"Well now you don't have to, do you?" His voice cracked, confirming the heartbreak beyond the front of anger.

"Michael, I'm so sorry…" She reached for him, but he jerked away, stormed down the hall, and slammed himself in his room.

She peered at the document in her hands, the police report she'd read so many times and knew from memory:

Infant male was retrieved at 4:11 AM on June 3, 1994, from cardboard box next to the dumpster on the property of On the House located at 2631 Jefferson Street, Madison, Wisconsin. Birth mother: Unknown. Birth father: Unknown. Estimated day of birth: June 3, 1994. Infant was wrapped in green towel and appeared to be unharmed. Infant was found to be a Child in Need of Protection and Services and ordered to be placed in the custody of Dane County Social Services.

He knew everything. Every painful detail, every sordid fact spelled out like a rote grocery list. No sitting down with him and explaining gently, no tender words to soften the blow. No dicing the ugly, indigestible truth into manageable pieces.

When Eric came home from work and coaxed Michael out of his room, they flanked him on the couch and reminded him of their love and God's bigger plan. He only sat stone-faced, rage burning in his eyes. Beth sat drowning in her failure. Even her fierce, consuming mother love couldn't ease the sting of rejection he felt.

In the days that followed, Michael talked to Eric but refused even to look at her. That was OK. She could take it. If he needed her to be the scapegoat, if that's what it took for him to work through the hurt and pain of his birth mother's rejection, then that was OK with her. But she missed him. His teenage bouts of surliness and sarcasm aside, she missed him. Missed joking with him. Missed their simple banter as they drove home from school, when he'd recap some middle school antic, and she'd quote one of her kindergarten students just to make him smile.

The walls complete, she hammered the paint can shut and pushed the desk back into the alcove, making sure not to brush up against the walls. She went to her bedroom and dug out the new package of brushes and set of acrylics she'd shoved in the closet then sharpened a half dozen pencils and tied them all together with a piece of blue ribbon she'd found in the junk drawer. She set the bundle on his desk and took a step back to observe her work.

Oh boy, she hoped he liked this. Too late now.

An hour later, as she was frying ground beef for tacos, Michael came home. He dropped his backpack on the floor and helped himself to a handful of corn chips.

"Did you have fun with Evan?"

He nodded, his mouth full. He turned to head to his room.

"Wait!" she called out. "I have to show you something. One last birthday gift."

He turned around, his curiosity clearly piqued. She clicked off the stove and moved the frying pan to the back burner. She led him to his room and pushed open the door dramatically. "Ta da!"

He stepped inside and stared quizzically at the three, whitewashed walls surrounding his desk, three walls that didn't match the remaining bright green of his room. He looked at her and wrinkled his brow.

"It's your canvas."

His cocked his head, still not understanding.

She went to his desk and handed him the bouquet of supplies. "Think of these walls as your giant sketchbook. Draw, paint, sketch, whatever you want. Fill them up and then when you run out of room, we can repaint it and start again."

He took a step closer, his hand outstretched toward a wall.

"But don't touch it yet. It's still a bit tacky."

He spun around to face her, his mouth slightly opened, his eyes clearly processing.

"What do you think? Do you like it?"

She'd struck gold. She could tell from his expression. She'd tuck away this moment forever. File it away in her mind and let it sweeten with time.

He started toward her and once again she marveled at his stature. He'd exceeded her by a good inch and was still shooting up like a tree. "Mom," he said, giving his head a little shake, "this is the *coolest*."

"You're a good artist, Michael. I thought it might be fun for you to sit at your desk and doodle whatever you want."

All of a sudden, he seized her, the swiftness of his motion catching her off guard. It took a second for her brain to register that *he* had hugged *her*. She rubbed his sinewy back, her fingers tracing the shoulder blades that used to stick out like dolphin fins but now seemed proportioned and too, too mature.

He let go of her just as abruptly as he'd grabbed her and ripped open the package of brushes. "I can't wait until it dries."

After dinner that night, while she and Eric puttered in the kitchen, Michael holed himself in his room. In between the songs blaring from his CD player, she heard soft, scratching sounds against his wall.

12

May 2012

Ginny opened the envelope with Lizzie's return address across the top and her heart sank. Lizzie's signature sprawled across the bottom of the note card, as whimsical as ever, the only marking on the stationary. Only that. No note, no greeting, just her name written across a blank field of snow. So this was what it was like to grow old.

For some time now she'd noticed Lizzie seemed off but chocked it up to her eccentricity. Lizzie had always been unconventional. But last week, as they'd chatted on the phone, Lizzie uncharacteristically interrupted her in mid-sentence. "I can't find my purse anywhere. I think the cat stole it."

Ginny had chuckled but wondered now if the accusation had been spoken in earnest. And Lizzie didn't own a cat.

As Ginny maneuvered up the walkway, she sighted the growing assortment of potholes and cracks beneath her feet. She really ought to see about getting the path fixed. But of course repairs cost money and as resourceful and creative as her granddaughter was, she didn't think Amber knew anything about pouring cement. The porch steps creaked in rhythm with her hips as she climbed to the top. The porch needed a little work too, a little lift and tuck of its own.

She decided to fetch her address book and cordless phone right away. For years Amber had insisted she get a cell phone, but for what? "For driving, for one thing," Amber said just last week and then demanded to know what she'd do if she ever slid into a ditch.

"Sit and wait for help like I've done for the past seventy-five years," Ginny had retorted. "I've never slid into the ditch before, and I don't plan to start now. I don't need a cell phone."

That was the problem with young people these days; they always wanted a snap, crackle, pop solution. An easy out. If she ever did slide into a ditch, she had a blanket and flashlight, and if they failed to save her, maybe a ditch was the way the Good Lord intended her to go. Bottom line, she didn't like the idea of people being able to get a hold of you every second of every day no matter where you were, and apart from Amber and Lizzie and her ladies prayer group at church, she wasn't in that high of demand. Certainly not to warrant a seventy-nine bucks a month cell phone plan.

Cordless phone and address book in hand, she returned to the porch and settled in her chair. She adjusted her bifocals and scanned the R section until she found Lizzie's son. She dialed, and after exchanging pleasantries, told him about the blank card she opened today.

He sighed into the phone. "The doctor thinks it's the beginning stages of Alzheimer's. We're beginning to investigate nursing homes. In the meantime we've hired a nurse."

After she told him how very sorry she was and if there was anything she could do to help, please call, they said good-bye. Ginny sat staring at the brilliant late spring greenness of the trees. Fall would come, blazing with color, and then the leaves would fade and wither and disintegrate under her feet.

She shuffled into the kitchen, replaced the phone, tucked away the book, rinsed out the etched crystal pitcher, and filled it with water halfway to make a fresh batch of lemonade. She returned to the porch and squeezed the life from the cheerful fruit, mourning the loss of her friend's mind, mourned her own loss of confidant and mentor. Her keeper of secrets. Her partner in petty crime. The thought of Lizzie—only a decade older than herself—sitting vacantly in some nursing home, staring into space, left her feeling heavy with dread. She hadn't seen Lizzie face to face in over a year, and although she fully intended to keep her plans to fly out to Boston in the fall, she wondered how different their visit would be. Conversation between them always flowed like a brook. What would it be like now? A dog chasing its tail?

Without measuring, she dumped sugar into the pitcher and stirred. She sampled the concoction and trickled in more sugar. Life here on earth was but a house of cards, she mused, and the older she grew the more she longed to fly to her true home. Tomorrow, thankfully, Jackie and the other girls would fill her living room for prayer group. She needed them, needed her small circle of women friends to hold her up, to be her Aaron and Hur who propped up Moses' weary arms, because if she sat and thought too long about Lizzie's demise, Amber's turbulence, and Margaret's animosity, she'd feel as frail and broken as kindling.

ॐ

Amber barreled down the interstate, hoping Grandma wouldn't mind an unannounced visitor. She didn't trust herself to talk on the phone with anybody right now.

A year and a half of her life flushed down the toilet. As if she and Paul had never been together. From the beginning she thought Paul would be different, and to some extent, he had been. He was never violent, and he could hold down a job, and ever since he'd sidled up to her at the bar, she couldn't get her fill of him. That was the problem; she loved him more.

After she moved in with him, she'd occasionally joke about tying the knot, but he dodged the subject like a politician, claiming he wasn't ready. A charming Peter Pan complex, she'd thought. She didn't push commitment; she didn't want to lose him. But at thirty-seven, she wasn't getting any younger. It didn't matter, she'd say. They were together and that's what mattered.

She'd been stupid enough to believe it. Until today. Until the truth broke through her world like a rock shatters a window.

"We've been growing apart for months and you know it," he'd said simply, after mixing a can of tuna fish with mayonnaise and slathering it on bread. He actually served her a tuna-fish sandwich first. Before demolishing her.

No, she *didn't* know, she wanted to say but couldn't get her vocal chords to work. She *didn't* know they had been growing apart. If anything, she thought they'd been growing together, like two trees that lean into each other and almost turn into one.

"Tracie and I have something good going, and I

don't want to mess that up," he said and took a bite.

She looked down at her plate, at the pale, gummy white-bread sandwich because Paul preferred infantile white bread instead of wheat. So she never bought wheat. Only white. Even though she hated it. She stared at her colorless sandwich, two triangles that stared back at her like a pair of albino, jack-o-lantern eyes on a round plate.

"I never meant to hurt you," he went on. "I know you and Tracie are friends, *were* friends, but this thing with her just sort of happened. We didn't plan it." And then he asked, between bites, if she thought she could be out by tomorrow. No need to rush or anything, he'd said, she could finish her lunch before packing. They could part amiably, right? They were adults.

She looked at him, at her poor excuse for a lunch, then stood to her feet and Frisbeed the plate across the kitchen. It smashed into the wall above the sink. Tuna fish slid down the ivory wall. She glared at Paul. "Buy your own disgusting bread!" Then she started throwing things into her truck. She wouldn't wait until tomorrow. She'd be out of his hair tonight.

Amber tightened her grip on the steering wheel and peeked at the speedometer pushing ninety. She slowed down, a sign promising Elkin forty-six miles ahead instantly igniting her craving for gelato. That's what she needed—a big serving of pistachio delight to drown out her sorrows. To save herself from a speeding ticket, she set the cruise control.

Would Paul really call the police on her, she wondered? Like he warned when she threw the last of her belongings into the bed of her pickup and then calmly approached his bike, his precious Harley Davidson, clutching her set of keys in her fist, one key protruding? She looked straight at him before she did it, before she scraped the small silver key across the shiny black chrome of his bike. His jaw dropped in disbelief and then he deluged her with profanities. She only smiled. Good. She'd hurt the thing he loved most.

"No wonder it's over between us," he shouted. "Why I ever hooked up with a broad like you is beyond me. Expect a bill. Expect a call from the cops."

But even as she scrambled into the cab of her truck and threw the vehicle into reverse, she couldn't help watching him, waiting for him to crack his lopsided grin and say it was all a big joke. A big misunderstanding that they could work out. The thing with Tracie was just a fling. But he only turned away and stormed into the duplex, stepped back into his life that now didn't include her.

And what about her life? How did she get on with her life without him? A year and a half together. Gone. Just like that.

Amber approached the exit for the highway leading to Elkin and made a snap decision. Turning up on Grandma's porch, like a ticking time bomb, would only lead to more conflict, and right now she couldn't stomach one of Grandma's lectures, no matter how well intentioned they were.

Flicking on her blinker, she veered off to the right. Maybe something better awaited her in Elkin.

❧❧

A half an hour later, Amber pulled up alongside the shop with the green-and-white awning and scowled at the For Sale sign mocking her from the window. She left the truck running, jumped out, and pressed her face against the window. She peered into the lifeless building and banged on the glass with both fists. Of course it had gone out of business. The stars were set against her tonight.

She heaved herself back into her truck and rambled through town, driving up and down streets flocked with couples and families, until she came to a rinky-dink hotel just on the outskirts of town, one of the few blemishes among the picturesque bed-and-breakfasts and lodges. She booked a room and asked the pimply teenager working the desk if she could borrow the newspaper splayed across the counter. He gathered the loose papers and tapped them together before handing it to her. "Knock yourself out."

On her way to her room she passed a vending machine and treated herself to a bag of candy and a soda, then flopped down on the unyielding bed. She found a pen in the nightstand drawer next to a pristine Gideon Bible and circled anything from the classifieds that seemed remotely interesting. Waitressing jobs were easy come, easy go. She certainly wouldn't cry over leaving the one she had behind. An ad on the top of the second column caught her attention. *Apply in person* it read. Tomorrow. She'd check it out tomorrow. Right now she needed to hunt down some food and drink, something more substantial than a bag of sugar and stronger than a soda.

13

Beth pushed open the door to the downtown pub and scanned the area for Gretchen. The music was loud, the lighting dim, and the decor mirrored that of an old-time saloon, but the place served the best deep-fried Walleye and rough-cut coleslaw for miles around. Spotting her sister, she waved and made her way over to a corner table.

It was later than she usually ate dinner—close to eight—but with both Michael and Eric out of town for the weekend, she'd jumped at Gretchen's invitation to meet up for fish fry, even if Gretchen could only meet late. More than that, Beth had detected an irregular quality to her sister's voice, a suppressed excitement beneath her words. Beth pulled out the slat-back chair and sat across from Gretchen who was grinning like the cat who caught the canary.

"So," Beth said. "What's the news."

Gretchen let out a soft gasp of indignation. "What do you mean? What news?"

"You look like you're going to explode."

"Just because I invited you to dinner doesn't mean I have *news*."

"Fine. There's no news, then." Beth picked up her menu and skimmed the entrees even though she'd already decided on the Friday special.

Gretchen slapped the table with her hands. "OK, fine. So there's news."

Beth lowered the menu and smiled.

Pressing her lips together, Gretchen leaned forward, her eyes shimmering. "I'm going to be a grandmother!"

"What? Really?"

"Sarah's pregnant!"

Beth grabbed her sister's hands. "That's wonderful! Fast, but wonderful!"

"I know. They've only been married four months. Tyler didn't say so outright, but I think this has knocked them for a loop. They're happy but stunned. And trying to figure out where in the world they're going to put a crib in that little shoebox of an apartment of theirs."

"They'll figure it out."

"I mean, Tyler's only twenty-three, and I don't know if he makes enough to support the two of them, let alone the three of them, if Sarah plans on staying home with the baby."

Gretchen's face clouded in worry. "Do you think they're too young? I mean, not that it matters, but do you think they're too young to handle all the responsibility?"

"No," Beth said. "I don't think they're too young. Ovaries can be fickle things." She took a sip of water. "This is a blessing, Gretchen. Be happy for them."

Gretchen's features relaxed. She nodded and sat back. "I am happy for them."

After the waitress set down heaping plates of fish and chips, and after they'd exhausted Gretchen's list of suitable grandbaby names, their attention shifted to the boys' graduation party less than two weeks away. Beth had already ordered the cake and would start on baking and freezing other treats this coming week. The boys had requested a taco bar. Gretchen had promised to provide all the ground meat if Beth agreed to host the whole affair at her house.

"Of course all of this planning is contingent on Evan passing English Comp," Gretchen said irritably. "At least we can count on Michael. I suppose he's counting down the days."

Beth let out a small laugh. "Sometimes I think he'd skip summer all together and go straight to fall if he could. He's so ready to high-tail it to Madison."

The university offered the courses needed to pursue graphic design, but Beth knew Michael's true reasons ran deeper. His birth city held some kind of spell over him. It always had. Last spring, when she and Michael and Eric drove down for college preview day to take a guided campus tour, she teetered between excitement for her son, for this new chapter in his life, and full-fledged terror. So many opportunities. So many temptations. Was he ready for it all? Co-ed dorms. Fallacious professors. Infinite beer.

After exploring campus they traversed down State Street, the white dome of the Capitol building luring them like an oversized moon. They gaped at the marble rotunda and climbed to the observatory deck and back. After stepping outdoors again, they wordlessly set course to their next destination, Michael leading the way. She and Eric trailed a few steps behind, and although she hadn't been able to see Michael's face when he stopped just across the street from the small back lot of the building on the corner of Jefferson and Illinois, she saw the slight droop of his shoulders, as if he were crumpling into himself. He hadn't wanted them near, she sensed, so she gripped Eric's hand to keep her feet planted, to keep herself from swooping in like a mother bird.

"Madison does have a lot to offer in comparison to Elkin," Gretchen said, breaking through Beth's reverie. "He'll love it."

"I hope so."

An eruption of laughter caused her to glance at the bar. A woman with a long blonde ponytail slapped her hands against the bar and cackled again. Beth turned back to Gretchen and dunked a chunk of walleye into her tartar sauce. "He found a summer job. Did I tell you that? He's bussing tables and washing dishes over at Winston Hill, hoping to work his way up to waiting tables. Not his dream gig but it's something."

"Good for Michael. Tell him to light a fire under Evan. Apparently flipping burgers for summer tourists is beneath my child." Gretchen shook her head. "I worry about him. It's like he expects someone will knock on his door one day and hand him a paycheck for strumming his guitar. And presto. He'll be a rock star. You know, for all the times I've urged my clients to use logical consequences with their children, I can't seem to make it work for my own kid, not this one anyway. Dave told him that if he doesn't get his act together and get a job by the end of the week he can forget about us chipping in *anything* for community college. That is, of course, if he manages to pull that elusive D in English Comp."

They finished up and headed for the cashier to pay their bill. Beth wondered, not for the first time, how the boys would fare without each other. What would happen to the comfortable equilibrium of the inseparable pair? Would Michael and Evan ebb and change and lose their dependence on each other? And was that just a necessary part of growing up, of filling out your own skin?

They stepped into the now dark street and strolled a few paces from the pub. Gretchen paused under a streetlight to fumble in her purse and pull out a pack of gum. She handed a stick to Beth and then unwrapped one for herself. "I didn't tell you. Lily's decided to come home for the summer. She's going to teach summer dance."

"Good for her. It'll be fun to have her back home for a few months. Is she still dating what's his name?"

The pub door burst open and the disheveled blonde from the bar stumbled out. She tottered toward Beth and Gretchen a few paces then stopped and eyed them. Instinctively, Beth drew her purse tighter to her side. The woman noticed and let out a snicker before staggering past them. She tripped slightly then steadied herself and continued lurching down the sidewalk until she stopped next to a white pickup truck parked along the street twenty feet away. She extracted something from her pocket—a key apparently—and struggled to fit it in the door.

Beth felt her sister clamp her arm. "She can't drive like that." Gretchen released her grip and turned to follow the woman, but Beth grabbed her by the hand.

"Just leave her alone," Beth whispered. "It's none of our business."

"None of our business? Just look at her!" Gretchen clipped down the sidewalk, the short heels of her pumps clicking rhythmically. "Ma'am, hold on a minute. Can we take you somewhere?"

Beth caught up and lingered behind her sister's shoulder. The woman narrowed her eyes and gave Gretchen the once over. "What for?"

Gretchen smiled, easily sliding into psychologist

role. "Looks like you've had a fun night. And maybe a little too much to drink? I'm parked right over here," she said, motioning to her car a block up the street. "It won't be any trouble for me to take you anywhere you need to go. Or I could call you a cab if you'd like."

The woman only stared at her.

Gretchen touched the woman lightly on the arm, but the woman violently jerked away.

"Let *go* of me!"

Gretchen's tone remained casual, unaffected. They were old friends. "Look, you're not fit to drive. You know that, right?"

The woman looked beyond Gretchen to Beth, and before Beth looked away she recognized something behind the glaze of intoxication, a familiar quality in those bleary, troubled eyes. The woman barked out a vulgarity. Beth took a step backward.

Gretchen held out her hand for the keys. "Come on now. We just don't want to see you get hurt, that's all."

The woman gaped at them. Her eyes narrowed, as if she couldn't believe Gretchen's audacity. For a second Beth expected her to drop her keys in Gretchen's waiting hand. The woman looked from Beth to Gretchen.

Then, without warning, her hands shot up and she shoved Gretchen. Gretchen fell back into Beth, her heel piercing the unprotected, sandaled toes of Beth's right foot. Beth yelped in pain, reeling backward until her head smacked the brick storefront behind her.

As they regained their balance, the woman climbed into the truck.

"You can *not* drive in that condition!" Gretchen shouted.

The truck roared to life and squealed away.

Limping, Beth grabbed her sister's hand. "Are you trying to get us killed? There's nothing we can do. Come on. Let's go." She felt the dampness of blood against her throbbing big toe.

"*Go*? We can't just go. That woman could barely walk. She could *kill* someone like that." Gretchen sprinted to her car, and Beth hobbled after her. "Hurry up and get in. Find your phone and call 9-1-1."

Beth sighed and obeyed. As Gretchen barreled down the street, Beth probed her pockets in search of her phone. Then she delved her hand into the cavity of her purse and felt around.

"*Beth*?"

"I'm trying! I'm trying!"

"I can't make out her license plate. Did you get it?"

"No. Slow down! What are we doing? Just what do you plan to do if you catch up with her anyway?"

Gretchen hooked a left, about thirty seconds behind the pickup. "I don't know. Just find your stupid phone."

Hands shaking, Beth checked the side zipper compartment of her purse as Gretchen turned into a motel parking lot. Beth's hand triumphantly hit something hard and rectangular. "Found it."

Gretchen slowed. "Hang on. I think she's stopping."

The woman parked the truck, fell out, and stumbled toward the lobby doors. "Should I call? What should we do?" Beth whispered, her heart in her throat.

They watched the woman disappear through the hotel doors. Gretchen exhaled. "Pray that she stays put for the night, I guess. I am going to report that pub, though. There are laws about serving to someone who's clearly tanked, and if there aren't, there should be." Gretchen let out a wild laugh. "Well that added an element of excitement to our girls' night out, huh?"

"My toe is killing me."

Gretchen shifted into park and clicked on an overhead light. She winced when she peered down at Beth's foot. "Oh, honey, I'm sorry. Do you think it's broken?"

"No. I can wiggle it. It's just smashed from your pointy little heel."

Gretchen found a napkin in the glove compartment and handed it to Beth. "Let's get you home. You can pick up your car tomorrow."

Her chest still prickling with adrenaline, Beth held the napkin against her toe, feeling like the proverbial little sister. What had just happened? Who was that woman? Who was Gretchen? Who was she, herself? Something gnawed at her, something she didn't like. The whole exchange with the wild-eyed drunk woman triggered some insecurity in her. Here she was, inching toward fifty, and she still wanted to flee from the things of this world she didn't like. Not fight, flee. Not only flee, but pretend they didn't even exist. Like that woman.

Gretchen pulled into Beth's driveway. "You OK?"

"I didn't like what happened tonight," Beth said.

"Wasn't a picnic for me either."

"No, that's not what I mean." She shifted positions to face her sister. "I didn't like who I was back there. You were ready to take on the world and wrestle the keys from that woman. I wanted to slink away and hide. I've never been brave like you."

Gretchen looked at her. "Brave? Or stupid?"

"Brave. Mostly brave. Maybe a little stupid."

Gretchen shrugged. "I get a crazy rush from conflict sometimes. But look, you're brave in other ways. You deal with a classroom of squirrelly five- and six-year-olds day in and day out. I couldn't do that. You were out of your comfort zone, that's all."

"We both were out of our comfort zones. I don't like who I was back there."

Gretchen let out her breath impatiently. "You're being too hard on yourself, as usual."

Beth propped her elbow on the side window and peered out. "Maybe I'm not being hard enough."

"Don't get all cryptic on me. What are you talking about?"

She felt overwhelmed with emotion, with shame and fear and disappointment. She fought to corral her thoughts and pin them down with words. "Sometimes I think my life is too small. I don't like that I was paralyzed with fear when something out of the ordinary happened. Makes me feel sheltered. Ineffective. Like I should be able to handle life's curve balls more effectively, you know?"

"Life's curve balls?"

"You know what I mean."

"OK, fine." Gretchen chuckled. "I'll pray that life throws you more curve balls. So you can handle them. But, boy, are you asking for it."

14

Amber rolled to her side and reached out an arm. No warm body met her expectant fingertips. Remembering, she threw the hotel blankets over her head, hoping to block out yesterday and the arrow of light that streamed through the window and pierced her between the eyes. Apparently, she forgot to pull the drapes last night. She couldn't remember most of last night but did recall flirting with the bartender and then somehow making it back to the hotel. Traces of someone else, a woman's face, attempted to assemble in her mind. Someone she'd wanted to throttle. Tracie? No, it couldn't have been Tracie. Someone at the bar, maybe? She couldn't remember.

Swinging her legs over the bed, she reached for last night's bottle of soda and took a swig of warm carbonation then stood, pulled the drapes, and started the shower. The scalding water needled her skin as she told herself again and again she was better off without Paul.

After dressing and grabbing a doughnut from the meager continental breakfast, she made her way to Winston Hill where she smiled and shined before one of the managers and was offered the job on the spot. She followed him for a quick tour, shook his hand, and then made her way back into town, back to her empty motel room that seemed as dismal as a shelter for unwanted dogs.

In desperation she called Grandma who seemed to be out of sorts herself. Lizzie had Alzheimer's.

"Lizzie? Oh no, not Lizzie."

Her grandmother sighed. "I've noticed she's been off, even from across the country."

Maybe she could bolster Grandma's spirits. "Well maybe this will cheer you up. I left him."

"Paul?"

"Of course, Paul."

Ginny was quiet for a minute. Probably doing cartwheels. "I'm sorry, honey."

Amber grunted. "No, you're not."

"Of course I am. I'm sorry you're hurt."

"Who says I'm hurt? *I* left *him*." Grandma didn't need to know she left because he kicked her out.

Ginny sighed. "OK, then. You're not hurting. So where are you?"

"Elkin."

"*Elkin*?"

"I had a hankering for gelato. I ended up getting a job here waiting tables at this real swanky place. I start tomorrow." Grandma made a sputtering sound, and Amber broke in before the lecture ensued. "I'll explain everything when I come up in a few days."

Hopefully by that time she'd be able to make sense of the whole thing herself.

かくが

With its honey brown floor, sandstone fireplace, and white linen-draped tables, Amber could see why Winston Hill attracted hordes of summer tourists. The lake shimmering behind the generous west windows merited the over-priced food. Without a doubt the nicest place Amber had ever worked. A shiver of anxiety coursed through her, but she calmed herself with the fact that the job was just like any of the greasy spoons and truck stops she'd worked in over the years. Taking orders and serving food of course, but more importantly, filling the role, playing the so-happy-to-see-you game. Even though she swore some people ate out for the sole purpose of venting bottled up frustration on an easy target.

Ernie handed her a white apron and motioned to a curly-haired blonde. "Brenda will help you if you have any questions."

As promised, tips were good. Within a couple of hours Amber had made more in tips than she sometimes made in an entire shift at the diner where she used to work on 51. She tucked another ten into her apron and studied the one-page menu in the after lunch lull. Ernie expected the wait staff to memorize the daily specials, and she'd already tripped over some of the entrée descriptions: *Baked Duck with Wisconsin Brie with local cranberry gastrique and black pepper crème fraîche.* She knew little about what she was offering, but the aromas circling the kitchen left her mouth watering.

"Chef likes to cook with the seasons," Brenda said, suddenly beside her. "Usually the menu's never longer than a page."

Amber took in the perky waitress who looked to be a good fifteen years her junior and suddenly felt old and flabby. "The shorter the menu the better the food." She went back to memorizing.

"Can you give me a hand with these?" Brenda asked a moment later.

Amber glanced up to see Brenda assembling a tray

of pork tenderloin in rhubarb chutney sauce. "I'm stuck with a rehearsal dinner in the banquet room. Can you help me get these out? If you're not busy, I mean?"

Amber set the menu aside and smiled. Better not to make an enemy on her first day.

She filled her tray with entrees and followed Brenda to the banquet room tucked behind the mammoth double fireplace. After doling out the dishes, they returned to the kitchen and began assembling trays of asparagus stuffed chicken in hollandaise sauce. With her full tray over her shoulder, she exited the kitchen and rounded a corner. Too quickly. Suddenly her chest was on fire.

Dishes clattered. Her chest burned. She peeled her soaked blouse away from her skin. Spotted a pair of horrified, blue eyes. She had to get this shirt off. She bit down on her lip to keep from crying out and darted toward the bathroom.

Burning. Burning.

Inside, she yanked open her blouse. A button clinked to the tile floor. She cranked on the faucet and splashed herself with cold water. Brenda entered, wide-eyed. "Are you OK?"

"No, not really."

Brenda ran a terrycloth towel under cold water, rung it out, and handed it to her.

Amber pressed the towel to her chest and exhaled, the fire cooling slightly. "Thanks." She peeled back the cloth to reveal a red mark resembling a splotch of strawberry jam.

Brenda winced. "That looks pretty bad. You might want to see a doctor or something."

"I'll be fine. Some first day. Or last day, I should say."

Brenda leaned against the counter. "Oh, no, don't worry about that. Ernie would never fire you over something like this. Especially with high school graduation this Sunday. The place will be swarming. Poor Michael. He feels horrible."

"Who's Michael?"

"The guy who crashed into you."

She recalled a young, male face jumbled in the mix. "Oh, *him*."

"Yeah, poor guy."

"Don't think I've met him yet. Not officially."

Brenda crossed her arms and leaned into her. "I think he's adorable."

"I think he needs to watch where he's going." She peered at the mark in the mirror again. "Guess I've sealed my reputation here."

"Oh, we're a pretty friendly bunch. We won't hold it against you." Brenda's face lit up. "Hey, I have an idea. Come to my party a week from today. A lot of us will be there and you can meet everyone for real. You know, make a better first impression."

Amber studied the girl. "You know I'm a bit older than you, right?"

Brenda gave her shoulders a shrug. "Yeah, so what? You seem cool. My brother and some of his friends will be there and he's, like, nine years older than me. He's getting a keg. Here." She pulled out an order pad from her apron, scribbled something, and handed the slip to Amber. "Directions to my place. Actually my parents' place, but they're on a cruise in Alaska. Not that they'd care. Next week. Friday night, June third."

Amber swallowed against the sudden nausea, her face burning hotter than her chest. She ran the cloth under cool water again and rang it out, pressing it to her forehead before holding it to her burn again.

"Who knows?" Brenda said, leaning into the mirror and running her pinky under her heavily eye-lined eye. "Maybe you and my brother will hit it off."

Amber tucked the slip of paper into her apron and smoothed her ponytail. "I'll think about it."

She had a standing date with Jack Daniels on June third anyway. Maybe this year she'd let Brenda foot the bill.

15

Elkin High School gymnasium was packed. Perched halfway up the middle section of the bleachers, Beth joined dozens of other parents fanning themselves with programs. She scanned the throng of graduating seniors donned in navy caps and gowns and searched for Michael. Spotting him, she nudged Eric.

The orchestra attempted "Pomp and Circumstance," and Gretchen leaned into her. "I don't see Evan."

Beth surveyed the sea of bobbing navy square caps again. "I'm sure he's here. He passed English, right?"

"Right."

"Then stop worrying. He's not going to miss his own graduation."

Gretchen let out a grunt of doubt. From behind them, Beth heard a soft moan and the rustle of plastic. She turned around and smiled at Sarah who sat fumbling with a baggie of Saltines. Tyler sat next to her, rubbing her back.

By the time the selected teachers took their place on stage, Gretchen was heading toward panic. While the valedictorian asserted that this class was the voice of the future, Beth systematically scanned the rows of students for her nephew. The speech concluded and a guitar strum resonated throughout the room. Beth peered at the small band to the left of the stage, hardly visible from their vantage point, and squeezed Gretchen's knee. "There he is. In the band."

Gretchen sighed. "He might have mentioned he was playing and spared me the heart attack."

Beth readied her camera and waited for the presenter to call the graduates whose last names started with *D*. Michael filed in behind the line of students waiting at the bottom of the steps to the stage, a blond tuft of hair peeking out from under his cap. Beth felt a thrill of pride at the pronouncement of his name, at his broad swimmer's shoulders and long-legged gait. He crossed the stage and she furiously clicked her camera, until the image in the lens grew blurry. She set the camera in her lap and swiped away the moisture under her eyes. Before jaunting down the steps, Michael glanced up at them in his shy, proud way, and Eric squeezed her knee.

When the ceremony ended, Beth positioned the boys on the school's lawn in front of a glorious lilac bush and snapped a half dozen pictures until Evan feigned fainting. If he didn't get something in his stomach soon, he claimed, he was going to die. Beth snapped one more of Evan languishing on the grass before they made their way home.

Earlier that morning, she and Gretchen had chopped five heads of lettuce and mashed twenty avocados into guacamole. The beef and chicken simmered in the slow cookers, and the cakes and brownies were spread out on the card table next to the patio door. Beth handed Gretchen a can opener for the six cans of black olives.

"Do you know Miranda Dodds? From church?" Beth asked.

"The one with all the kids?"

"Yes. Five, I think. Anyway, she called me the other night and asked if I'd host this study she's teaching this summer. It starts next week."

Gretchen drained a can of olives over the sink. "That's short notice."

"Apparently whoever was planning to host broke her foot and had to back out."

"Why not have it at church?"

"She really wants to have it in a home. It's just for women, mostly neighbors of hers. Mine, too, I suppose, since we only live a few blocks apart. She doesn't want anyone to think they have to be a part of church to attend."

"What's the study on?"

"The Gospel of John. It's specifically for anyone who's never cracked open a Bible before."

Gretchen dumped the olives in a bowl and eyed her. "This seems a bit out of the box for you."

"Under the circumstances, I feel like I can't say no." She went to the refrigerator and took out a colossal bag of grated cheddar.

"So you're going to do it?"

"She said there was no way she could teach it at her house, not with five little kids to tend."

"The hand needs the foot needs the head."

Beth opened the bag of cheese and dumped it into a bowl. "I suppose so."

"See. Braver already." Gretchen popped an olive into her mouth.

"Gret, I'm just *hosting*."

"Beth, some people would rather jump out of a plane. To you having people over is no big deal. To me this"—she motioned to the taco contents that had overtaken the kitchen—"is the stuff of nightmares."

While Sarah went to lie down for a while in the guestroom, Gretchen convinced Tyler to go pick up his grandmother for the party. Michael and Evan initiated the taco bar, deemed it awesome, and within the hour a steady stream of relatives, friends, and neighbors began to trickle through the house. Beth couldn't help notice the attention that Lily attracted; Evan and Michael's friends flocked to her like moths to a lantern, much to Evan's incredulity. One hopeful graduate went so far as to boldly ask her out, right there next to the punch bowl. Lily cocked her glossy auburn head, said something about being a junior at Concordia, and glided away as only a dance major could.

Beth admired her composure. "That one's going to be hard to capture," she said to Dave who stood eyeing the roomful of boys tripping over each other for his daughter's attention.

"Fine by me."

Beth grinned and went to check the salsa supply. She passed Michael and a group of kids on the sofa paging through a yearbook, and felt a twinge of sadness, a tight, pressing feeling of something ending soon. Too soon. Something sweet and fleeting and impossible to prolong.

16

June 3, 2012

Every year the day crept up on Amber like a thief. Her day of penance. The day the memory she tried so hard to submerge pushed boldly to the surface of her mind.

Amber stepped onto Brenda's sprawling country house lawn. Brenda was right about the place being secluded; the nearest neighbor seemed to be a quarter of a mile down the road, too far to be cognizant of the happenings on this wooded lot. Shoving her hands deep into her jean pockets, Amber scanned the faces of the twenty-somethings peppering the lawn. What was she doing here? New to town and free drinks aside, this was ridiculous.

Recalling the liquor store she passed on her way, she spun on her heel and headed back to her truck, until Brenda called out her name. The girl flitted over, linked arms with her, and pulled her back to the party.

After some chatter, Brenda's smile turned into a pout. "Michael hasn't shown up."

"At least there's no chance of me getting run over tonight."

Brenda's brother showed up with a girl on his arm, a rowdy thing crammed into a tube top. Brenda introduced Amber to him and then led her to a keg, all the while prattling like a bird. She'd have a drink or two, Amber decided, for etiquette's sake, and then sneak off. Brenda chattered and Amber nodded periodically and poured herself a beer. When she emptied her cup, Brenda was still talking. So Amber refilled.

Sometime later, someone from work, a heavyset cook, playfully pushed her onto a picnic table bench and said she was in for a round of beer pong. Her team lost. But who cared?

Brenda appeared again and asked above the blare from the subwoofers in the garage, if she was having a good time.

Amber stuck her thumbs up. Magical. She was having a magical time.

Head swimming, she let Brenda babble while the lawn and everything on it began to spin. She felt fuzzy and giddy and glad she stayed until she heard a word, a familiar phrase. "What did you say?" she interrupted Brenda.

Brenda looked at her blankly. "About what?"

"About where you work."

"Where I work? Oh, you mean during the school year. On the House. In Madison."

Amber cursed and took a swig of beer.

"Why?" Brenda said. "You've been there before?"

"I hate that place."

Brenda seemed to take this personally and wanted to know why.

Why? Because she'd left something there, something she'd never get back. She left it—on this very day come to think of it—and now it was gone, so she hated that place.

Brenda said something, asked her a question, but Amber's head throbbed too loudly to make sense of the words. And then Brenda waved to someone and flitted away and attached herself to a guy with spiked hair. Amber finished her drink and fished out her keys and wondered why she'd come to this stupid party to begin with, with these flighty kids and their stupid games. She clambered into her truck and started the engine.

Later, she toppled through her apartment door, one unit out of many in a mammoth but sagging Victorian. The day of the burn incident, Ernie sent her home, probably freaked out about the possibility of having a lawsuit on his hands, and on her way back to the motel she spotted the For Rent sign in the lawn, called the number, and signed the lease that day.

The numbness was fading. But it was too soon, too soon to feel again. Her senses prickled back to life, and she remembered what she was fighting to forget. More liquor. She found a half a bottle of tequila in the refrigerator, pulled it out, unscrewed the cap, and caught a glimpse of her reflection in the kitchen window. She hoisted the bottle in the air. *Here's to you. Here's to your life.*

The life she fought for, the life she couldn't give up. She took a drink and then another, reminding herself with each swallow that she was nothing, nothing, nothing. Not worth the air she breathed. She lowered the bottle and glared at the haggard woman staring back at her in the window.

Murderer.

Downing the last of the tequila, she staggered out of the room, the walls around her growing fuzzy, the faint sound of crying ringing in her ears. She stepped into her bedroom, the gray world dimming to black, and felt herself fade and crumple like a leaf.

కావొ

To her disappointment and relief, Amber woke the next morning, head raging. She gingerly fingered the left side of her head and felt a bump. She must have whacked herself on the doorframe the night before.

She shuffled to the bathroom and assessed the damages in the mirror. A purplish bruise had already materialized. She opened the medicine cabinet, shook out two Tylenol, and swallowed them with tap water. She started a pot of coffee, cranked on the shower as hot as it could go, and climbed into the steamy sanctuary, chiding herself for staying at Brenda's for as long as she did—for even going at all. Once dressed, she filled up a travel mug and secured a baseball cap and a pair of oversized sunglasses then headed to Grandma's.

An hour later, Grandma embraced her on the porch. When they broke apart, Amber removed her sunglasses without thinking.

Ginny gasped. "Honey, what happened?"

"Nothing."

Ginny's fingers hovered over her bruise. "Did Paul do that?"

"No. Paul didn't do this. I haven't seen Paul in weeks. I collided into some kid at work, remember? I told you about it." Half true, anyway. Between the bruise and the burn, she was starting to look like a prisoner of war.

Grandma continued her inspection. "Really, Amber?"

"Really, Grandma."

"It's good you left him."

Fury surged through Amber. "I *told* you. It wasn't from Paul. Drop it already!" She galloped off the porch toward her truck, her pulse throbbing at her temples, and unhooked the back. She grabbed the potted plant and carried it to the side of the house. "I brought you a Bleeding Heart. I thought it would look good in that bare patch over here."

"That was thoughtful of you." Ginny trotted down the porch steps and disappeared into the garage and came out with a shovel, a trowel, and a pair of gardening gloves. She set them on the bottom step. Amber picked up the shovel and trowel, not bothering with the gloves.

With her foot on the ridge of the shovel, Amber pierced the ground and dug a hole, then carefully freed the Bleeding Heart from its temporary container and settled it into the earth. Her knees pressed into the soft ground as she packed down soil around the plant, the black coolness soothing the rage coursing through her. Minutes later, she stood back and examined her work, satisfied that she'd actually done something right. The lawn would never measure up to Harold's meticulous standards of course, but Grandma's yard certainly never lacked color.

She slapped her hands together a few times to clean them, unconcerned about the dirt embedded in her fingernails and in the creases of her palms, proof of her accomplishment. She bent to pluck a few weeds sprouting along the front walk.

"Don't worry about those," Ginny called from the porch. "Sam will take care of those on Saturday."

"I don't mind."

After pulling a half dozen dandelions, Amber filled the watering can, showered the Bleeding Heart, and then washed her hands at the spigot. She swung her hands in the air to dry them, climbed the porch steps, and dropped into the swing.

"Sure is an unusual looking flower," Ginny said, gazing down at the Bleeding Heart. "Reminds me of a pair of clip-on earrings I once owned."

Amber sat forward, took a lemon from the wooden bowl that sat on the table beside a paring knife, and with her palm, rolled the fruit back and forth on the tabletop.

"I do think it's for the best, Amber," Ginny said. "That you broke things off with Paul."

Amber clutched the lemon to her chest like a small treasure, a smooth stone washed up on the beach, and sank her leftover anger into the lemon's thick skin. "I don't think you gave him a chance."

Grandma's words were quiet but resolute. "Yes. I did."

Amber took up the paring knife and sliced the lemon lengthwise, the air instantly bursting with fragrance. Cupping half of the lemon in her hand, she positioned it on top of the glass dome of the juicer and pressed down, twisting at the wrist. Press, twist. Press, twist. Pale, cloudy juice trickled to the bottom of the jar.

Ginny rolled her own lemon across the table. "I didn't like the way he treated you."

Maybe not, but he never hit her.

"I only want what's best for you, and I don't think Paul is it."

Amber squeezed the last drop from the lemon. "It's not like men are lining up at my doorstep."

"Maybe they're all in Elkin," Ginny said, a smirk playing at her lips. "So why there? Why Elkin?"

Amber shrugged. "Why not?"

"It is a pretty little place, bustling in the summer. Where are you staying?"

"I found an apartment downtown in this big old house. High ceilings. Hardwood floors. Built-ins. Partly furnished. Not much room but lots of character. I'm going to ask the landlord if I can paint the rooms."

Ginny nodded and rocked for a moment. A monarch fluttered near the porch. "So what does your mother have to say about your move?"

Amber snorted. "Nothing yet."

Ginny stopped rocking and looked at her.

Amber sighed. "Don't worry, I'll call her. You've trained me too well."

"Leave the ball in her court. That's all I've ever said."

"Right. Just in case she wants to take me out for a mother-daughter lunch."

"Just in case." Ginny disappeared into the house, and returned with a glass pitcher, already filled with sugar, water, and ice. Amber added the murky lemon juice and Ginny swirled the mixture until it looked like a twister. She poured two glasses and handed one to Amber who held it up to the sky until the concoction glowed like liquid sunlight. She took a sip. The sweet-tart fluid burst on her tongue. All was right with the world with a glass of Grandma's lemonade in hand.

Ginny leaned forward to brush her fingers lightly across Amber's wound. She cringed. "Whoever bumped into you the other night must be a real bruiser if he managed to leave you with that."

"Just some kid. I go back in tonight."

Ginny kissed the tip of her finger and touched it to Amber's head. "Well, watch out for what's-his-name."

❧❦

Even though Amber had done her best to camouflage her bruise with a heavy coat of makeup, Brenda noticed immediately. "What happened to your head?"

"Bumped it after your party."

The girl giggled and lowered her voice. "I got *so* drunk. I don't even remember when you left."

That made two of them. Amber clipped off to introduce herself to a couple at table six, rattled off the specials of the day, and then headed to the bar to retrieve their drinks, conscious of the busboy's frequent glances. While she waited for her merlots, he approached her.

"Got any more dishes you want to throw at me?" she tossed over her shoulder.

The boy's mouth fell open. "I'm...I'm so sorry about that."

She instantly regretted her sarcasm; poor kid looked like he might pass out. "I'm kidding. It was an accident."

He released his breath and shook his head. "Man, I don't even know what happened. I guess I wasn't looking where I was going. I'm really sorry."

She shrugged. "Well, apparently I wasn't looking either. Guess you can't take all the credit for our little comedy act."

"So you're OK, then?"

"Oh, I'm fine. Just a little burn." From the look of it, she might be left with a tiny scar, just north of her heart, but she'd keep that to herself. "What about you? Were you hurt?" She hadn't thought to wonder until now.

He shook his head. "Just covered in asparagus."

The bartender set her wine glasses on the bar, and Amber placed them on her tray. "Good. I'm Amber, by the way."

"Michael."

"Nice to officially meet you, Michael. From now on watch where you're going, OK?"

"Sure thing." He spun on his heel and walked away, but turned to grin over his shoulder. "You, too."

She chuckled as she made her way back to table six. Seemed like a nice enough kid.

17

Sometimes Beth thought it'd be easier to corral squirrels than teach the last week of school. At three o'clock on the last day, Beth congratulated her students for being big first graders now and waved them out the door in a mixture of relief and melancholy.

The following day she was back in the classroom, peeling nametags off cubbies, scrubbing down tables, organizing puzzles, filing away IEP's, and cleaning out the fish tank. No one wanted Bubbles for the summer, so he'd vacation on top of her bookshelf and probably wouldn't make it to fall. She carried Bubbles in his Ziploc bag to her car, the newfound freedom of summer so sweet she could taste it.

That night Gretchen and Dave rolled in on their bikes, an ice-cream pail of strawberries nestled in the wire basket attached to the back of Gretchen's ten-speed. Beth easily talked them into staying for supper. Eric was just firing up the grill for a late supper, and she was feeling practically giddy. A late night dinner on the deck. Fresh berries. And no school tomorrow.

After they assembled a tray with all the hamburger fixings, Beth and Gretchen joined the guys in the backyard. Beth's phone trilled, and Miranda's name flashed across the screen. She stepped away to answer and chatted for a few minutes before closing the phone and returning to the patio table. "The study starts on Monday, and she still doesn't have a firm count yet. Heaven knows who will show up here."

Gretchen shot her a look. "That's kind of the whole point, isn't it?"

A puff of smoke shot up from the grill, and Eric flipped the burgers.

"Miranda seems like a sweet gal," Gretchen said.

"She is sweet. Sweet and persuasive."

Gretchen patted down her jean shorts. "Think I left my phone in my basket. I'll be back in a sec." She stood and headed for the front yard.

Beth dealt out paper plates and napkins and heard the rumble of a nearby engine. Didn't sound like Michael's car, yet he should be home from work by now. Eric transferred the burgers onto buns and draped them with squares of Colby.

She was shaking up the ketchup bottle when she spotted Gretchen rounding the side of the house with someone by her side. Gretchen's eyes penetrated her own, and Beth sensed a message behind them, a warning.

"I'm sure Beth will want to thank you," Gretchen said, her eyes still locked on Beth's.

Beth set down the ketchup and made her way over to them.

"Michael needed a ride home," Gretchen said.

Beth smiled at the woman beside Beth. "Oh, thank you. I didn't know he needed a ride. What happened to his car?"

"Dead battery, he thinks," the stranger said.

Beth smiled into the woman's ocean blue eyes, eyes that tugged at her memory. Had they met before? Church? School? She glanced at Gretchen, who was smiling in an odd way, then turned back to her visitor. "I hope it wasn't too much trouble."

The woman shrugged. "No trouble at all. I was heading this way anyway."

In an instant, Beth knew. That voice. She knew that voice. She gasped softly and looked to Gretchen whose eyes were wide with silent admonition. *Play it cool*, Beth read in her sister's stare. *Don't freak out.*

The patio door slid open, and Michael stepped out onto the deck. "Think my battery's dead, Dad.

"We'll take care of it tomorrow," Eric called.

Beth stared at the woman standing before her, lost in the blue eyes that had been filled with disdain only—when was it? A week ago? She glanced down at the women's hands, the hands that had shoved Gretchen and caused her own head to smack into the brick wall behind her, and realized she was fingering the tender spot beneath her hair. She quickly lowered her hand. "You..." she said but didn't know how to finish.

"Work with Michael." Gretchen finished. "Yes, Amber works with Michael."

"The least we can to is offer you a burger, Amber," Eric said. "You've probably been on your feet all day. Take a seat." He tipped his head in the direction of the patio table.

Gretchen smiled and pulled out a chair for her. The woman, seeming surprised, mumbled a thank you, and sat down. Beth looked from her husband to her sister to the woman.

"I can help you with those drinks now, Beth," Gretchen said.

Beth followed her sister across the deck, past Michael, into the kitchen.

"Can you believe it?" Gretchen whispered once the patio door was shut. "I thought I recognized that truck when it pulled into the driveway. When I glanced inside, I knew it was her. I mean, what are the odds?"

Beth stared at her sister for a minute. Then she went to the Tupperware drawer, found a plastic pitcher, and thudded it to the counter.

Gretchen squinted up at the ceiling. "I don't think she recognizes us. Maybe she doesn't remember that night at all."

Beth silently filled the pitcher with water.

"What?"

"*What?*" Beth said, turning to look at her. "What is she doing here? In my backyard?"

Gretchen's shoulder rose and fell. "I figured you'd want to thank her. For bringing Michael home."

Beth crossed her arms. "No you didn't. You wanted to create a scene. You wanted to see the look on my face when the drunk from off the street showed up on my deck. I know you. If anyone else was sitting behind that steering wheel, you wouldn't have bothered inviting them in for dinner."

"I *didn't* invite her for dinner. That was Eric."

Beth let out her breath.

"OK, fine. Yes. A part of me couldn't help myself. I mean come on! She shows up at your house? How could I *not* invite her in?"

Beth turned to the refrigerator and dislodged the root beer stuck in the door. "Don't you remember how completely *inebriated* she was? How she swore and *pushed* us? And now she drives my *son* home from work?"

Gretchen shrugged. "She's not drunk now."

"You might have considered my feelings."

"I was. Thought I'd throw you a curve ball."

"Oh, don't even start with that." Beth removed the tray of ice from the freezer and began pitching cubes into glasses.

Gretchen opened a powdered iced tea mix and sprinkled it into the pitcher. She stirred the mixture with a plastic spoon, apparently trying to hide a smile. "I just mean that maybe this is your chance to be brave."

By the time Beth and Gretchen rejoined the group on the deck, Michael was retelling the story of his work collision. "At least Amber here has a sense of humor about it," he concluded.

Beth set the root beer down on the table. "This is the waitress you crashed into?"

Michael nodded.

The blonde woman looked at her. "Worst first day ever."

Gretchen sat down and propped her elbows on the table. "This just keeps getting better and better."

"Michael," Beth said, "you didn't mention that accident happened on someone's first day."

"I didn't know. Give me a break. I'd only been there a week myself." Michael doused his cheeseburger with ketchup and devoured a quarter of it in one bite.

Gretchen handed Amber the bowl of strawberries and asked, "So, Amber, are you new to Elkin?"

"Moved here about a week ago."

"Welcome," Gretchen said. "What brought you to our little corner of the world?"

"Gelato." Her cheeks went pink, and she took a drink of tea.

Gretchen laid a piece of iceberg lettuce across her burger. "Well, Beth and I have lived here forever. Grew up about three miles from here and never did manage to escape. So if you need anything, you know, find a good hair stylist or mechanic or whatever, we're the girls to ask."

Amber nodded. "Nice to know not everyone's a tourist."

"They tend to disappear in the winter," Dave said.

"Yeah, I didn't realize how they'd be swarming around my place when I signed the lease to my apartment."

"Where do you live?" Gretchen asked.

"In that old Victorian on the corner of Clark and Franklin. That big white one."

Gretchen nodded. "Yes, I know that one. Only about a mile from here, right? Better get used to the tourists. That house is in the middle of all the summer action."

"I'm beginning to see that," Amber said and bit into her burger.

"I'm sure it can be hard moving to a new town," Gretchen went on, glancing at Beth before looking at Amber. "Getting to know people, getting used to the area. Probably can feel overwhelming."

Amber shrugged. "It's been OK so far. Although most of the people at work are kids, like Michael here."

Gretchen peered at Beth in a pointed way.

What? She'd had it with these theatrics.

"Yes," Gretchen said, "Getting to know people in a new town can be difficult." She shot Beth another look.

Beth shifted in her chair and pierced a strawberry with her fork. Seconds later she felt a foot nudge her own. Beth glared at her sister whose eyes darted to Amber, and then settled back on her. Beth took a sip of tea.

"Hey, you know what?" Gretchen said and instantly, Beth knew. "Beth, you should tell Amber about this get-together you're having on Monday night. That'd be a wonderful way for her to meet some people in the area. Especially since she lives so close."

Beth forced a smile. "Of course. You're more than welcome to join us Amber, if you'd like. Right here on Monday night at seven."

Amber stared at her, her fork in midair. "Do you sell Mary Kay or something?"

Beth let out a laugh. "No. I'm sorry. A friend of mine is leading a Bible study here on Monday nights and I'm hosting. It's nothing formal."

"Oh." Amber popped a strawberry in her mouth.

"Our first meeting is this week if you're interested. We'd love to have you." *Would* she? Would she love to have this woman in her living room?

Amber wiped her mouth on her napkin. "I don't really go to church."

Beth leaned forward. "That's perfect. I mean, the study is designed for women who aren't a part of a church and simply want to investigate the Bible. Sort of like a book club. We'll be going through the Gospel of John."

Amber opened her hamburger bun, shifted a pickle around, and closed it again. "Not sure you'd want me with all my questions."

Beth studied the woman across the table, recalling the hatred and misery in her eyes the night outside by the bar. She was really quite pretty, tonight anyway, with her hair in an up-do, a few loose strands framing her face, her wide-set eyes so much clearer and brighter than they were that night. Beth set down her fork, her compassion unfurled. "Sure we would. It's simply a group of women reading the Bible together and discussing it. We'd love to have you and welcome any questions you have."

Amber's eyes flickered over Beth. Beth smiled, picked up her burger, and glanced at her sister who was grinning in triumph.

18

Ginny swallowed her nightly heart pill and set the glass of water on her bedside table. Sometimes, in the middle of the night, her throat felt as dry as the Sahara, and she liked knowing she could quench it without leaving bed. Of course that meant getting up anyway for an extra trip to the bathroom. Getting old was no picnic.

After turning back the quilt, she eased herself into bed and switched off the lamp. An unruly cricket serenaded her from the backyard. She debated if she should end the performance by shutting the window, but a caressing breeze convinced her to stay put. Nothing like fresh air to soothe you to sleep.

But she couldn't sleep. She watched the red numbers on the digital clock ruthlessly climb until she sat up, peeled off the covers, and knelt beside her bed. Her knees creaked in protest, and she slid a pillow under them. For some reason her thoughts, which at times rolled around like marbles on a linoleum floor, were easier to corral while on her knees. Perhaps it was the pain that kept her on track. Even though one of these nights she might be forced to yell through the window for the neighbor to help her back up, she refused to wear one of those emergency buttons around her neck like a noose; she'd rather expire on the floor with her dignity intact.

Closing her eyes, she silently recounted the day's

mercies: her house and food, the clement weather. The increasingly rare gift of a lucid phone conversation with Lizzie. Lizzie *knew* her today, had even asked after Margaret and Amber.

She turned her attention to her daughter and granddaughter and pleaded like a child for God to *do something*. She was not too proud to beg. Minutes later, she moved on to her friends and their laundry list of health concerns, upcoming surgeries, family struggles, and travel plans. She prayed for each of the women in her prayer group by name. Jackie. Barbara. Denise. But her thoughts U-turned to Amber.

Taking a breath to refocus, she prayed for Janet, her neighbor from across the street, who told her just a few days ago that her eldest son had been diagnosed with cancer. Which type, Ginny couldn't remember, but the Lord knew. She prayed for him and his wife, for their two little boys, and for Janet. But once again, her thoughts zigzagged back to Amber.

Amber was starting over in a new town. Again. Wounded from another relationship gone sour. Again. She loved that girl with every fiber in her being, but the way she hopped from bar to bar, boyfriend to boyfriend, waiting for any fellow to swoop down and rescue her, made Ginny want to slap some sense into her. Thank the Lord this Paul fellow was out of the picture. Nothing but an overgrown boy if you asked her.

She'd only met him once when he and Amber stopped in for a visit months ago, and it was enough. Clearly, her porch was the absolute last place the man wanted to be. She'd tried to draw him into conversation, but Paul refused to meet her eyes. He fidgeted and paced and after only a few minutes, barked to Amber that they needed to get going. When Amber protested lightly, he stomped off the porch like a bratty toddler and waited by his Harley Davidson.

Where did Amber *find* these men?

Burying her face in her hands, she went before the throne like the persistent, demanding widow she knew she was. *Knock, knock, knock. It's me again.* Yet she trusted that her King did not grow weary of her petitions but welcomed them, even longed to hear them and, she still believed, longed to grant them. Once more, she held out Amber. Her precious, life-weary, girl.

And Margaret. Yes, even after everything, she still loved that girl, too. How could she not? She remembered the box she'd uncovered in the attic a week ago and the thought came to her to give it to Margaret, a possible peace offering. Why not? What did she have to lose?

Yes, she'd stop in tomorrow before she had a chance to change her mind. And she wouldn't call first either.

Depleted and drowsy, Ginny hobbled into bed and drifted effortlessly to sleep.

❧

The next morning, Ginny clutched the box and secured a smile as she rapped on the door to Margaret's mobile home. The door nudged open and Margaret stood there, eyeing her suspiciously. "You didn't tell me you were coming today."

Ginny held tight to optimism. "Just passing through and wanted to give you this."

Margaret glanced at the box with disdain. "What

is it?"

"Can I come in?"

Margaret stared at her for a moment before her shoulders sagged in resignation. She took a step back. Ginny stepped into the front room, thick with smoke. Reagan presided in the Oval Office the last time she'd indulged in a cigarette, but the years hadn't completely stifled the itch.

"I found this in the attic. I thought you might like it," Ginny said and set the box on the couch.

Margaret sat on the other side of it and pulled back a cardboard flap. Her brow wrinkled in puzzlement as she pulled out a faded blue piece of construction paper. She turned it over and squinted at a snowman made of cotton balls and red yarn. She looked up at Ginny quizzically.

"Your school projects. From kindergarten on up. I forgot I'd kept it all. Look at this." Ginny riffled through the papers and pulled out a yellow envelope and removed a card. "Even your report card from first grade." Her eyes scanned the teacher's assessment before she handed it to Margaret. *Margaret is quiet and respectful but sometimes has trouble making friends.*

For the first seven or so years of school, the comments from Margaret's teachers were mostly positive. Then high school hit. Then words like *belligerent*, *discourteous*, and *easily distracted* began to appear. What had happened? Boys, for one thing. Margaret bloomed early and Ginny never did figure out a way to approach the whole birds and bees thing. Although time would prove that Margaret had figured that out for herself.

Ginny looked at a crayon drawing of a dog and wondered, again, how much of Margaret's quest for attention stemmed from her iceberg of a father. Even when Margaret was little, Harold hardly ever gave her more than a pat on the back. Whenever he sat down to read the paper and Margaret attempted to scramble into his lap, he'd heave her off and tell her to find something to do. Who would her daughter be had she been raised with an affectionate father?

Of course she couldn't blame everything on Harold. He wasn't the only culprit. Heaven knew all the ways she'd failed this child, this woman.

Margaret took out a thin sheet of lined paper. Ginny knew the paragraph by heart. *My mother makes pie. I help peel the apples. We eat the pie together.* "I didn't know you'd kept all this stuff."

"I'd forgotten all about it until Amber and I were digging in the attic a few weeks back, when I was looking to hang out the flag."

"I have a box of Amber's stuff somewhere around here."

"You do?" She hadn't meant to sound so surprised.

Margaret shot her a look. "Yeah. I do."

"She probably doesn't know you've kept any of that. You should show it to her. She'd like that."

Margaret tossed the sheet of paper back into the box. "I was wondering how long it'd take."

"What?"

"For the lecture to start."

"I was only—"

"Why don't I just send the box with you? Then you can show it to Amber yourself. Another warm fuzzy moment for the two of you. Sound good?"

"Margaret, I wasn't trying to tell you what to do."

Margaret let out a sharp laugh. "Of course not!

You've never told me what to do, especially when it comes to Amber. You know best. She certainly doesn't need me when she has you."

"I've never tried to get in between the two of you. I wish the two of you would spend more time together. Why do you think I'm always calling you to join us?"

"Oh, I don't know. Maybe so you can feel the joy of telling me I'm doing everything wrong?"

"Margaret, I don't want to be like that with you anymore."

"Oh please. That's how it's always been. From the very beginning. *Margaret*, that's not how you pin a diaper. You're going to stab the child. *Margaret*, that bath water is too hot. What's wrong with you? *Margaret*, don't you even know how to swaddle a baby?"

Ginny bit her lip. How many times were they going to have this conversation? "Yes, I took over too much. I know that now. I was only trying to help."

Margaret stood and paced to the other end of the room. "You know what really gets to me? You know what the real joke is? That you were the one who wanted me to get rid of her."

Ginny froze.

"Remember that, Mom? You even drove me to the clinic, told me it would be for the best. Said I was too young, and—what was the word?—*foolish* to take care of a baby."

Ginny closed her eyes and gripped her hands together in her lap. "Margaret, I was wrong. So very, very wrong. I don't know what else to say to you. Thank God you had the sense not to listen to me."

"That's not what you thought at the time. No, when I decided I didn't want to go through with it, didn't want to burn up in hell, you waited until she was born and took her away from me anyway."

"Honey, I wanted you to finish high school. Who else was going to watch her while you sat in geometry? And how could I not fall in love with her? She's one of my greatest joys."

Margaret stood looking out the window. "How lucky for you. How nice that the baby you wanted me to get rid of turned out to be your greatest joy." She turned, her eyes glinting in anger. "Thanks so much for stopping by, Mother. You know how I live for our little chats." She grabbed her pack of cigarettes and disappeared down the hall.

Ginny stared at the box of memories beside her, blurred from her sudden tears, then collected her purse and let herself out.

19

The landlord granted permission for Amber to paint the apartment and, miracle of miracles, didn't ask what color. On Sunday night, after enduring the brunch crowd, she accomplished the first coat in the living room and finished the second coat and touch ups by late afternoon the following day. After showering, she plopped down in the one chair that came with the place, a ratty, pea green monstrosity that seemed to be stuffed with packing peanuts, and devoured a turkey sandwich on wheat bread. The grainiest wheat bread she could find at the store.

She'd expected Paul to call by now, after nearly a month. Could this thing with Tracie really be more than a fling? It couldn't last, could it? Not after what she and Paul had shared together. But of course, that was the problem; she always fell harder, hung on tighter. And in the end, when it all came crashing down, she was the one left licking her wounds.

She finished her sandwich, washed the few dirty dishes gathered in the sink, blow dried her hair, and peeked at the clock. A quarter past six. She clipped her toenails and scrubbed the bathtub, then figured, while she was at it, she might as well scrub the toilet and archaic tiled floor. When she shoved all the cleaning supplies back under the sink, it was a quarter to seven.

She frowned at herself in the mirror. "Pathetic," she said out loud. Pathetic that her one prospect to do anything social came in the form of a straight-laced Bible study. What did they even *do* at such a thing? Sit around and polish their halos while discussing how the rest of the world was headed for hell in a tired old hand basket?

Still, it was something.

Giving in to her curiosity, or boredom, or loneliness—or whatever it was that had set off this gnawing restlessness—Amber smeared on lip gloss, found her keys, and headed out to what would surely be the dullest night of her life.

Beth seemed surprised to find her at the doorstep, and for a second Amber wondered if she'd gotten the day wrong. But then a smile overtook the petite woman's face, and she stepped aside and extended her arm in welcome.

"Amber! I'm so glad you could make it. Please. Come in."

The house smelled of cinnamon and candles, and Amber followed Beth to a living room where women stood clumped together, sipping from coffee mugs or goblets. She shouldn't have come.

Beth asked her what she'd like to drink. Vodka, she wanted to say. She settled for coffee.

As soon as Beth was out of sight, Amber made for a cream-colored chair tucked in the corner. She sat and surveyed her environment. A collection of pillar candles surrounded by smooth stones glowed on the coffee table, soft acoustic guitar music droned in the background. She scanned the walls, passed over reproductions of a Monet and a Thomas Kinkade, and then her eyes fell over a framed watercolor positioned above a bookshelf.

Beth returned and held out a mug. "Cream and

sugar are on the table." She sat down beside Amber with her own cup, smiled in a sheepish sort of way, and seemed as though she was going to say something. She didn't.

Amber took a sip. This was a mistake.

Just then, a woman with unruly brown hair introduced herself as Miranda and asked if each of them could go around the room and tell a little bit about themselves. Beth started. She taught kindergarten, she said, and her son would be leaving for college come fall. The woman to Beth's right flipped her hair back and announced that she was a real estate agent and was recently divorced. Next was Miranda's next door neighbor and running buddy. Following her was a stay-at-home mom who lived down the street.

Amber drank her coffee, prepared with her one-liner when her turn came: "I just moved here, and I waitress at Winston Hill."

When Miranda picked up a Bible from underneath her chair and asked everyone to turn to the Gospel of John, the fourth book in the New Testament, Amber felt a trickle of perspiration slide down her side. Beth nudged a book onto her lap.

Amber mumbled a thank you, certain she had a Bible somewhere. Grandma had given her one years ago; she just didn't know where the thing was. Still at Paul's maybe?

Miranda read the first chapter out loud while Amber followed along in the borrowed Bible and tried to make sense of the strange words. Light and dark. The Word becoming flesh. Some crazy fool shouting in the desert. Miranda asked questions. Some of the women responded. Miranda explained who John was.

Some of the women asked questions. Amber kept her eyes glued to the page as if she were back in math class and hoping to deflect the teacher's attention.

At eight o'clock Miranda said a short prayer, after which Beth disappeared to the kitchen. She returned with two plates of some kind of strawberry dessert crowned with cream. Beth handed her a plate, and Amber passed it to the stay-at-home mom next to her. "Can I help you get these out?"

Beth blinked before she smiled. "That'd be wonderful."

Amber followed her to a brightly lit kitchen, grabbed two plates and napkins, and served Ms. Real Estate and the neighbor with the Texas accent.

"Thanks for your help," Beth said once they sat back down with their own desserts.

Amber shrugged, and ruptured the pastry with her fork.

"I hope there haven't been any more mishaps at the restaurant," Beth said after awhile. "Michael hasn't mentioned anything."

"We've managed to steer clear of each other. So where is he headed in the fall?"

"UW Madison."

Her insides gave a little twist. "I spent a couple of semesters there. Years ago. Never finished, though."

Beth nodded. "Is that so?"

"What does he want to go into?"

"He loves art and wants to do something like graphic design, or maybe web design. I guess it shouldn't matter the first year, with all the generals to get through."

Amber peered at the framed watercolor. "Is that one of his?"

Beth followed her gaze and smiled, visibly proud. "Yes."

Plate in hand, Amber stepped over to have a closer look. It was a depiction of the sea, sapphire and gray and turquoise meshed and swirled together to represent the crashing and tumbling of ocean waves. A white sailboat struggled in the distance, and the sky held a storm. The flawless balance of light and darkness and sense of motion revealed Michael's skill. "Watercolor is tricky. It can get away from you, surprise you. This is good."

Beth beamed. "Thank you. I'll tell him you said so." She glanced down at Amber's hands and crinkled her face. "It looks like...you paint too?"

Amber stared, her heart racing. How did she know? She remembered her stained cuticles and grinned at the traces of orange. "Oh, this. Just my apartment. I finished today."

"Looks like a fun color. I've been meaning to repaint my kitchen and dining area for years. Takes me forever to decide on a color. Maybe you can inspire me. Want to take a look?"

Amber followed as Beth led the way to the kitchen "I'm kind of a neutral gal," Beth said. "I'm worried that if I do something too bold I'll regret it. And yet I'm tired of plain old beige."

The room was tediously safe. Amber ran her hand along the wall, noted the warm grain of the kitchen cabinets and the cream-colored countertop. "What if you did a glaze? A subtle two-toned effect. That way you could stick with neutral but add depth, like sand on top of cocoa brown. Then add pops of color here and there. Like a red tea kettle or a ceramic rooster or something."

Beth nodded, surveying the room. "I'll think about that. Of course I have no idea how to do a glaze."

"It's not hard. I want to do one in my bedroom. Blue on blue."

Beth looked at her, her face bright. "You want some help? I'd be happy to give you a hand so I could see how it's done."

The offer caught Amber off-guard. "Sure. If you want."

Someone from the living room called out a good-bye. Beth touched Amber's arm to excuse herself, and then disappeared. Amber dawdled back to the living room, admired Michael's ocean painting again, and then stood before a collection of photographs lining the mantel.

A little boy, leaning up against a tree, smiled at her from behind a white, wooden frame. Sunlight poured over his white-blond hair, and his eyes sparkled impishly, as if he'd just been caught digging up flowers or had finished rattling off some childish joke. She could almost hear Beth gently scold him from behind the camera, speak his name in that way she'd often heard mothers do, with equal measures of amusement and warning.

Amber picked up the picture of the boy. His freckles had all but disappeared, his hair had darkened, and his teeth had grown in, but it was Michael all right, same slightly protruding ears and wide-set blue eyes. There was something familiar about the way he grinned at her, something about the gleam in his eyes tugged at her...

"First day of school," Beth broke into her thoughts. "Kindergarten. I love that picture. I can hardly believe that little boy is now six feet tall."

Amber returned the frame to the mantel, the room suddenly too quiet. She turned around, flustered to see that she and Miranda were the only two remaining. She retrieved her purse from under the chair in the corner. "I should get going."

Miranda smiled at her. "Will we see you next week?"

Amber fumbled with the straps on her purse. "Not sure. I'll have to check my schedule."

Beth showed her to the door and said it was good to see her again.

Amber stepped out into the night air under a smattering of stars and drove home, her mind turning over the words she'd heard tonight. Words about light coming into darkness, and the darkness not understanding it.

☙❧

The following Monday, Amber dashed through Walgreens on her way home from work to restock her supply of toilet paper and paper plates, and then zipped through a drive-thru for supper. As she followed Center Street she decided what the heck? She hooked a right into Beth's neighborhood, still unsure if she was irritated or glad that Ernie had scheduled her to work from eleven until six on Mondays. Now she couldn't use work as an excuse not to show up. Was that a good thing or a bad thing?

Clutching the brown fast food bag and cylinder of soda, she rapped on Beth's front door. "I'm a little early."

"That's fine," Beth said, letting her in.

Amber sat at the kitchen table gnawing on french

162

fries while Beth pulled a pie from the oven, a golden circle of glory that, from the looks of it, could rival the desserts served at Winston Hill. "Smells good," Amber said.

Beth transferred the pie to a wire rack. "Peach."

Amber took a drink of pop through her straw. "I've never made a pie."

Beth glanced at her. "The secret is to not overwork the crust."

They chatted as Amber worked on her burger, and within minutes, the other women began to trickle in. The living room was soon buzzing with chatter, and Amber tossed her leftovers in the garbage and slinked to her corner chair while Beth began serving coffee and iced tea.

Miranda led the group through chapter two, a surprising account of Jesus turning water into wine at a wedding and then later driving out corrupt salesmen from the temple with a hastily made whip. Like the first week, Miranda posed questions and the group fell into discussion while Amber sat silently.

She knew little about this Jesus, only what Grandma had tried to tell her; that He was God and He died to save people from hell. That was about it. For the sake of preserving their relationship, they'd been forced to draw an invisible line and not cross it. Certain subjects—religion and men primarily—were off limits. Amber only took Grandma's preaching in small doses. She accompanied Grandma to church a couple of times a year, on Christmas and Easter, to placate her, and of course endured plenty of meal-time prayers. The woman could do whatever she wanted to in her own house. But Amber wouldn't put up with regularly scheduled sermons. She didn't need to hear about forgiveness that couldn't possibly include her.

She didn't doubt Grandma's sincerity, only her perception; the woman didn't know she was fighting for a lost cause. If Grandma knew Amber's secret, she'd give up. But she didn't know, had no idea how far her granddaughter had fallen, how she was miles beyond forgiveness, God's or anyone else's.

Yet these first two chapters in John—these words about light and dark and water and wine and rage and mystery—captivated her. This Jesus who lived on the pages of Beth's Bible intrigued her.

The next morning, when Amber chatted on the phone with Ginny, she didn't mention anything about the study. With the bus schedule in front of her, Amber promised to pick her up at the station in downtown Elkin at two o'clock on Thursday afternoon.

"Whatever for?" Ginny said. "I just got the oil changed on the Buick."

"Grandma, we've been through this before. You should take the bus. I'll buy the ticket for you online."

Ginny huffed indignantly. "I have triple A. My license is valid. I have just as much right to the road as anyone. I don't need to take a bus."

Amber squeezed her temples and thought about what good AAA would be if Grandma was stuck in the middle of nowhere without a cell phone. She held her tongue. "Fine. Have it your way."

"I'll see you on Thursday," Ginny chirped and hung up.

❧

On Thursday afternoon, Amber plopped out little lumps of refrigerated cookie dough onto a baking sheet as she cast frequent glances out her kitchen window. She slid the cookies into the oven, heard a car rumble up, and turned just in time to witness the front wheel of Grandma's Buick mount the curb and lop back onto the street. Amber wiped her hands on a towel. Next time she'd insist on the bus. Barefoot, she jogged outside.

When Ginny stepped into the living room she gave a little yelp. "Mercy me, I should have worn my sunglasses!"

Amber withered. "Too much?'

"No, no. It's bright and cheery. Makes me feel like dancing the samba." She shimmied her shoulders playfully.

Amber surveyed the *Arizona sunset* walls. "Mom said it reminded her of a Mexican restaurant."

Grandma stopped dancing. "Your mother stopped by?"

"Last week, on her way to the casino. She stayed for a whopping ten minutes."

Ginny lowered herself into the pea green chair. Just this morning, Amber had vacuumed the thing as if she could suck out the ugliness, but it still reminded her of an oversized Muppet. Maybe an orange and green throw pillow would help. Or a sheet.

"That was nice of her to at least stop. Did she bring anything with her?"

"Mom? No. Why? Was she supposed to?"

Ginny waved the air. "No. I just… Never mind. I stopped in a week or so ago but things didn't go so well."

"Why do you even bother? You know she's not going to change."

Ginny gazed at the birdfeeder hanging from the

window outside. "She does have a right to her anger, I suppose."

"Why do you defend her?"

"Amber, there are things in our past that, to your mother's credit, you don't even know about. She's done a lot of things wrong, yes. But she has done a few things right."

Amber plopped onto the floor with her oversized pillow. "She's not in jail, and she's not strung out. She's not worth your time."

"I don't want to hear that." Grandma's eyes held fire. "I turned my back on her once. I'm not going to do it again. She's still my child. No matter what, I can't give up on her. I can't give up on my own child."

With her elbows on her knees, Amber lowered her head and stared at the nicked hardwood floor.

"I understand your anger toward her, I really do. But I can't stop trying to set things right between us..."

Her abruptness caused Amber to lift her head.

Ginny's wrinkled her nose. "Honey, what is that smell?"

Amber sniffed. "Paint?"

Grandma shook her head.

Amber bolted to the kitchen. She pulled out the sheet of blackened circles from the oven, tossed it into the sink, and swore. Even this. She couldn't even manage refrigerated cookie dough. "I forgot to set the timer."

Ginny chuckled. "Oh, don't worry about it. Just make some coffee."

Ginny scooped grounds into a filter as Amber rummaged through the cupboard for a half-eaten package of Fig Newtons. Once the coffee was percolating, she persuaded Ginny to sit down in the living room. For once she needed to do something right, even if it was merely serving store-bought cookies and pre-ground coffee.

Minutes later, Amber carried two mugs into the living room and found her grandma examining the Picasso print she'd hung last night. Some people didn't appreciate Picasso, but for Amber, he spoke straight to her soul. The cacophony of color and shapes, his disturbing, often distorted characters—he was on to something. Life wasn't always a bowl of fruit or a pastoral meadow. Sometimes it was downright ugly. Terrifying. In fact, the kaleidoscope of colors in *Woman in Front of the Mirror* served as the impetus for the orange walls.

"Such a troubled soul," Grandma said.

Amber wondered if Grandma meant the woman in the painting or Picasso himself. Ginny ran her hand over the orange wall. "I do like this color, Amber. It ties everything together. So do I get the grand tour?"

"You've already had it for the most part. Here's the bathroom." She took three strides and extended her arm then took two more steps until she was in her room. "And the bedroom. That's about it."

Ginny poked her head into the room. "Small but cozy."

"I hope to paint this room, too."

"What color?"

"A glaze, in different shades of blue. A friend of mine wants to learn how, and she said she'd give me a hand with it."

They walked back to the living room. Ginny reclaimed the chair, and Amber handed her a mug. "Someone you met at the restaurant?" Grandma asked.

"No. Just someone I know."

"That old high school friend you were thinking of calling?"

Amber sat on the floor and leaned against the wall. "Just someone I met in a class I'm taking."

Ginny's eyes grew large. "Are you going back to school? That's wonderful!"

For a brief second Amber basked in the warmth of Grandma's pleasure, loathing to disappoint her. "No, Grandma. I'm not going back to school."

Ginny's face fell slightly. She leaned back in her chair. "Well, what class, then?"

Amber set her mug on the floor. "Believe it or not, a Bible study." She glanced up at her grandma, saw a flash of disbelief, and looked down at her hands in her lap.

"Oh?"

Amber inspected her thumbnail. "The woman who hosts it, Beth, wants to learn how to do a glaze."

Ginny helped herself to a Fig Newton from the plate Amber had set on a TV tray. "How did you meet Beth?"

"You know the kid who crashed into me at the restaurant? Beth is his mom."

Ginny's eyebrows rose in surprise. "Well, I'll be. The Lord works..." She fell silent, took a bite of cookie, and after a moment asked, "How many are in your group?"

"Eight. Only women. So don't get any ideas about me snagging a husband or anything."

"I love women's studies. Sometimes men just clutter up the place. You know that's how Lizzie and I met and became such good friends, at a study in her house. What is your group studying?"

"John."

"Wonderful." Ginny popped the remaining half of her cookie into her mouth.

Amber grabbed a cookie for herself, baffled by her grandma's lack of reaction. "We've met twice so far. We do a chapter each time."

"So next time you'll be in chapter three?"

"Yeah, I guess so."

Ginny nodded. "Well, you already know a verse from that chapter."

Amber stared at her. "I do?"

"John 3:16."

The series of numbers sounded familiar and suddenly Amber recalled the framed picture Grandma had given her for Christmas years ago, of a satellite picture of the earth with the verse imprinted along the bottom in gold lettering. She'd never hung it up. "For God so loved the world..." she began and looked to Ginny to finish.

Grandma merely sipped her coffee.

A couple of hours later, Grandma treated her to supper at an Italian restaurant downtown, and then the two of them strolled to Ginny's Buick. "You know I pray for you every day," Grandma said, her eyes suddenly somber.

In Amber's mind, praying was a small step from talking to oneself, yet Grandma's words wrapped her in comfort. "I know."

"And I'm glad you're going to this Bible study and you're meeting other women. Maybe you'll make some good friends."

Amber felt herself bristle. "I'm not twelve, Grandma. Don't worry about me. I have you, right?"

"I won't be here forever, you know."

"Don't talk like that."

"I worry about what will happen to you when I'm gone." The older woman broke into a smile. "I sound like I think I'm the center of the universe, don't I? That's not how I mean it. But I do wonder who you'll turn to. If only things were different with your mother...Well, it is what it is." She looked off into the horizon, where the sky was glowing almost as orange as Amber's walls.

"I'll put an ad in the classifieds," Amber said. "Wanted. Good-looking, twenty-five plus man to take care of pathetic, thirty plus waitress when Grandma's gone."

"That's not what I mean. I'm not even talking about marriage."

Amber crossed her arms. "Then what are you talking about?"

"I'm talking about having someone in your life you can depend on. Someone you can trust, besides me. A true *friend*. Oh, I know you have friends. I don't mean to imply you don't. But I just can't help but wonder who will be your family when I'm gone. And I don't necessarily mean a husband and kids. Lord knows I wouldn't be anywhere without my church family."

Amber shifted under the sudden weight of the conversation. "Grandma, you're a tough lady, and you know it. You have years ahead of you."

Ginny placed a warm, weathered hand on Amber's cheek. "Honey, I'm an old woman."

Amber peered into the love-etched, weary blue pools and had to look away. She took two steps backward and focused her attention on the dilapidated front porch that wrapped around the old Queen Anne like a skirt. In her mind's eye she saw the house in its glory, before it had been divided up like a sheet cake, before the assortment of metal mailboxes clung to the siding like leeches. She imagined the paint on the house smooth and pristine, the porch level, the disparaging trellis cascading with roses. She envisioned the house as it was meant to be. A queen.

"You know me," Ginny broke into her thoughts. "I'll keep praying for you. Can't help myself. What else is an old woman to do?" She ducked into the car and secured her seatbelt. "And now if you don't see any cops around, I'll see if I can make it home in record time."

Amber leaned into Ginny's open window. "You be safe. And call me when you get home."

Grandma promised she would.

Amber stood on the curb and watched the Buick disappear around the corner. Then she trudged back into her apartment, went straight to her bedroom, and pulled out a box of odds and ends she hadn't opened for months, not since before Paul. She loosened the packing tape and rummaged through the mess until she found it. Blowing dust from the frame, she carried the world to the living room, set it on the built in bookshelf, and read John 3:16 out loud.

If only it were that simple.

20

Beth never missed the Lakeshore Drive neighborhood garage sale. Every year the waterfront property owners purged themselves of furniture and clothing, most of which sported brand names that rarely glimpsed the inside of her closet. Last year she snagged a charming antique bookshelf, and this year she was on the lookout for an area rug. She usually came home with an assortment of treasures, and even if she didn't, the excursion was worth it simply to ogle the houses.

She called Gretchen the night before to see if she wanted to tag along.

"Lily wants to go, too," Gretchen said. "She found a killer little black dress last year, and I'm on the hunt for a loveseat. We might need a van. Who do we know?"

"Amber has a truck," Beth said, thinking out loud.

"Good idea. Call Amber."

"Do you think I should?"

"Sure, why not? She'd probably love to join us."

To Beth's surprise, Amber had appeared every Monday night for the past month, often still in her work clothes, clutching a sack of fast food. While Beth brewed coffee and cut dessert, they chatted. About Amber's grandmother. About Beth's students. About Amber's ex-boyfriend Paul. But then as soon as study started, Amber shut down and didn't utter a word.

Beth hung up with Gretchen and dialed Amber. "I need to get another chair for my place anyway," Amber said, sounding genuinely pleased.

"This is the place to look." Beth took a breath. "I wanted to ask you, would you mind if we took your truck? I just don't know what we're all going to find."

There was a beat of silence. "Oh. So you're just after my truck."

"No, not at all. I just thought—"

"I'm kidding. Of course we can take my truck. I'll pick you up at eight."

The next morning, Beth climbed into the cab of Amber's white Chevy and directed her to Gretchen's house. Clad in shorts and sandals, Gretchen and Lily clambered in as Beth slid tight up against Amber.

"This is cozy," Gretchen said and insisted they stop for Starbucks. "And donuts. My treat."

"Amber might not appreciate all of us eating in her truck," Beth said.

Amber shrugged. "I eat in here all the time."

They whipped through Starbucks' drive-thru then pulled up alongside Eddy's Bakery where Gretchen jumped out, ran inside, and returned with an assorted box of powdered sugar, apple turnovers, and cream filled. After a few minutes of finger licking and lip smacking in the parking lot, they crammed back into the truck and set off. "Now we're fueled and ready to roll," Gretchen said, clutching her Grande Americano.

Amber parked in front of a stately Tudor with a trampoline for sale in the front yard. As they made their way up the driveway, they rummaged through Christmas decorations, flipped through racks of dresses, and perused kitchen gadgets. Lily found a pair of red patent leather heels and a matching purse, and

Gretchen snagged a pair of curtains still in the original packaging.

As they approached the second house, Beth spotted a beige recliner and clipped over to claim it, just in case. She waved Amber over. "Look at this. Pristine condition."

Amber slid into the chair, leaned back, and closed her eyes. "Sold." She paid the owner, backed her truck into the driveway, and the owner helped heave the chair into the truck's bed.

Beth spotted a table crowded with dishes and lost herself in porcelain and china. She examined a delicate dessert plate trimmed with blueberries. Perfect for summer.

"Pretty," Amber said, coming alongside of her.

Beth set the plate down and sighed. "Like I need more dishes. Gretchen says I could set the table for three hundred people and still have leftover plates."

"I get it though," Amber said picking up a dish. "It's art. Functional art. You should get them."

Beth grinned. "Should I?"

"Absolutely. As long as you promise me blueberry pie for Monday night."

"You've got it." Beth clutched the stack and moved on down the table, setting down her loot to run a hand along a smooth, cedar box. She opened the lid to reveal a set of ornate silverware. She traced the stem of a fork and glanced at Amber. "How do you like John?"

Amber stared at her, her brows knit together. Then her expression loosened, and she tossed her head back and forth. "Oh, *John*. For a minute there I wondered if I'd met your brother and forgotten about it or something."

Beth smiled and waited, not wanting to give up before the conversation began.

"Interesting, I guess." Amber turned back to the table and picked up a fingerbowl. She glanced at the price tag and set it down. "I'm not sure if I buy all of it though."

"Like what?"

Amber turned to her and looked her dead-on. "Like God wanting to forgive everyone. Sounds like make-believe."

"Yes," Beth said, nodding. "I suppose it does seem hard to believe. But that's grace."

"Well, like I said from the get-go, I've never been religious."

Beth set down the candlestick she was holding and spoke softly. "It's not about being religious. It's about realizing we're broken. It's about repenting and being set free."

A flicker of what looked like longing passed through Amber's eyes before she turned away and tucked a strand of hair behind her ear.

The wind picked up, setting off a high-pitched tinkle from a wind-chime. Cherry blossoms sprinkled over them and the dishes like snow. A few landed in Amber's tousled blonde hair as she toyed with the fingerbowl, her eyes downcast, her cheeks as pink as the tiny flowers. Beth felt a twinge of empathy and wished Amber could see herself. She was really quite lovely; right now she seemed to be the antithesis of the woman she'd encountered at the pub.

"Fifty cent wicker baskets at the next house down!" Gretchen hollered, striding up the driveway.

"We'll be right over," Beth said.

Amber gave the fingerbowl a little nudge and

finally met Beth's gaze. "Sounds too good to be true." She turned and clipped off after Gretchen.

Beth carried her stack of blueberry plates to the cashier table, wondering if Amber's statement was prompted by Gretchen's declaration, or her own.

☜☞

Beth offered to help Amber get the recliner into her apartment, but Amber assured her she could handle it on her own. Box of treasures in hand, Beth hopped out of Amber's truck and thanked her again for driving before making her way to the house. Down in the basement, Beth cleared off a space on the dish shelf for the blueberry set, then emptied the contents of the dryer into a laundry basket and headed up. She rapped on Michael's door, the item she bought for him on top of his clean clothes. Saturday or not, it was nearly eleven.

She set the laundry basket on the floor and twisted his blinds until sunlight pierced the room. He groaned and pulled the covers over his head.

"Found something for you today," she said.

He propped himself up on his elbows. "What?"

She held out a black duffle bag. He sat up and took it from her and examined the red Wisconsin Badger on one side and the bright, collegiate W on the other.

"Cool. Looks new. Thanks."

She admired his art wall surrounding his headboard. Some time ago he had switched out his desk for his bed and now an assortment of images surrounded him as he slept. She spotted several depictions of Evan—a striking one of him laughing with his head thrown back, his curly hair springing from his head like coils—and any other friend who happened to cross Michael's threshold. From the looks of it, a few of the kids had added their own drawings, although Beth could distinguish her son's in a heartbeat. She was biased of course, but Michael's talent shined above the rest. The eyes in his faces held light and life; even his silly doodles seemed alive.

Over the years the wall had been covered with caricatures, doodles, algebra problems, hangman nooses, trees, and phone numbers. It had touted every imaginable color, been brushed with oil and watercolor alike, marker and pencil. She caressed one of the alcove walls lovingly, longingly, wishing somehow she could preserve it. The wall's constant forward motion, its unstoppable evolution, was the only unforeseen downside. It couldn't be saved, couldn't be tucked away in a box, and a photograph captured only so much.

What would they do with this wall after Michael was gone? Leave it? Paint over it again? Paint the room a new color altogether?

"Make sure to take a picture soon," she said and turned to the laundry basket. She sat down on his desk chair and tossed a few of his clean socks in her lap to couple. Usually she made him do this, but the weeks with him home were dwindling, and right now she wanted to couple his socks and stuff them into his top dresser drawer for him. "We still need to go through your closet. I'm making a trip to Goodwill today anyway. Let's get through it this afternoon."

When he didn't answer, she looked at him. A pencil in his grip, his right hand pressed against his wall. He glanced at her, then back at the wall, and back at her.

"What are you doing?" she said and side-swept her bangs.

"Hold still."

The soft scratches and tapping from his pencil sounded like the gentle pecking of a bird. He turned to study her, his head tilted to the right, his eyebrows furrowed in concentration, a look he'd practiced since toddlerhood. He scratched at the wall, then glanced back at her and sketched some more. Beth sat quietly, contentedly, and wished, like so many times before, that she could arrest this moment in time, hold it in her hand like a jewel.

21

No way around it, the chair was stuck.

Amber stood outside her apartment—*trapped* outside her apartment—and glared at the beige recliner wedged in her doorway. She took a breath, grasped the bottom of the chair, and pushed with all of her might. The thing didn't budge.

Defeated, she stood back. She supposed she could call Beth since she'd offered to help earlier, had even offered Michael or Eric's help, but she loathed being the damsel in distress. She'd gotten herself into this mess. She'd get herself—and this chair—out.

Hands on hips, she exhaled and examined the impasse as rationally as she could. The problem was, she'd started off all wrong. Instead of tilting the chair forward so it was almost upside down, she'd tried to shove the thing in front ways. The only thing to do was shimmy it loose and start over.

Gently, she tugged and nudged, tugged and nudged, until millimeter by millimeter, the chair loosened. Then she tipped it forward, angling it slightly, and coaxed it through the doorway. It moved easily now, and in her elation, she gave it one final push through the doorway, and heard the rip of fabric.

She set the recliner upright and cringed when she spied the one-inch slash on the side upholstery. Apparently, the fabric had snagged on the door hinge. Why hadn't she taken the time to take the door off?

Why hadn't she taken her time, period? She gave in to her anger and spewed profanity.

Next time, she'd take the help.

She left the chair right where it was, just inside the door, and trudged to the fridge for a beer. With the hem of her shirt, she twisted off the bottle cap and gulped down a quarter of the brew then collapsed into her new, now marred, chair. Maybe Grandma knew how to sew it. She'd call and invite her over for a sewing lesson and promise un-scorched cookies. She yanked the side lever and the footrest popped up. At least she hadn't broken *that*.

Broken. She recalled Beth's words from this morning: *It's about realizing we're broken...*

Beth's words and tenderness left Amber nearly paralyzed. For a moment she'd wanted to spill everything, right then and there. Dump out all the broken, jagged pieces before Beth and say, you want broken? I'll show you broken. Now what? Some things were too broken to be fixed, not for all the king's horses and all the king's men.

As pious and sweet as she was, Beth didn't have a clue about broken. She didn't understand real life. Maybe God forgave sins like cheating on your taxes, but to claim that anyone could somehow wriggle their way into God's affection, no matter what they've done, that was just plain naïve. Even forgiveness had its limits. Last Monday when Miranda read words from John about the evil done in secret coming to light, Amber kept her head down, her hair falling at the sides of her face like a shield, hopefully hiding her burning cheeks. Miranda said God had bought their salvation with his own blood. Amber saw a bloody bathtub and a bloodstained towel. Miranda said God wanted them to come to him and admit their failings. Amber saw a girl running in the darkness. Miranda said God longed to forgive them and grant them new life, new birth. Amber shut her eyes, wishing she could shut her ears to the faint sound of a newborn's cry.

No. Such forgiveness didn't extend to her. Besides, she was fine on her own. Yet something seemed to be sprouting inside of her, fighting to break free. Some restlessness she couldn't conquer, some longing she couldn't gratify. She was merely missing Paul, she told herself with little conviction.

Her phone jingled. She answered and immediately regretted it. Margaret sounded drunk. Her speech garbled and disjointed.

"Mom, I can't understand a word you're saying." She was about to hang up but heard her mother choke back a sob. She wasn't drunk. She was crying.

"She's had a stroke," Margaret said.

"Who? Who are you talking about?"

But she already knew.

22

Beth was jotting out a grocery list when Amber called. "Did you get your chair in?" she asked as she checked her flour supply. "Looks like a storm's coming."

Amber made a strange sound and didn't answer.

"Amber?"

"It's my grandma."

Beth set down her pen. "What happened?"

"She's had a stroke."

"Oh, Amber. Are you alone?"

A long pause then, "Yes."

"I'll be right over." She sent a text to Eric, grabbed an umbrella, and headed out.

Minutes later, when Amber opened the door to her apartment and let her in, she almost tripped over the beige recliner. She thought she noticed a small tear on one side, an imperfection she didn't remember seeing before.

Amber paced the length of the small room. "I need to see her."

"I'll drive you. You shouldn't go by yourself."

Amber didn't protest.

❧

The rain drummed the roof of the car like nervous fingertips as Beth considered all the things she could say to Amber, all the greeting card quips she had both heard and spoken with good intentions. Right now, no words seemed adequate. The rain intensified and she switched her wipers to high.

Amber lit up a cigarette. Within moments, the car was thick with smoke and Beth rolled down the window a fraction. Raindrops splattered her thighs.

"Sorry," Amber said. She rolled down her own window a few inches and attempted to exhale through the space. "I wasn't thinking."

Beth glanced at her. "It's OK."

Miles passed in silence.

Amber shifted in her seat. "There's so much I need to tell her," she said. She drew her cigarette to her mouth with trembling hands. The windshield wipers ticked off the seconds and Amber said nothing else.

"I'm sure you'll be able to." Beth regretted the words as soon as she spoke them. She wasn't sure. She wasn't sure at all.

સ્

The elevator door parted on the third floor of St. Mary's, and Amber took off for the nurse's station. Beth followed.

"Virginia Swansen," Amber said to the woman behind the desk.

A woman who seemed to be around her own age, with frizzy grayish blonde hair and a splotchy pink face approached them and clutched Amber's arm. "You're too late."

Amber glared at the woman and jerked her arm free. She addressed the nurse again. "Virginia Swansen's room please."

"She's *gone*, Amber," the frizzy haired woman said in a raspy voice.

Amber slammed her palms against the counter and Beth jumped. *"Virginia Swansen!"*

The nurse tipped her head, her eyes sympathetic. "I'm so sorry."

Beth stepped forward and gently placed a hand on Amber's shoulder. Amber startled then gaped at Beth, her eyes wide and frenetic. She took a step backward, her eyes darting from Beth to the nurse to the other woman, until she backed into a row of gray chairs, collapsed into one, and dropped her face in her hands.

∂∽∅

Amber directed Beth to her grandmother's house in a quiet almost mechanical voice. After telling Beth to make herself at home, Amber shut herself in one of the bedrooms. The rain let up and Beth went outside for a walk. She dodged puddles and called Eric.

"I think she wants me to stay," she said halfway into their conversation. "Through the funeral and everything."

"Has she asked you to?"

"Not in so many words."

"Then stay," Eric said. "Michael or I can drop off whatever you need. I'm in your corner, babe."

How had she gotten so lucky? "And I'm in yours."

After listing out the things she'd need Eric to bring, she hung up and climbed Ginny's porch steps and sat down on the hanging swing. What she really wanted to do was crawl into bed and call it a day. Was it just this morning she and Amber and Gretchen and Lily had hopped from yard sale to yard sale, sipping

Starbucks? Her stomach growled, and she realized she'd missed lunch. The last thing she'd eaten was an apple turnover courtesy of Gretchen.

Closing her eyes, she pushed back with her feet and recalled the look on Amber's face when she returned from viewing her grandmother's body. Beth remained in the waiting area, thoughtlessly flipping through magazines, until she spotted Amber coming down the corridor, face ashen, eyes haunted. For some reason, Michael's face flashed to her mind. Something in Amber's shattered expression mirrored Michael's when he'd uncovered the truth of his abandonment.

She'd wanted to embrace Amber, but not only had Amber made no move toward her, she seemed to cower into herself, with her arms crossed tightly over chest, her spine curved. Beth knew what to do with a sobbing friend, but this stoicism baffled her. So she patted Amber's shoulder and then, at Amber's request, drove her here.

Beth's stomach rumbled again. The thought of wandering through a stranger's kitchen — particularly one who just died — filled her with unease, but necessity and hunger won out. They needed to eat. She slipped into the house and tiptoed down the hall to Amber's room to make sure it'd be all right if she cooked something but thought better of it. The woman was swimming in grief. She probably couldn't care less what Beth did.

As she crept back to the kitchen, she scanned the photographs lining the wall. A pretty little girl with deep blue eyes and long blonde braids smiled at her. Beth paused to study the picture. Over the last month, Amber had tossed out bits and pieces about her past and family life and from what Beth could fit together,

her childhood sounded far from idyllic. After meeting her mother today, the picture came into clearer focus. Beth studied the little girl on the wall, wondering how deep the hidden wounds ran.

She made her way to the kitchen and took inventory of a stranger's fridge. A bag of carrots. A few stalks of still crisp celery. An onion. She opened the freezer and struck gold with a package of frozen chicken breasts. Scanning the kitchen, she determined where she'd keep the baking supplies if she lived here. Hopeful, she opened a pantry door and found a canister of flour, salt, and baking powder. Perfect. Everything she needed for chicken dumpling soup.

While the chicken defrosted in the microwave, she filled a stockpot with water and noticed a note-card with a handwritten Bible verse taped to the windowsill above the sink. She read the verse and felt a thrill of connection. As the water heated to a boil, she chopped vegetables. Once the chicken was simmering, she set about making the dumplings. By the time she was dropping the dumplings into the boiling soup, Amber emerged.

"Were you able to sleep?" Beth asked.

Amber nodded. "A little."

"I hope this is OK," Beth said, nodding at the disarrayed kitchen. "I thought you might be getting hungry."

Amber sat at the table and rested her chin in her hands.

Beth secured the lid on the soup and turned the heat down to simmer. "I'm more than happy to stay here with you, but I don't want to be in the way—"

"No," Amber said quickly. "Stay. If you can. I don't want to be alone with her."

Beth could only presume she meant her mother. "Do you think she'll mind?"

"I don't care if she does."

When the dumplings had swelled into doughy sponges, Beth found bowls and ladled out two and carried them to the table. She slid into the chair across from Amber, who sat pushing around a carrot with her spoon.

"My dad died three years ago," Beth said after some time. "It felt like I'd gone to bed and woken up in a different world. It was so strange to think of life without him. I'm so sorry, Amber. I know there aren't words."

Amber lifted her spoon to her mouth and took the tiniest taste. "How did he die?"

"Pancreatic cancer." The words tasted like poison in her mouth. "And in a way, his passing came as a relief after all of his suffering, but that doesn't mean we didn't grieve."

She took a sip of soup, remembering how the disease had whittled her once brawny father into a gnarled shadow of a man. In his final moments, as she and Gretchen and their mother clung to each other, encircling Dad's hospice bed as he passed from material to eternal, heaven seemed as tangible as the house next door. And at the same time, losing him felt like someone had ripped off a patch of her skin. And she had Eric to lean on. And Gretchen, and Michael, and her mother. She glanced up at Amber, alone at the table. Where *was* everyone?

Amber took another sip of soup and looked out the window.

By the time Margaret shuffled through the door, Beth was looking for a container to store the leftovers.

Amber still sat absently at the table. Margaret peered into the half-eaten bowl in front of her. "What's that?"

Amber looked up at her mother. "It's called soup."

Beth took out a clean bowl, ready to ladle. Margaret's eye's flashed over her. "I already ate."

"And drank, apparently," Amber said. She stood up, carried her bowl to the sink, rinsed it, then turned to her mother. "We need to figure out the funeral."

Margaret wobbled over to the table and sat down. She wiped at her nose with the back of her hand and let out a little cry.

Beth glanced at Amber, waiting for her to go to her mother. Speak a gentle word. Offer a gentle touch. *Something*. But Amber maintained her stance at the kitchen sink and crossed her arms. "The pastor said Tuesday would work. Not that any of this matters to you."

Beth felt a jolt of shock.

"Oh here we go," Margaret said, lifting her face from her hands.

"Would it have killed you to spend any time with her? That's all she wanted you know."

"You didn't know the half of it, Amber. You didn't know her like I did. Try growing up with her, with a mother who is never, *ever*, happy with anything you do, who tells you everything you do is *wrong*."

Amber's eyes narrowed. "Don't worry. I *have*."

"Oh, you think so? You think I was so terrible? Well I never left you with something like this!" Margaret pushed up her shirt sleeve, and Beth thought she could make out a small pink mark. A scar.

"How many times are you going to play that card, Mom?" Amber said. "She never pretended to be perfect. She never denied hurting you. She only wanted to fix things, and you wouldn't let her."

"Not everything can be fixed."

Amber spun around and gripped the edge of the counter. Beth stood frozen in the corner, feeling like an intruder, huddled next to a Peace Lily on top of a small shelf of cookbooks. The cuckoo clock on the wall *tisked* disapprovingly. Suddenly the phone rang, cutting through the arctic silence. Beth looked at Amber, then Margaret. Neither woman budged. The phone trilled again. Beth stepped toward it. "Do you want me to…?"

Amber nodded.

Beth answered and after a minute covered the receiver with her hand. "It's the pastor. He'd like to talk about funeral arrangements."

Amber's attention darted to Margaret who had covered her face with her hands again. Sighing, Amber took the phone. After awhile she hung up and turned to Margaret. "The funeral's on Tuesday at eleven. The church will provide a lunch afterwards."

Margaret sat back in her chair. "We don't need their handouts."

Amber slammed the phone down. "*Fine. You* tell them. If you want something different then *you* talk to them."

"You couldn't pay me to talk to those people. Nothing but a bunch of self-righteous hypocrites."

"Everything is a soap opera with you, Mom."

"This is the same church that practically kicked me out when they found out I was pregnant. You think I want their charity now?"

"That was thirty-seven years ago!" Amber pinched the bridge of her nose with her thumb and forefinger. "Look, I'll talk to the pastor about the funeral arrangements. I don't want to get into this now, OK?"

Margaret's eyes flashed to Beth. "Oh, sorry. Wouldn't want to upset the guest."

Heat flooded Beth's face. She took a step toward the door that led to the porch. "You two have a lot to discuss. I'll just..."

Margaret swatted the air as if the room suddenly stunk. "No, no. Don't worry. I was about to leave anyway. There's never been enough room for me in this house."

"Mom, you know that's not true. Grandma *wanted* you here." Beth heard a trace of vulnerability in Amber's voice and caught a glimpse of a girl who wanted her mother.

But the look was lost on Margaret. She grabbed her purse and made for the door. "Too late for that. I'll see you at the funeral."

Amber stood motionless, staring at the closed door as if waiting for someone to walk through it.

23

It seemed like a horrible prank gone wrong, a joke pushed too far. But in the narthex of the church, the simple oak box cradling Ginny's body cemented the truth. Amber stood beside her grandma who only appeared to be sleeping, grasped her hand, and wordlessly demanded the impossible. *Wake up, wake up!*

Hushed sounds of life surrounded her: the rustling of skirts, quiet footsteps along carpet, the organ droning mournfully from the sanctuary. Soon the pallbearers would arrive and carry Grandma into the sanctuary, away from her. Something like panic seized Amber, and she turned to the pastor standing a few feet away. "Can I have a minute?"

He nodded and strolled away.

Amber gathered Ginny's hands in her own, startled once more by their lifelessness. How could these hands—hands that produced fresh-squeezed lemonade, hands that cradled her face, often in love, sometimes in reprimand—be so unresponsive? How could life go on without these hands?

She felt as if she were drowning, as if water was rising around her and inside she was thrashing her arms and legs to keep her head above the flood of grief, to breathe. She forced herself to inhale and exhale and swallow down the emotion. The cosmetician had gone overboard, she thought as she studied Grandma's uncharacteristically glistening lips and rouged cheeks. Grandma only ever wore lip balm. She found a tissue in her purse and gently blotted Ginny's stained mouth, then turned the tissue over and blotted the unnaturally pink cheeks. Then, with her comb, she tamed down the pouf of hair and smoothed out her grandma's blouse, the soft rhythm of footsteps behind her.

No, she wanted to scream. She wasn't ready yet. She wanted to fling herself on top of Grandma and command the squad of pallbearers to march right out the door. But when she looked over her shoulder, she only saw an elderly woman donned in a black chiffon dress and a wide-brimmed hat, clutching an intricately carved wooden cane.

Lizzie. Vibrant, vivacious Lizzie. Now a hobbling old woman.

Lizzie approached the casket and grasped Amber's forearm with her free hand. Her head bobbled in Ginny's direction. "This is my dear friend!"

Amber covered Lizzie's vein rippled hand with her own. "Hi, Lizzie."

The old woman looked as surprised as a child. "You know me? Yes, I'm Lizzie!" She narrowed her eyes suspiciously. "Who are you?"

Amber wanted to weep. "Amber. Ginny's granddaughter."

Lizzie nodded but her face registered bewilderment.

Amber cleared her throat. She'd play her role, for Grandma's sake. "Thank you for coming. I know it would mean so much to Ginny to know you were here today."

"Oh, I wouldn't miss this day for anything. And doesn't she look charming?" Lizzie reached out a tremulous hand to touch the string of pearls circling Grandma's neck, pearls she'd worn on her wedding day. Pearls that Margaret would later unclasp and keep. "So, so lovely."

Lizzie stared vacantly at Ginny for some time. Amber glanced around, searching for a chaperone, her son or whoever had brought her, but found no one. She placed her hand on Lizzie's back. "Would you like to sit down?"

Lizzie looked at her as if she suggested she eat her cane.

"In the sanctuary?" Amber said. "Would you like to sit down? I think we're going to start soon."

A shadow of understanding passed before Lizzie's eyes, and her mouth parted slightly. She blinked a few times, as if waking from a dream, and suddenly she was Lizzie again.

She grasped Amber's hand. "Precious, precious girl. I have something to say. 'The Lord is compassionate and gracious, slow to anger and abounding in love. He does not treat us as our sins deserve nor repay us according to our iniquities. For as high as the heavens are above the earth, so great is his love for those who fear him. As far as the east is from the west, so far has he removed our transgression from us. Today if you hear his voice, my dear Amber, do not harden your heart. Repent then, and turn to God so that your sins may be wiped out.'" Lizzie pressed her thumb into Amber's palm, her eyes beams of fire, her mouth curved in a knowing smile.

Amber stood motionless, caught under the intensity of Lizzie's gaze, and she didn't dare look away. Lizzie was a doctor, scouting out a disease, and Amber was the patient pinned down by truth. Fear and hope boiled inside of her at the possibility that Lizzie could see right through her, see past the armor, beyond the wall of pretense to the hidden hope that had taken root deep in her soul this past month.

She looked away and groped for words. She wanted to ask Lizzie if it were true, if the words she'd spoken were true. True for *her*. She felt the throb of longing, of needing to know, and turned to Lizzie with the question on her tongue. But the moment of lucidity was gone. Lizzie had receded back into that secret, unreachable world of hers, staring vacantly at Grandma.

"I wonder if they'll serve popcorn," Lizzie chirped. "How I do love an organ!" And with that, she hobbled away.

When the service started minutes later, Amber sat next to Margaret, half expecting Ginny to sit up and insist she hadn't been sleeping, like she did whenever she dozed off on the porch, the wind chime dancing above them. If only Amber could lean over and gently nudge her now, bring her back to consciousness, bring her back to where she needed to be. Here on earth with her.

Amber smoothed her gray skirt and ordered herself to keep it together. She could fall apart soon enough, in privacy, when every eye wasn't boring into the back of her. Wondering about her. Judging her. Lizzie's words resounded in her mind: *Repent then and turn to God…*

Someone stood behind the podium and gave a eulogy. Someone else read a verse. Then a heavyset brunette wearing a purple floral dress bustled onto the stage and introduced herself as Jackie. One of the women in Grandma's prayer group, Amber recalled.

"We're going to miss Virginia around here," Jackie said. "One of the things I loved most about Ginny is how she loved to sing. Let's stand and sing one of her favorite hymns." Jackie sang out in a clear soprano voice:

To God be the glory, great things He hath done!
So loved He the world that He gave us His Son.
Who yielded His life an atonement for sin,
And opened the Life-gate that all may go in.

Amber stirred under the weight of the words as the congregation belted out the chorus before Jackie went on to the second verse:

"O perfect redemption, the purchase of blood!
To every believer the promise of God;
The vilest offender who truly believes,
That moment from Jesus a pardon receives"

The words echoed Lizzie's pronouncement. What if it were true? Amber wondered again. The small seed of hope reared up, stronger than ever. She regarded the face she loved more than anything and felt a jolt of realization; Grandma's body was but an empty shell. The truth settled within her like a rock. A fresh wave of grief crashed into her, threatening to uproot the tenacious bud of hope. Grandma was gone and she'd been abandoned. There was no hope. Not for her.

The hymn ended and the pastor read about streets of gold. He said God loved every single person. He spoke words about Christ's death and resurrection, redemption and eternal life, words Amber had heard dozens of times before from Grandma and Lizzie and Beth and Miranda. Words that warred within her as hope and despair dueled for control. They seemed too simple, these words. This preacher, just like anyone who touted this Jesus thing, glided through life as a

195

mere simpleton. Out of touch with reality. Or they were all hypocrites. Or selling something.

Except for Grandma. And Lizzie. And Beth and Miranda.

The service ended in a blur. The pallbearers carried Grandma down the aisle, and Amber endured the gravesite ceremony as if on autopilot, like an out-of-body experience. Sometime later, she found herself back in the church fellowship hall, pushing around globs of casseroles.

Jackie pulled out the metal folding chair beside Amber and sat down. She introduced herself as Jackie. "Your grandma loved you so much, Amber."

Amber nodded. She sampled a bit of a green fluffy salad but had trouble swallowing.

"We'll all miss her, her and her spunk," Jackie went on. "You be sure to let us know if you need something. Anything. This church is here for you."

Amber looked into Jackie's hazel eyes and nodded.

When the crowd thinned, the ladies working in the kitchen loaded Amber and Margaret with containers of leftover food. Amber and Beth drove back to Ginny's house in silence. Margaret mentioned she needed to pick up cigarettes and would stop by later.

When Amber stepped into the house, her stomach tightened. Never again would she see Grandma washing dishes at the sink or reading her magazines on the sofa in her raggedy slippers. Amber stepped out of her flats and wandered to her room. The Georgia O'Keefe print hanging over her bed greeted her like a familiar face. She changed into shorts and a tank top, leaving her skirt in a heap on the floor, and considered curling up in a ball and pulling the covers over her head. But the sounds of Beth moving about in the kitchen and the yearning of her soul propelled her out.

"You may want to freeze some of this," Beth said, sorting through baked goods at the table.

Amber poked a loaf of banana bread. "Way too much food."

"This is how people respond to grief, I guess. It's all done in love, you know."

Amber went to the refrigerator and took out the lemonade pitcher, poured two glasses and set them on the table. "No milk, no bread, but she still has lemonade."

Beth took a sip, and Amber watched her lips curve into a surprised smile. "Tastes like the real deal. I haven't had this kind of lemonade since I was a kid."

"That's all she'd drink." Amber cleared a trail through the condensation along the glass pitcher. "I think I'll keep this."

"You should."

Amber took a drink, her stomach tumbling. "I'll show you something else," she said on impulse and bolted out. She returned holding a framed cross-stitch. "This has been hanging in her room for years. Not much to look at, I guess."

Beth lightly traced her finger over the image of the daisy-filled basket. "She made this?"

"We both did. For some reason, she thought I should know how to cross-stitch. What a joke. I spent more time untangling knots and pulling out my hair than anything." Poking a needle through a pinprick of a hole over and over again to create some predestined, cliché picture had driven Amber crazy. Where was the creativity in that? One night, after realizing she had made a chain of x's a row too high, she hurled the hoop across the room and let the curses fly. Without a word, Grandma walked over, picked up the fabric, and set to work. *Finish what you start, Amber.* Yet in the end, Grandma was the one to finish it.

"Bet you can tell which half is mine," Amber said.

Beth studied the needlepoint for a moment then looked up and shrugged.

"Oh, come on. You're too nice for your own good. See this part, all sloppy and loose? That's mine. Here's Grandma's half. Perfect stitches."

"I think it's beautiful. It holds a piece of both of you."

Amber took the frame back and swiped the dust from the bottom ridge with her index finger.

"Everyone had such wonderful things to say about her at the ceremony," Beth said and began transferring brownies into a plastic baggie. "The more I hear about her the more I wish I could've met her. The music was beautiful, too. That church sure does love to sing."

Amber set the cross-stitch aside, her pulse accelerating. "Grandma used to blast out these old hymns on her CD player like a teenager. Old stuff. Honky-tonk pianos and everything. I don't think I've ever heard that one song, though, the one the soloist sang."

"To God be the Glory," Beth said, not looking up. "That's a good one."

Amber took a gulp of lemonade. She felt shaky and volatile, like a kettle of torrid water inching toward boiling point. Needing something to occupy her, she paced to the refrigerator, slid out one of the crisper drawers, and set it on the counter. "I can't get one of the lines out of my head. Something like, the vilest offender who truly believes…"

"That moment from Jesus a pardon receives," Beth finished.

"Yeah. That's the one." She tossed out a bag of overripe cherries and a sack of wilted lettuce, then carried the crisper drawer to the sink and filled it with warm water and dish detergent. She scrubbed the bin as her soul raged. She rinsed and dried the container and returned the still fresh food, then slid the drawer back in place. Now what? Sunlight poured into the kitchen. "Let's go out to the porch. I need some air."

The porch's worn, smooth floorboards welcomed Amber's bare feet like old friends. She sank into the embrace of the swing and watched Beth settle herself into Grandma's sturdy, oak rocking chair, surprised that the gesture didn't bother her. She'd considered taking the rocking chair back to Elkin with her but decided against it. Removing it from the porch seemed as severe as an amputation. The chair belonged here.

They rocked silently, fragments from dozens of conversations tumbling over each other in Amber's mind, words Grandma had longed to impart, but Amber had swatted away like flies. The chains on the porch swing groaned in remorse. What would she give to sit here with Grandma one last time? What would she say? What would she reveal? She closed her eyes, grieving the lost opportunities, and opened her eyes to Beth.

"How is your heart?" Beth asked.

The question struck Amber as odd, one she'd never been asked before. Shattered, Amber thought of saying. Shattered into a million pieces. She grasped the chain of the swing, her fingernails digging into her palm. "It's strange seeing you in her chair."

Beth ceased rocking and looked at her, stricken.

"I'm sorry…I didn't think…"

"No, it's fine. It works, seeing you there. Grandma and you…you're a little alike somehow." Heart racing, she contemplated letting that being the end of it, letting the moment sail past. There was so much to do, so many tasks inside needing her attention, so many papers to sort though. But her soul wouldn't let her. She couldn't turn this ship around now.

"I'll take that as a compliment," Beth said.

"Grandma loved God, talked about Him like He lived next door. Lizzie, too. And you, I see that in you, too. But I have some questions." She felt a rush of foolishness, as if she were a child trying to ride a bike for the first time, shaking and wobbling and not sure how to make the thing go. Yet at the same time, something compelled her forward, urging her to release the questions whirling around in her head. She had to chase down the truth of Lizzie's words. "You all talk about how much God loves us, how He wants to forgive us. I want in on that. How does that work? How do I ask for God's forgiveness?"

Beth leaned forward and smiled. "You simply ask."

24

Coffee mug in hand, Beth crept to the porch, hoping not to disturb a still sleeping Amber. She slid into Ginny's rocking chair, warmed by the bond she felt to the woman she'd never met, and took a sip of the strong brew.

She leaned her head back, the sweet perfume of summer mingling with the rich aroma of her coffee. Cumulus clouds billowed across the blue sky, the kinds of clouds she'd imagine living in as a kid. Soft cotton castles with ever-shifting walls. Today she envisioned angels bursting from them, still celebrating the events of yesterday. After rising from her knees on the porch, Amber's face had glowed in a kind of bashful surprise, and Beth couldn't stop herself from throwing her arms around the girl in joy.

The porch door rattled open, and Amber stepped out in her pajamas.

Beth smiled up at her. "Good morning."

Amber raised her coffee mug in greeting, nestled into the swing, and pulled her knees up to her chest. "I slept like a rock."

"Good. You probably needed it."

Amber ran her hand across the white chipping paint of one of the porch pillars. "I really need to give this thing a makeover."

"I love these big old porches. It's a pity new houses are seldom built with them."

Amber took a sip of coffee, her eyes scanning the structure. They swayed in comfortable silence for a while. "Can we leave by noon?"

Beth nodded, longing for home. "I'll be ready."

⤙⤚

A few hours later, packed and on their way, Beth set the cruise control and flipped down her visor as the sunlight poured in through the car window and toasted her legs inside her jeans. A mere sixty miles separated her from home yet she felt like it was six hundred.

"Do you mind?" Amber said and held up her pack of cigarettes and gave them a slight shake.

Beth shut off the air conditioner and rolled down her window. "No, it's OK."

"I'd love to quit," Amber said after exhaling through her open window.

"Have you ever tried?"

"Yeah, once. I was doing pretty well, down to just one or two a day, and then I moved in with Paul who smokes like a chimney. Hard to quit when you're inhaling secondhand smoke all day long. I'll blame it on him." She exhaled out the window. "Grandma was right about him. I don't know how it happens, but I always seem to pick the biggest loser in the bar, some jerk who doesn't think twice about shacking up with my supposed best friend on the sly."

Beth tightened her grip on the steering wheel, her thoughts scrambling for a point of reference, for a way to relate, but came up with nothing. Eric had his share of bad-boy stories, but overall, her life was pretty boring. Even her teenage years. Once, at camp, she and her cabin mates got busted for skinny-dipping. But that was forty years ago.

"Is that why you moved to Elkin?" she asked. "To get away from Paul?"

"What? You don't believe my gelato story? I'll take gelato over any man."

Beth scanned an approaching billboard. "How do you feel about cheese curds?"

"They're right up there with gelato."

Beth decelerated and waited for an Amish buggy to clop past before turning into the parking lot of the family-owned cheese factory. Gentle green hills surrounded them like a billowed blanket, polka-dotted with white and red barns. Amber finished her cigarette and flicked it in the trashcan before they made their way inside.

Beth purchased two pounds of curds, still warm in the bag, and Amber bought two bottles of flavored water. They settled back in the car, the bag of curds in the cup-holder between them.

"Can I pick you up for church on Sunday?" Beth asked after she turned on the highway.

Amber shrugged. "I don't know."

Beth glanced at her. "What? What's wrong?"

"Just the whole church scene."

"You'll know a few of the women from study. Gretchen and her family attend, as well as Miranda and her family."

Amber reached for a curd. "Right. Families."

"It's not all families," Beth said, understanding. "There are students and singles and senior citizens, the whole mix. The single's group is pretty active. I think they meet on Thursdays."

Amber glared at her. "You're not planning on

fixing me up are you?"

"No. I'll hold off on that for a while. But I think you should at least give it a shot. Church, I mean. I think you'll like it." Beth extracted a curd, the cheese squeaky fresh in her mouth.

"I don't fit into church. There's so much about me you don't know. So much from my past..." She let the sentence hang and took a drink of water. "I just don't fit in. Not even after what happened yesterday."

"We're all works in progress. Everybody struggles with something."

Amber made a sniffing sound. "Yeah. OK."

"No, really."

Amber turned to her. "OK. What do you struggle with?"

Beth fought the urge to backpedal. She might have glided through an idyllic childhood, graciously spared from teenage heartache, but she certainly battled her share of vices: Pride. Jealousy. Depression. Feeling the need to control every last detail. The crisis of Ginny's death had thrust her and Amber into a deeper friendship, forced intimacy, but even so, she wanted to hold back. Friendship took time. Complete transparency was earned. "I'm a control freak," she said finally. "When Eric folds the bathroom towels I re-fold them because he does it wrong."

Amber sat silent for a moment. "Your man folds towels wrong? *That's* your biggest struggle?"

"No, I'm talking about my need for control. It's crazy, I know, but I like all the towels to face the same way in the linen closest, seam side out. See. Control freak."

"Golly, Beth. Maybe you can find a support group for that." Amber erupted with laughter.

Even though it was at her expense, Beth welcomed the sound. "Maybe that was a bad example."

"No. That's a perfect example. You've proved my point."

"I know we've led very different lives, but I struggle with sin just like anybody." Beth rounded a curve, an old REO Speedwagon song playing softly in the background. "What happened between your mom and your grandmother?" she asked after a while. "If you don't mind my asking."

"*I* happened." Amber unscrewed her water bottle, took a swig, and recapped it. "Mom got pregnant with me when she was fifteen. She didn't tell Grandma and Grandpa for months and when she did, Grandma went ballistic, threw Mom out of the house. They had problems before, I guess, but this was the final straw for Grandma. Mom lived with a friend until I was born and then we moved in with Grandma until I was five. I don't remember a lot, but I do remember the fighting. Eventually Mom stormed out in a rage, took me with her, and I didn't see Grandma for fourteen years. Then one day, out of the blue, Grandma called and invited me over for dinner, and after that, she wouldn't leave me alone. She was going to love on me whether I liked it or not, she told me later."

Beth digested the story. "I bet you're glad of that."

"I wouldn't be here if she hadn't." Amber turned to look out her window. "You don't know how lucky you are, to have the family you have. Your sister, your husband. Michael. What you've told me about your parents. You don't know how lucky you are."

Compassion surged through Beth. Even after three years, she still sometimes expected to see her father under the hood of a car in her mom's driveway.

Whenever the loss of him pierced her afresh, whenever a memory swept over her, knotting her heart in her chest, she called Gretchen or her mother and they remembered together. She leaned on them, and they leaned on her. Who did Amber have?

A half an hour later, Beth pulled up beside Amber's apartment and carried in her suitcase. "I'll call you tomorrow," she said at the door and gave Amber a hug.

Amber locked eyes with her when they parted. "Thanks. For everything."

Beth nodded and returned to the family she had been reminded to cherish.

25

The trill of a bird pulled Amber from sleep, yet she fought against waking, sensing a reason lay behind her desire to linger in the nothingness. Her mind began shifting pieces together, and all at once, she remembered, and just like every morning since Grandma's funeral five days ago, she fought to return to sleep, to that sweet oblivion that divided dream from wakefulness, that fleeting place where her brain tricked her into thinking Grandma was still with her. But morning after morning she awoke anyway, and her heart plummeted once more.

Amber opened her eyes. After tucking a pillow behind her back, she sat up and reached for the Bible on the nightstand. She propped the book against her raised knees and traced the gold engraved *Virginia Swansen* on the worn leather cover. She lifted the book to her nose and inhaled the earthy scent of leather, with hints of lemon, and longed for Grandma.

The enormity of the book overwhelmed her. She could easily find the Gospel of John now, and Beth had suggested she dive into the book of Psalms and showed her where it was. With her thumb, she flipped through the tissue-thin pages, skimmed a section in the Psalms, then flipped ahead and randomly selected another chapter. David, the writer of these poems according to most of the chapter headings, seemed like a certified manic-depressive, vacillating between grief and joy, anger and remorse. A Van Gogh of words. She connected with his paradox of emotion. More than once, she'd wipe dampness from her cheeks these last few days and realized, with surprise, that she'd been crying. And then, in the midst of her grief, a jolt of happiness hit, like a lightning bolt.

Something had happened when she knelt on Grandma's porch beside Beth, when she grasped on to this crazy forgiveness thing. The words she and Beth uttered in prayer were simple, childish almost, and yet something happened, something loosened and opened inside of her. Sorrow plagued her, yes, but she also felt wrapped in a new kind of hope, as if she'd stepped out from a dark cave and into a room filled with light. Instinctively, she wanted to run to Grandma, tell her about it, explain how her soul had been taken out and shaken clean, and then sadness engulfed her when she remembered she couldn't. She'd lost her chance.

Yes, she connected to David and his conflicting emotions. She was heartbroken but healed. Lonely but filled. Back and forth, back and forth, her heart turning as swiftly as a fan. She couldn't predict her feelings from one minute to the next.

She turned a few pages ahead and stopped in Psalm 32:

"When I kept silent, my bones wasted away through my groaning all day long. For day and night, your hand was heavy upon me; my strength was sapped as in the heat of summer. Then I acknowledged my sin to you and did not cover up my iniquity. I said, 'I will confess my transgressions to the Lord'—and you forgave the guilt of my sin."

"May 20, 1983," was printed along the margin in tiny block lettering.

Amber reflected on Grandma's account of first meeting Lizzie, when she joined the new pastor's wife's scandalous Bible study. This date brimmed with meaning. And now Amber had her own date to mark.

She found a pen in her nightstand drawer and underneath Grandma's handwriting printed, "July 19, 2012." Five days ago. The day she silently confessed the darkness of her soul. The day she crumbled and began to let her heart mend. The day she'd knelt on Grandma's porch as a hopeless beggar and risen as a child of God. The day commemorating Grandma's death and her new life.

In a flash, she knew exactly what she wanted to do today. She'd suppressed the desire for so long, pushed it under guilt and denial and daily survival, but today she'd give in. Today was a new day. Marked by loss and grief, yes, but also liberation.

She closed the book and jumped out of bed. Riddled with anticipation, she rummaged through her closet until she found the cardboard box, pulled it out, and picked at the packing tape with her fingernail until it loosened. In one fierce tug, she ripped the tape from the box, sending the cardboard flaps springing upward. Then her hand plunged inside the box, diving past the crumpled newspaper. Her fingers touched the soft, familiar heads of her brushes. She removed the bouquet fastened together by twine and slid out her favorite—a flat camelhair—and tickled her forearm. Soft as baby hair. Like a caresses from an old friend.

Time to give in to her soul's desire. Time to paint again.

The portable easel snapped together in seconds. She positioned it beside the window then squirted out dollops of rainbow on her artist's palette, dipped her brush in the brilliant yellow, and felt as if she was breathing again for the first time in a long while. Her eyes pricked with tears at the first stroke against the white canvas. She painted, stood back, reconsidered, painted over. That was the beauty of paint, its mercy, its magnanimity. Any mess could be fixed, painted over again and again, layer upon layer, until even the most ghastly of mistakes disappeared under a liquid blanket of color.

A breeze rustled in from the window, stroking Amber's arms as she gave herself to her work. Time disappeared as she lost herself in the sweeps of gold and crimson and russet, unconscious to everything but the colors and shapes materializing before her eyes.

She was alive again.

⇝⇞

The following Sunday, Amber waited for Beth outside the front doors of Elkin Community Church and indulged in a cigarette. She owed it to Beth, she supposed, after everything she'd done for her, staying with her through the funeral and all. Besides, it was only an hour on Sunday.

Amber exhaled over her shoulder as a high-heeled churchgoer glanced her way and wrinkled her nose. Amber took a deep drag and blew smoke in an exaggerated way as the woman disappeared behind the glass doors. Maybe she'd tattle on her. Maybe she'd luck out and they wouldn't let her in.

Her agitation growing, she considered calling Beth and making up an illness but spotted Miranda and her flock of children approaching. A curly-haired boy perched on Miranda's hip while she clutched the hand of a little girl. Three older kids trailed behind with a man Amber assumed was Miranda's husband. Miranda gave her a quick, one-armed hug. "Come in with us."

"I'm waiting for Beth."

The small girl tugged at Miranda's arm. "OK, I'll see you in there. I need to get these monkeys checked into nursery."

Amber watched them topple through the door and turned and saw Beth clipping toward her, Eric and Michael close behind.

"You're here!" Beth said, breathless.

Amber exhaled over her shoulder. Sometimes the woman beamed a little too brightly. "I'm here."

Michael offered a quick wave and passed through the doors. Beth glanced at her watch. "Sorry, we're a little late."

Amber looked at the cigarette between her fingers, scanned the area for a receptacle, but found nothing. Eric nodded toward the rocks. "We'll pick it up on our way out." He breathed in deeply and shook his head. "Man, every now and then I still get the hankering."

"You smoked?" Amber asked.

"A lifetime ago." He swung his arm around Beth's shoulder. "Before Beth here reformed me."

Amber dropped the butt on the cement and crushed it with the toe of her shoe before nudging it into the stones.

She followed Beth and Eric through the church's foyer and into the sanctuary where, mercifully, they sat toward the back. Within seconds, the band on stage came to life. Everyone stood, and Amber followed suit, the music so unlike Grandma's church. Pulsating. Modern. After the songs, the pastor took the stage and talked about the power of the tongue. He didn't shout once.

When the service ended, Gretchen appeared and gave Amber's arm a soft squeeze. "I'm so sorry to hear about your grandmother's passing."

Amber felt a strange stirring as she looked into Gretchen's kind green eyes, a sense of déjà vu. She mumbled, "thank you" and twisted the church papers in her hand.

Gretchen turned to Beth. "So, what are you all doing for lunch?"

"I don't know," Beth said. "We haven't planned that far."

"Let's go to your house and order Chinese."

Beth clicked her tongue. "Why my house? My house is a disaster."

"Fabulous. I spent all afternoon cleaning mine yesterday, and I don't want it messed up."

Beth gathered her purse. "But it's OK to mess up *my* house."

"You just said it was a disaster so what difference does it make?"

Gretchen gave Amber a conspiratorial wink, and Amber wondered, not for the first time, what it would have been like to grow up with a sister. Or a brother, for that matter.

"Fine," Beth said. "My house it is. You'll join us, right, Amber?"

"You have to," Gretchen said quickly. "We always order way too much food and besides, you can give us the inside scoop on Michael and this Brenda girl he works with. I've heard she is something else."

Standing a few yards away with a group of kids, Michael eyed them.

Beth elbowed her sister. "Stop."

Amber shrugged. "The scoop? Brenda thinks Michael is the best thing since liquid eyeliner. And that's saying something because she has a thing for liquid eyeliner."

Michael turned to her and shot her a look. Amber only smirked.

❧❧

Beth's house *was* a mess. A far cry from dirty, but the family room was nothing like the *Better Homes and Gardens* display Amber witnessed on Monday nights. Amber felt a wave of relief.

"Michael had friends over last night," Beth explained. "Apparently they all forgot where the garbage can is." Beth tugged out a fresh trashcan liner from a kitchen drawer, snapped it open, and called for Michael. He tromped in, surveyed the area with something like surprise, and began collecting empty soda cans and grease-stained paper plates.

Gretchen introduced Amber to her husband, Dave, and her son Tyler and his wife Sarah. A grinning redhead stuck out his hand and introduced himself as Evan. Amber instantly recognized him from one of the photos on Beth's mantel. While Beth and Gretchen cleared off stacks of newspapers from the table, she helped Lily pour drinks. When the food arrived, they divided up egg rolls and snapped apart chopsticks. The men heaped their plates and retreated to the family room while the women circled the kitchen table, the white takeout boxes clustered in the middle like a centerpiece.

"I felt the baby move for the first time this week,"

Sarah said. She ran a hand across her belly, confirming Amber's inkling. Beth and Gretchen erupted in coos of delight.

"Let us know if you get any hard kicks so we can feel too," Beth said.

"So far it's been pretty light, like something's squirming in my stomach."

"Something *is* squirming in your stomach," Gretchen said. "My grandbaby."

She helped herself to Cashew Chicken and passed the carton to Amber.

"I'm just glad the morning sickness has passed," Sarah said.

Beth turned to her sister, her chopsticks pinching a bamboo shoot in midair. "Well Grandma Gretchen, when did you get so *old*?"

"Look sister, if I'm old, you're old. But I'm not. I'm seasoned. Mature. Not old."

Lily rolled her eyes. "You're in denial, Mom."

"Absolutely not! I'm thrilled to pieces about this baby. I merely refuse to accept that he or she means I'm old."

"Are you hoping for a boy or a girl, Sarah?" Beth asked.

Sarah blushed prettily. "It doesn't matter. We'd be thrilled with either."

"The first time around, I wanted a girl," Gretchen stated. "Once I finally accepted the fact that I was going to *have* a baby, that is. But when Tyler was born, I fell so completely in love with him I forgot pink existed. Until I had my little Tiger Lily, of course." She swept her hand down her daughter's auburn mane, and her gaze drifted to the living room. "And now my baby boy's going to be a dad? Oh, hang it. I *am* old."

"A baby is the sweetest gift you'll ever receive," Beth said, leaning forward in that earnest way of hers. "Savor every minute."

Amber excused herself to get some water. She filled her glass at the kitchen faucet, the striped curtains fluttering as a breeze blew in from the open kitchen window. She drank slowly, trying unsuccessfully to block out the words filling the room.

"You think you've been tired before, but honey, you don't know tired yet."

"Sure, he *says* he'll get up with the baby in the middle of the night, but trust me, men can sleep through anything."

"Don't bother reading too many baby books. They only mess with your mind."

"Holding your baby for the first time is pure magic."

Amber glanced at the circle of women, at Sarah who maintained a protective hand on her small bulge. Amber took a sip of water and focused on the backyard while images from the past flashed in her mind like scenes from a movie.

How could she have dismissed the signs all those years ago? Ignored what she knew to be true, deep down? Pushed reality aside until it—until *he*—could no longer be denied?

An eruption of laughter sounded from the family room where the men sat. The women at the table glanced in their direction and shook their heads. Scents of garlic and peanut sauce filled Amber's senses, and she couldn't help but wonder, what was she doing here? With this family? She liked Beth, liked all of them actually, but she was an outsider. A criminal. Forgiven or not, guilt stabbed like a dagger.

"Amber, are you in?" she heard Lily ask.

She glanced over at the table. "What?"

"Trivial Pursuit," Beth said.

"OK." She topped off her glass and returned to the table. She helped Beth clear while Gretchen closed up the leftovers and stashed them in the fridge. Sarah wiped rice from the table.

Lily came in from the hall, holding the game. "Guys against girls? The teams would be even."

"Numerically maybe, but not cognitively," Evan said.

"Says the kid who graduated by the skin of his teeth," Gretchen said.

Michael came into the kitchen, and Evan karate chopped him across the back. Within seconds, they were engaged in full combat until Gretchen told them to cut it out or go outside.

Amber grinned at the boys. "They seem to be close in age."

"Only a month apart," Beth said.

Amber looked from Beth to Gretchen. "Must've been interesting for you two to be pregnant together." She wanted to kick herself. They'd just steered clear of that topic.

Beth smiled as she unfolded the game board. "Actually, Michael was adopted."

Amber looked at Michael. No wonder he looked nothing like tiny little Beth, or Eric for that matter. She felt a ripple of curiosity. But before she had a chance to respond, the brightly colored pie pieces plunked to the table and the game was underway.

26

August arrived and so did Beth's depression. She was used to it, this heaviness that draped across her like a cold, wet sheet each year whenever she counted down the last days of summer. Although this year it seemed worse. It wasn't merely the end of summer and the start of school that weighed her down, it was Michael's looming departure. The end of parenthood as she knew it.

"Maybe you should go back on Prozac," Eric suggested one morning.

She loathed the idea. She'd been off for years now and wondered if maybe God wanted her to walk straight through the darkness, groping for His hand before running to the drug store. Even so, the cloak kept pressing. "No. Not yet. Aren't I supposed to be depressed? Isn't this normal when your child flies from the nest?"

"You know, you don't have to teach, Beth," he said.

"But I *love* teaching! Most days. How could I stop teaching? What else would I do?"

Eric looked at her as if he wanted to say something more, but he closed his mouth.

To get her mind off of herself, Beth called Amber and asked when she wanted help painting her bedroom. Amber told her she'd picked up a gallon of paint earlier that week and planned to start the following Saturday.

Later that afternoon, Gretchen stopped by on her bike, noticed Beth's glumness and persuaded her to ride down to the lake. After the three-mile trip, they leaned their bikes against a tree and sat at a picnic table overlooking a public beach, catching their breath and chugging bottled water. Beth mentioned she was helping Amber paint her room and asked if Gretchen wanted to join them.

"Lily and I are heading to the Renaissance Fair that day. I've been meaning to ask. Do you think she remembers?"

"Amber? You mean what happened at the pub? I don't think so. If she does, she's never mentioned it. I'm not about to bring it up."

"Of course not. I was just wondering." Gretchen turned back to the water lapping the shore. "It's ironic though, isn't it? How one thing can lead to another? I mean who would have thought that after that night we'd even see her again, let alone have her show up at your house and then come to Miranda's study, and now the two of you are good friends? Crazy."

"It's called a curve ball, Gret," Beth said and took a drink of water.

Gretchen smirked. "Yeah, I've heard of them."

They finished their water, stretched their backs, hopped on their bikes, and headed home, the breeze cooling Beth's cheeks and lifting her spirits.

❧◈

On Saturday, Beth rapped on Amber's apartment door and let herself in, following the beat of a bass-heavy song to Amber's bedroom. Amber noticed her standing in the doorway and turned down the music. She was dressed in a faded *Point Beer* t-shirt and cut-off shorts. A sheet of plastic already covered the hardwood floor. "Can you believe this pink?" she said. "Thanks for agreeing to help me paint over this nightmare."

"Sure. You'll be helping me with my kitchen soon enough."

Amber pried open a can of paint revealing a blue-gray liquid.

Beth read the color title printed on the lid. "*Stormy morning*. Pretty. Very soothing."

"I have a thing for light blue. Who thinks of these names anyway?"

"Wouldn't that be a job, looking at color swatches all day and coming up with clever names?" Beth thumped one of the pink walls. "What do you think they called this? Bubble gum?"

"Cotton Candy Overdose?"

"Maybe this used to be a little girl's room."

"Well it's time to move on," Amber said and tied a bandana over her hair.

Beth picked up a small box of odds and ends sitting under the window and carried it over to the closet. As she bent down to set it on the floor, a flash of color caught her eye. She straightened and looked at Amber. "Is this one of yours? This painting in here?"

Amber glanced in the closet and her face reddened. "Yeah."

Beth waited for her to take it out and show it off, but Amber only stirred the paint around.

"Can I see it?" she finally asked.

Amber looked at her shyly, scraped off the excess paint from the stick, and laid it across the can. She wiped her hands on a rag and went to the closet and pulled out the canvas. She held it in the same self-conscious way that one of Beth's more timid kindergarten students might, before propping it on the windowsill. Then she walked back to the paint can and continued stirring.

Beth regarded the painting. The composition consisted of whimsical shapes, reds and yellows swirled together like fire and possessed a certain movement, as if a wind blew across it, sweeping color into color, shape into shape, darkness into light. "Amber. This is lovely."

Amber's face flashed pleasure before she shrugged. "Doesn't feel finished yet."

"When did you do this?"

"A few weeks ago. After Grandma died."

The painting spoke to that, Beth realized; somehow the abstract simultaneously captured death and life, hope and sorrow. "Beautiful. I can see why you studied art in college."

Amber gave a soft snort. "That was forever ago." She strode to the window, snatched the painting, and stashed it back in the closet. "We better get cracking."

Amber used a flat artist's brush to cut in the room while Beth followed with a saturated roller brush, covering the severe pink with a serene blue. A comfortable quietness settled over them. One wall complete, Beth reloaded her brush and scooted her step stool over to begin the next wall. "How is your mom doing?"

Amber didn't look up from the window she was edging. "Wouldn't know. Haven't talked to her since the funeral. She's decided not speak to me for a while. Lucky me."

"Why?"

"Grandma split the inheritance between the two of us. Not that there's much, but Mom thinks every dime should go to her. Just another way I've messed things up for her."

"She said that?"

Amber nodded. "Nothing I haven't heard before."

"I thought you said she's hardly had anything to do with your grandmother for the past twenty years."

"She hasn't. So you'd think she'd be happy with half, right? She's just bitter. Whenever anything goes wrong, somehow it's my fault. It's been like that forever."

"What do you mean?"

"It was never any secret that she didn't really want me in the first place. I came along and ruined everything. Can't really go to prom with a baby on your hip. She missed out on a lot of life because of me. She likes to remind me on a regular basis."

Beth stopped painting and looked at her friend, half expecting the hidden wounds to materialize in black and blue. "Amber, I'm sorry."

Amber kept her eyes on her work. "She's not all bad, I guess. She did feed me, clothe me. There are worse mothers out there, much worse. She never left me..." She stepped off the chair and set her brush in the tray. "I'm getting a headache," she said, sitting down against one of the still pink walls.

Beth went into the bathroom and came back with a box of tissues. "You've been through a lot these past couple weeks."

"I'm not crying."

"Well maybe you should. Crying is good for the soul, you know. Trust me. I do it all the time." Beth lowered herself on the floor next to Amber and handed her the box. "You have to know that you're not responsible for how your mother's life turned out."

Amber set the tissue box aside and used her fingernail to scrape off a paint splotch on her knee. "I know everyone has something from their past that they wish they could change, things that haunt them." She looked at Beth, her eyes pools of regret. "But I'm *ruled* by them."

From her years of teaching, Beth knew that children felt innately responsible for whatever trauma or hardship their family suffered. And Margaret had told Amber outright that she was to blame. For everything, it sounded like. How did a child get over that? How did Amber break free from that kind of shame? She hadn't, apparently. "Can I ask, what do you know about your father?"

"Hardly anything. Growing up, I learned not to ask about him. Mom said he denied I could be his. He was a high school senior, she a sophomore. He lived on one side of the tracks, and she lived on the other. He was a basketball player, and by the time I was born had already left for college. Mom never saw him again."

"So you've never met him?"

"Never. In his world, I don't exist." Amber let out a bitter laugh. "When I was a kid, I used to dream about meeting him. I'd imagine him battling all sorts of crazy things to get to me: dragons, storms, my mother. But he never came. I used to think it was all Mom's fault, that she was keeping him from me on purpose. Until I was old enough to learn what men are really after."

"Not all men."

Amber turned to her with a smirk. "Yeah, you found one that folds your towels."

Beth laughed. "There are lots of good men out there."

"Sure, for women like you."

Beth searched for words. "You're forgiven now. Your past has been wiped clean, your sins gone."

"But the guilt isn't."

"The guilt *is* gone. The feelings may not be."

Amber looked down at her hands in her lap. "I can't help wondering if God feels like He's made a big mistake with me. Like He sees all of my baggage and says, 'Eh, not worth it.'"

"Amber, that's not who God is. He won't change His mind about you. You're His child and He's promised to never leave you. When we adopted Michael, it was completely by our initiative. He couldn't do anything to make it happen. He couldn't be good enough or sweet enough. He was powerless. We chose him to be our son and that can't be undone. And that's merely my human love. God's love is perfect. God will never change His mind about you. He'll never stop loving you."

Amber seemed to absorb this. She peeled the bandana from her head, untied her hair, and gathered it in ponytail again. "What made you want to adopt?"

"We weren't able to have biological children."

Amber studied her. "Was that hard?"

Beth had to look away. She still mourned it at times. She wouldn't trade Michael for a dozen children of her own flesh and blood, but a loss remained a loss, regardless of the blessings that followed. Life was not one giant math problem; one blessing didn't cancel out a loss. Even now, after all these years, sometimes when she cradled a newborn or congratulated a blushing mother to be, she felt a wistful lump climb her throat, and all at once, her failure to conceive struck her anew, stung as sharply as it did the day she walked out of the doctor's office with the diagnosis her ovaries had shut down.

"It was devastating," she said quietly. "Having a baby was the only thing I ever wanted. I was furious at God for a long, long time. I sunk into depression. My marriage went through the wringer. Honestly, I didn't know if Eric and I were going to make it." She fell silent, the dormant emotions rising in her like smoke. "We got through it somehow. God pulled us through."

"And gave you Michael."

Beth turned and smiled. "And gave us Michael."

"He's a great kid."

Beth nodded. "My pride and joy."

"How old was he when you adopted him?"

"Just a couple of months. And the cutest little cherub you ever saw. Big blue eyes. Big chubby, cheeks. I couldn't stop kissing them the day we got him."

"Must have been something," Amber said.

Beth nodded, seeing the day and all of its facets like a prism dangling before her. She, clammy and trembling in her yellow sundress. Eric, an uncharacteristic mess of nerves. And Michael. Beautiful Michael dressed in white. Her angel, rescued and set apart for her. She remembered how his warm little body melted into her arms the moment she first held him, how the intoxicating sweetness of his fuzzy head left her dizzy. How later, after the three of them bonded for a few minutes, his foster mother patiently told her everything she could—about his sleeping and eating patterns, about how he liked to be rocked, how he liked his tummy rubbed during his fussy times. His foster mother had tears in her eyes when she kissed Michael good-bye, and it struck Beth in that moment just how much this baby was loved. No doubt, he came into the world on the wings of tragedy, but he'd been rescued by love. For even in that first moment, with only her little toe in the sea of parenthood, she knew she would lay down her life for this child. The love pulsated through her, thick and irrevocable. Pulsated through Eric, too, she trusted, and through Michael's foster parents. And that was merely in that room. Dozens of people waited outside those four walls to love Michael: Gretchen and Dave and their children, and her parents and family and friends and co-workers. Surely if they could harness all that love it would outweigh the evil committed against him. Such love would break the scale, for in those first few seconds with him, her heart alone felt like it might burst from the magnitude of such fierce and sudden devotion.

"Best day of my life." Beth set her brush down and reached over Amber for a tissue. She gave a little laugh. "Look at me. I'll be a puddle on the floor when he leaves for college in a couple of weeks."

"He'll do great in Madison," Amber said. "He felt the need to spread his wings and try out a bigger city, huh?"

"Yes. He's been drawn to that city for years."

"They do have a good arts program."

"Yes, but it's more than that." She stopped to consider if Michael would mind her sharing this one inconsequential detail. She didn't think so. "He was born in Madison."

Amber was quiet for a moment. "Does he have any contact with his birthparents?"

"No. None. It wasn't that type of adoption."

"Does he ever hope to? Contact them, I mean? I thought that was pretty common nowadays."

Beth let out her breath and thought carefully about her next words. She wanted Amber to know that they, too, had dealt with their share of heartache, but Michael's story was Michael's story; his to tell or not tell. Only a handful of people knew the details. "His birth story is...unusual. Tragic, in many ways. Maybe someday he'll let me share it with you."

They sat silently for a moment. After a while, Beth stood, took up her brush, and continued painting.

"How old is he?" Amber asked, still sitting on the floor.

"Eighteen. He turned eighteen on June third."

27

The floor beneath Amber shifted.

Beth continued to paint, transforming the walls with a new color, a new reality. The old swept away by a new concept, a new truth.

June third.

Michael's birthday.

The two facts collided into one another, birthing a new thought. Amber watched Beth, who had her back toward her, her brush making soft steady sweeping sounds against the wall. Then Amber raised herself to her feet and mumbled she needed a bathroom break and closed herself in the small room and sat on the tile floor. The coldness against her bare legs made her think of another time, long ago, when she'd lain on a bathroom floor and tried to extinguish the truth of what happened, the reality that she'd given birth.

She stood and hovered over the sink, splashed cold water to her face. She reached for her towel and blotted. Holding the cloth just under her eyes, she stared at her reflection. She'd smeared her mascara and tiny crow's feet stamped along the corners, but her eyes were still her best feature. Dark and blue, like the deepest part of the ocean.

Grandma's eyes.

Michael's eyes.

The towel cascaded to the floor. The color drained from the face of the woman in the mirror, and she clutched the countertop before sinking back to the floor.

෧৵৵৶

Amber knew if she didn't do it quickly, she'd fail at doing it at all. She slipped through the back door of Winston Hill and headed straight for Ernie's office. Someone—Brenda she thought—called out a hello. Without even turning her head, Amber kept her course.

She found her manager huddled over his desk, rapped on the doorframe, and waited for him to look up. "Amber! Glad to see that you fought your way through the stomach flu."

Somehow, she conjured up a smile. "Yes. All better."

"I'm assuming you came in for this?" He picked up an envelope and gave it a little wave in the air.

She nodded and slid the paycheck into her purse. "Thanks."

He bent over his work again.

She stood in the doorway, the storm in her stomach growing, and blurted out, "I can't work here anymore." She despised the way her voice hitched and wished she could take the words back and start over.

Ernie looked up. "Did something happen that I should know about?"

"No. Nothing. I just need...to spend some time with family right now, after my grandma's death and everything. I just need to get out of Elkin for a while. I'm sorry."

His face scrunched in what looked like concern. "I'm sorry, too. Take care of yourself, Amber."

She nodded and backed out of the room, grasping her keys purposefully as she stepped out into the parking lot and headed for her truck.

Suddenly she heard someone call her name, and the sound of it sliced through her heart.

"Amber. Wait up!"

She commanded herself not to turn around, to keep walking. Keep walking and don't turn around. Facing him would demolish her. She pretended not to hear and picked up her pace, but he caught up to her, his breathing audible from the sprint.

She turned and looked at him. Her breath caught. Here he was, standing before her. The beautiful impossible.

Michael held up his cell phone. "My battery's dead. Can I borrow yours?"

She swallowed, felt herself nod as she lost herself in the depths of his eyes. She broke her gaze and looked into her purse and rummaged for her phone. Finding it, she held it out and noticed the pale ridge of his knuckles as he reached for it, like jagged mountains. He tapped in a number, and the afternoon sunlight set his hair on fire, exposing the hidden gold accenting the sandy blonde. He stepped away and turned, offering his profile. She noticed the fair stubble peppering his jaw, a man's jaw, not a boy's, saw the way his hair curled slightly at the base of his neck. She wanted to reach out and loop her finger around one of those c-shaped curls.

"Well, that stinks," Michael said, jarring her out of her reverie.

She hadn't digested a single word of his conversation. "What's wrong?"

"I was hoping to head to the Twin Cities

tomorrow night to hear my friend's band play, but I'm supposed to be at this lame family shindig my mom is throwing."

She wanted him to keep talking, so she could stand there and drink him in, but forced herself to respond. She knew about the party. Since painting the bedroom together, Beth had left two messages in the last three days, one about the party and one to see if she was feeling better, to see if the sudden stomach bug had run its course.

"You should go," she said to Michael. "To your mom's party. She probably wants to spend time with you before you leave for school." Somehow, inexplicably, words were stringing themselves together and making sense.

"Geez, how much did she pay you to say that?"

Something inside of her reared up. "Your mom loves you. She loves you *very* much." Her fierceness startled her.

Michael raised his eyebrows and held his palm to her in surrender. "Chill. I was kidding. I'll go, I'll go." He glanced behind him at the restaurant. "Gotta run. I'm on break. Thanks."

He dropped the phone into her hand, the tips of his fingers grazing the inside of her palm, and she forced herself not to hang on to the very thing she thought was lost forever.

She drove home and began packing up her bedroom closet. When she came across her latest painting, she set it on her easel and dipped a fine point brush into ebony and went to work, suddenly knowing what the piece lacked.

❧❦

The day Beth had set aside for one last summer hurrah defied her. The fellow on the radio warned she'd need an umbrella, but how often was he right? She'd clung to optimism until lightning shattered the sky and her plans to eat out on the deck.

Eric looked at her, as glum as the weather. "You still want me to grill?"

"Unless you have a better idea. Do you want to order pizza for everyone?"

Eric made a small growling sound and pulled out a cookie sheet of thawed hamburger patties from the fridge and thudded the pan to the counter. "How many should I make?"

"All of them. Michael and his friends eat like horses."

"I'll get some hay."

"Lovely mood." Beth slid a pan of chicken wings into the oven to keep warm. Michael's latest craze. She'd spent part of yesterday scouring the Internet for a five star recipe since she'd never made her own before.

Minutes later, Gretchen and her family burst through the door, water droplets sliding down the ends of their hair. Miranda and her brood arrived shortly after. Her children wriggled out of their shoes, and Miranda lined them up along the wall. Thunder shook the house causing Miranda's three-year-old to scream and cling to her legs as a throng of Michael's friends toppled in.

Eric appeared wearing a scuba mask and poncho and tossed a rain jacket to Dave. "You've been drafted," he said to his brother-in-law.

Beth snapped pictures of the two huddled around

the grill, trying to stay dry underneath the overhang. Then she slid out the Buffalo wings and set them on the counter alongside a bowl of bleu cheese dressing.

Michael's face lit up. "Mom, you rock!" he said, draping an arm around her shoulders.

She smiled. Food was pure magic. Only this morning he'd sulked about the house, griping about how he was eighteen and how she needed to let him live his life. Now she rocked.

Michael and his friends filled plates and fled down to the basement while the adults spread out in the kitchen and family room. By the time Beth started coffee, the rain had let up and the party happily moved outdoors. Eric wiped down the patio furniture, and Evan tossed a football to Michael, prompting a full-fledged mud football game.

"I'm going to miss this," Gretchen said, plopping down beside Beth with a cup of coffee in hand.

"Me too."

Miranda's oldest, a boy around ten, watched the game from the sidelines. Michael went over to him, tousled his hair, and positioned him on defense. Beth prayed for protection. Most of the kids were barefoot, shards of green clung to their glistening wet feet.

Suddenly, Gretchen gripped her wrist. "You'd better lock your doors. Can you imagine your carpets if they tromp through like this?"

Beth shrugged. "They'll know better."

She didn't care about her carpet right now. She was floating on a sea of bitter-sweetness. She'd miss these messy, teenage laden events, miss Michael's friends barreling through her house uninvited, devouring all her food, calling her *Mrs. D.*, raving about her cooking. She had never really cared about carpets, not like Gretchen. Carpet could be replaced. These years, this moment, could not.

Eric, Dave, and Miranda's husband approached the game.

"Looks like the old dogs have something to prove," Gretchen said.

Beth yanked the lens cap off her camera and zoomed in. Eric intercepted a pass, ran with a fervor she hadn't seen in years, until Michael tackled him facedown. Beth winced.

"Way to go, Michael!" someone said from behind her.

"Hey, take it easy on the old man!" Gretchen shouted.

Michael extended his hand to help up Eric, who, to Beth's relief, popped up like a spring. He draped his arm around Michael's shoulders, and Michael did the same. With their backs to her, they turned to each other and grinned. Beth snapped a picture.

"Awww," the same female voice cooed. "He's so sweet."

After letting a minute pass, Beth nonchalantly turned around and surveyed the gathering of kids on the deck, searching for Michael's admirer.

"She's got it bad," Gretchen said under her breath once Beth was facing the game again.

"Who?" But she already knew.

"Please. Isn't it obvious? That Brenda girl he works with. That chick's been hanging on him all day. Don't tell me you haven't noticed."

Beth took a sip of coffee. "I've been trying not to."

Gretchen leaned into her. "How old is she?"

"A college student, I think."

"Oh boy. Does he like her?"

Beth shot her a look. "I don't know. Do your sons tell you everything? Mine doesn't." She chanced another glance at Brenda. "He must like her a little. I mean *look* at her. How could he not? She's darling."

Gretchen sniffed. "Sure, in a bimbo-ish sort of way."

"*Gretchen.*"

"That girl's a predator. A dolled-up predator. I'm sorry, but she's a little too bouncy and bubbly, a little too aggressive. Girls like that make me nervous, especially around my boys."

From the other side of Beth, Miranda chuckled. "A couple more years, and I'll have to worry about bouncy bimbos around my boys," she said.

"Hold on to your hat," Gretchen said to Miranda. "It's a wild ride."

Beth finished her coffee and went inside to set another pot to brew. While it percolated, she dashed to the basement for a stack of threadbare towels she'd saved. Gretchen labeled her a packrat, but times like this left her feeling a little smug.

By the time she returned with the coffee and towels, a light drizzle trickled down, too gentle to coerce anyone indoors. The football players tilted their faces upward, seemingly grateful for the refreshment. It was a peculiar rain, falling from a sun-lit sky, and Beth relished the mist on her face, breathed in the earthy, musty scent from the storm, and savored the eruptions of laughter from her son and his friends.

"I thought Amber was coming today," Miranda said. Her youngest was tucked into her lap like a little bird, sleeping beneath the shelter of her mother's jacket.

"I left her a couple of messages, but I never heard

back," Beth said. "She was sick the last time I saw her." Beth set the towels on the picnic bench and refilled Miranda's and Gretchen's mugs before setting the pot on the picnic table.

"Is she OK?" Gretchen asked.

"I don't know. We were painting her room, and all of a sudden she got hit with some stomach bug, said we'd better call it a day. I've tried calling to check on her, but she hasn't returned my calls. Which isn't like her. I'm beginning to worry."

The child in Miranda's arms stirred. Miranda repositioned the girl and rocked from side to side. "You could drop by. You're good enough friends for that, right?"

Beth tossed a towel to a dripping teenager on his way to his car. "Yes, I think so."

After an hour, the game fizzled out. The players cleaned up at the hose, grabbed towels, and dispersed. Gretchen gathered stray cans of soda and forgotten plates while Beth sliced off a generous piece of cake and constructed a tinfoil tent to protect it. Gretchen went home, and Beth headed to Amber's.

A surge of dread swept through her as she turned onto Amber's street. She clicked off the radio and listened. For what, she didn't know. So much to do awaited her at home, so much to clean up and put away, that she considered turning around. Yet something pressed her forward.

Beth pulled up to Amber's apartment. She shrugged out of her windbreaker and got out of the car, the sun blazing as if it had never rained. As she walked up the path to Amber's door, she happened to glance at Amber's truck and stopped short.

A blue tarp, puddled with water, stretched across

the contents in the bed of Amber's truck. Perplexed, Beth walked over, hesitantly peeled back a corner, and peeked in. Boxes and totes surrounded Amber's beige recliner.

Her dread increased. She hurried to Amber's door, poised to knock, but the door fell open and there stood Amber, clutching a cardboard box. Her eyes flickered over Beth in—*fear*? No. Terror. Amber was staring at her as if she were a trapped animal. As if Beth was the hunter.

Beth held out the cake wrapped in tinfoil. "I thought I'd stop by, see if you were feeling better and bring you some cake. We missed you at the party."

Amber stood speechless.

"How are you feeling?"

Amber's eyes flitted over the mound of tinfoil. "Fine."

Beth nodded, taken aback by the coldness. She hooked her thumb over her shoulder in the direction of the truck. "What's going on? Did you...are you...going somewhere?"

Amber stared at the box in her hands. "Yeah. I am."

Beth waited for an explanation. When Amber offered none, a burst of laughter bubbled out. This was all so absurd. "Well, where?"

Amber's gaze shifted to the truck, to the cake, to the box, anywhere but to Beth's eyes. "I just need to get out of here." She sidestepped Beth and headed for the truck. Beth watched her open the passenger side door and set the box on the floor.

Beth stood, stunned. Had she stepped into the Twilight Zone? "Why? Where are you going? What happened?"

Amber walked past her, re-entered the apartment, gabbed the duffle bag slouched next to the door, closed and locked the door, and headed to the truck again.

Beth trotted after her, recalling the night outside the pub. "Amber, wait a minute!"

Amber tossed the duffel onto the passenger seat and walked around to the driver's side.

Beth caught up and touched her arm. "Is this about...?"

Amber's eyes met her own for a brief second. "What? About what?"

"About that night. At the bar. When you pushed Gretchen."

"*What*?"

"That night downtown, when you had too much to drink? Because if it is, it doesn't matter. We've forgiven you for that. It's no big deal, really."

Confusion overtook Amber's features. "I have no idea what you're talking about." She stood blinking for a moment then climbed into the truck.

Beth clutched her open window. "Amber, please. Tell me what's going on."

Amber stared out the front window. "I can't. I'm sorry."

"But we're *friends*. Friends don't just wake up one day and decide to leave without an explanation, without saying good-bye." All at once she felt the swell of victory. "*Paul*! You're going back to Paul, right?"

Amber looked at her, crestfallen. "No. I'm not going back to Paul."

"Well what am I supposed to think? You're not telling me anything. Whatever's wrong, whatever happened, we can work it out."

"No. Not this." She started the engine.

Beth felt a rush of panic, and she involuntarily stepped into her teacher role. "You can't run away from your problems, Amber. Now shut off the truck, and tell me what's going on."

"Beth, I *can't*."

"Yes, you can," Beth said, her voice softening. "We're friends. Friends help one another. Friends don't shut out each other for no reason at all. Please. Let me help you."

Amber sat motionless for a while. Then her chin began to quiver. She was beginning to break. Soon all of this would make sense.

Amber flung open the door and walked around to the other side of the truck, took something out, and stood before Beth. She was clutching a canvas to her chest. "Here. I want you to have this."

"Amber, I don't want your painting. I want to know what's going on."

Without warning, Amber thrust the painting at her. Beth stumbled backward.

"Here," Amber said. "Take it! Take it and *see!*"

"Amber, you're not making any sense—"

"Tell Michael I'm sorry. Give the painting to Michael and tell him I'm sorry."

"*Michael*? What does this have to do with *Michael*? What are you *talking* about?"

Amber climbed into the truck. The vehicle jerked backward, jarred to a halt, and then squealed out of the parking lot. Beth stood, holding the painting, watching Amber disappear down the road pockmarked with puddles. She looked at the painting in her hands, the one she'd admired days ago, the one with the autumnal hues and sense of motion.

See what? What was she supposed to see?

Slowly, she walked to her car, carrying the canvas at arm's length, searching it. She considered the colors, the brushstrokes, even checked the back of the canvas for a clue, but saw nothing. They'd talked about the possibility of Amber going back to school to get her degree, but why wouldn't Amber simply tell her? Amber knew she was all for it. In fact, Eric had mentioned he could help her wade through the muck of financial aid.

Once at her car, Beth propped the painting on the top of the trunk and took a few steps backward. For clarity's sake, she gave her head a little shake and examined the painting once more, sounds of life surrounding her.

A door opened and shut.

An ice-cream truck jingled in the distance.

A child zoomed past on a bike.

And then she saw it.

28

Somehow, Beth managed to get in the car and start the engine. Somehow, she was driving through town, her foot compressing the gas, her hands gripping the wheel, maneuvering around corners and pedestrians and vehicles. All the while, a quiet voice counseled her to stop. To pull over. To let her body absorb the blow.

A light flashed red. She realized, vaguely, that red meant something, something important. By the time she remembered what, she'd already barreled past the stoplight and through an angry chorus of car horns.

The car automatically turned into her neighborhood. She suspiciously eyed the houses she knew so well. The manicured, predictable homes that lined the street like junior high girls, afraid to stand out but afraid to go unnoticed. On impulse, she hooked a left, disrupting the sequence of turns that would lead her home. At least she thought they'd lead her home. Then again, maybe if she went home she'd find only a massive hole in the ground. Who knew anything? Nothing was certain.

She depressed the gas pedal and sped out of her neighborhood, past city limits, until lush farmland rose up to greet her, a sight too green and pure and sure of its beauty. She drove for miles until she spotted an obscure turn off and jerked the wheel at the last second. The car rambled down the dirt course. Probably a private road, she considered. She was probably trespassing. But her foot refused to let up. If she kept driving, she wouldn't have to think. Just drive and drive and drive and forget what she saw. What she knew.

A cornfield stood before her, and it grew closer and closer until she had no choice but to slam on the brakes. The car jerked to a halt.

She shut off the engine and tumbled out, rows of cornstalks towering over her like wise, silent sages, their pointed, green arms flapping in the wind, gesturing her into their world. They beckoned her to enter, and she obeyed.

She stepped between two tight rows, pushing back stalks as she went along, surprised by the cool darkness of their hidden world. Their stiff leaves poked her legs and scraped her arms but she climbed further and further into their domain, deeper into their sanctuary, allowing their greenness to swallow her until she stood hidden, enveloped by plants bearing oblong pods, pregnant with sweet, ripe fruit. She could not see the outside world, and the outside world could not see her.

Amber is Michael's...

She was a speck among a multitude, a small child at a grown-up party who only sees knees and skirt hems. Even so, she felt the need to become smaller still and crouched down beneath the shuddering leaves. She sat in the strip of earth that separated row from row. The rain had rendered the ground a cold, soggy quagmire. She couldn't remember the last time she sat on wet ground without the protection of a blanket or tablecloth.

Amber is Michael's...

Beth closed her eyes and listened to the rustling of

cornstalks in the wind, the earth soaking her shorts and into her skin. She felt the urge to pray, yet pinning down words seemed too daunting. So she sat and slipped into an unspoken, uncensored prayer of the soul.

When her backside was numb from cold, she went home.

She removed her shoes by the garage door and surveyed the kitchen. Eric, of course, had cleaned up nothing. He sat at the table, his head bent over a newspaper, nibbling a piece of cake. She glanced out the window at the backyard then popped her head into the family room to verify its emptiness.

"Where's Michael?" she asked.

Eric didn't look up. "At a movie."

She padded down the hall to check Michael's bedroom. Nothing was for certain. Satisfied, she returned to the kitchen and clutched the back of a chair. Eric didn't look up.

The remains of the chocolate cake sat perched on the crystal cake plate in the center of the table. The cake plate was a gift, a wedding present from her aunt, if memory served her.

"So what's up with Amber?" Eric murmured, still reading the paper.

Beth stared at the cake plate and wondered how many cakes it had showcased over the years. How many birthday cakes, anniversary cakes, Easter torts and Christmas gingerbread houses had it hosted? A delicate piece she used often, with scalloped edging and a footed pedestal. Some people let their best china collect dust in the basement, but she had not sheltered this beautiful object. She'd shown it off, time and time again.

Eric shaved off another wedge of cake, picked up the clump with his fingers, and dropped it in his mouth. Crumbs sprinkled the table.

Beth watched him eat, and something inside of her snapped.

She lunged across the table and grabbed the crystal plate by the pedestal, the glass cool and smooth in her grip. She darted to the sliding glass door, flung it open, walked to the edge of the deck and with all of her strength, hoisted the plate over her head and hurled it over the railing to the concrete patio below.

The sound was magnificent, a symphony of a thousand particles breaking free. A wave of relief passed over her. But only for a moment. Then she looked at the disaster, the ruined thing of beauty, and felt sick.

Eric stood behind her, breathless. "Beth, what is *wrong* with you?"

What *was* wrong with her? Was this anger or insanity? Is this what it felt like to lose your mind? Her right shoulder ached from the pitch, and she rubbed it with her left hand.

A pair of her flip-flops sat beside the door, alongside the push broom. She slid into her shoes, grasped the broom, and descended the steps to the patio. She began gathering up the disaster with her broom, collecting the shimmering jagged diamonds mixed with brown sponges.

Eric galloped down the stairs. "Beth, what are you doing?"

She was cleaning up. She was the mom and the wife, and she was cleaning up.

Eric tried to wrestle the broom away. She tightened her grip on the handle. "*Stop* it, Eric. I need to clean this mess."

"Beth, what is going on? What happened?" He seemed to see her then, noticed her scratched arms and tousled damp hair, her mud-stained clothing. Fear clouded his eyes. "What happened? Are you hurt?"

She loosened her grip on the broom. "I was in a cornfield."

He gently took the broom from her and rested it against the side of the house then held her by the shoulders. "Beth, what's the matter? Tell me what the problem is."

And you'll fix it. Like a leaky faucet, like a flat bike tire, like her infertility. Like her depression. Weren't there some things that could never be fixed? This cake plate for starters?

She lifted her eyes to him, struck with a sudden desire to protect him and his blessed naiveté. He didn't know yet. His world was still intact. He had no idea of the earthquake rumbling beneath his feet. How would she prepare him for this?

How would she ever prepare Michael?

She yearned to ease Eric into the truth, but no segue existed. Showing him the painting would do nothing, not without Amber's cryptic words.

Too exhausted for preamble, Beth fixed her eyes on Eric.

"Amber is Michael's mother."

❧

Amber pulled into Ginny's driveway feeling like a refugee returning to her homeland. She dropped her suitcase next to the kitchen table and wandered to the living room, switching on lights and prying open windows as she went along, hoping a cleansing breeze might blow through and purify the stale, lifeless rooms.

It was the first time she'd been in this house alone, and the quietness unnerved her.

She stood in the middle of the living room and glanced at the things around her: the collection of bird prints hanging on the far wall, the curio cabinet housing the teacups, the worn burgundy Oriental rug at her feet. This was Grandma's home and her sanctuary, but it felt empty, hollow.

Amber stepped out of her sandals and curled up on the couch, the weight of her most recent failure crushing her. She'd planned to escape Elkin without anyone knowing, her secret intact. And now look what she'd done.

Would Beth see the truth in the painting? Had she pierced her friend through the heart? And what of Michael? Would his world be shattered beyond recognition? She couldn't even leave town right. Did Michael even know the full story of his birth, or had Beth and Eric sheltered him from that? What did they say to their son concerning his monster of a birth mother?

Michael. Precious Michael.

Closing her eyes, she pictured him and fought to catalog every nuance. She had no right to him, not even in her thoughts, but eighteen years ago she'd pretended he hadn't existed, and she wouldn't make that mistake twice. He lived, in the flesh, and he would live in her mind and heart, even if no one else knew of his existence.

She wondered, if Grandma were here, would she tell her?

Unknowingly, the past few months were a gift. Joking with Michael at the restaurant, enveloped by his very home. Tasting for herself the steadfast love that surrounded him. This knowledge that he was healthy and happy, should be enough to sustain her for her lifetime, fill her with joy. And it did. But also with heartache.

And now she'd compromised his perfect life.

She had the chance to bestow one gift to him and his family, leave them unscathed, but she'd ruined it. She'd shoved the truth at Beth and that truth, should Beth discover it, could destroy them all. Amber covered her face with her hands.

Why had God dangled Michael in front of her? Only to show her what could have been, to remind her of who she was and what she had done? Dangle him and snatch him away to seal the lesson. *See what you destroyed? See what you missed?*

A chill spread over her. She pulled the afghan from the back of the couch over herself and tucked it under her chin, the scent of Grandma still absorbed in the thick yarn flowers.

Grandma. If only Grandma were here to hold her hand and walk her through this mess…

Amber opened her eyes with a start, the heaviness of sleep threatening to pull her back under again. She had no idea how long she'd been out. Her growling stomach demanded she sit up and address it, and she realized that she'd survived the day on nothing but a granola bar and a soda.

Head cloudy, she staggered to the kitchen and yanked out the phone book, ordered a pizza and thought about calling her mother. Grandma had trained her well. Relocating meant calling Margaret.

Meet someone, fall for him, ruin it, move away, and call her mother. The pattern of her life. Although this time, she hadn't loved and lost a mere man. This time she'd loved and lost a whole family. A friend. A boy she presumed to be dead. A God she half believed loved her.

Amber punched in the number, desperate to hear a familiar voice, even if it belonged to her mother.

Margaret answered brusquely, as if the ringing phone had startled her from a nap of her own.

"I'm at Grandma's house," Amber said. She could hear the blare of the TV in the background. "I just wanted to let you know."

"Why? What are you doing there?"

"I thought I'd start sorting through everything." Partially true.

Margaret coughed. "It's not yours, you know."

"I know."

"Shouldn't even be half yours, really."

Amber shut her eyes. She couldn't play this game right now.

"I guess it was too much to hope that I, her daughter, would be the one to get her inheritance. I guess it's her last chance to stick it to me, show me who's boss. *You* should be happy."

"You should be happy, too."

"What's *that* supposed to mean? You probably think you should get all of it. Well don't get too comfortable. We need to go over everything in the house together. So it's *fair*."

"Fine," Amber said tersely. "When do you want to do that?"

"Soon. Maybe Monday."

"Works for me. I'll be here."

"Yeah, I thought you might. I've talked to a realtor. He'll come over and give me an estimate on what he thinks the house is worth. We should list it soon, before summer's over."

Amber rubbed her forehead. The thought of some stranger living in Grandma's house, her haven, left her almost nauseous. Her phone beeped in warning. "Mom, I gotta go. My phone's dying."

Twenty minutes later, when the lights from the pizza truck glared through the window, Amber found cash, paid the kid, and took the box to the kitchen where she devoured three slices with a glass of water. After refrigerating the leftovers, she wiped down the table and slumped back into her chair. The kitchen clock pierced the silence. Amber studied her ragged fingernails and tried not to think. Tried not to imagine what Beth was doing right now, tried not to wonder what she might be thinking or what she might be telling Michael.

Restless, she grabbed the afghan from the couch, wrapped it around her shoulders, and retreated to the porch. The swing, like always, welcomed her. She climbed into it and hugged her knees to her chest.

It didn't seem possible that a few weeks ago she'd knelt on this porch with Beth, her heart soaring even through the grief, because she'd been given a new lease on life, a chance to start over.

So much for that fresh start. So much for peace.

She tilted her head to the stars and trembled in her smallness. Who was she to think God would want to have anything to do with her? Solitude wasn't anything new. Given enough time, men wearied of her and left. Why would God be any different? Her mother always told her she needed too much time and attention. She knew she lugged around too much baggage.

The night grew darker, colder. Amber tightened the blanket around her shoulders, the ache for Grandma growing as the stars grew brighter. Maybe Grandma was the only one who could ever truly love her. The thought chilled her to her core.

Amber returned indoors. She dragged her suitcase into her bedroom and pulled out her pajamas, uncovering Ginny's leather, nutmeg-colored Bible, and eyed it warily. She lifted the book from the nest of clothes and cradled it in her arms like an infant. Then she went to the closet and opened the door and ducked inside. One tug on the string above lit up her blue haven like summer. She tucked herself into a corner, the blanket still shrouding her shoulders, and flipped through the weathered pages, paper as delicate as an empty chrysalis.

With no destination in mind, she let her thumb travel the edges of the pages, the leather scent a soothing tonic. She flipped around aimlessly until a flash of handwriting, toward the back, caught her eye. She opened the book to a page for note taking, and stared at the careful cursive she knew so well.

It was a list, a catalog of verses written out in Grandma's handwriting in various shades of ink, indicating its compilation had occurred over time. She skimmed the list, startled when she came across her own name. Her heart quickened. She read the verse Grandma had written for her.

"And we know that in all things God works for the good of those who love Him, who have been called according to His purpose."

Amber closed the book and wept.

29

The oil painting sat propped on Beth's dresser, striking against the soft butter yellow of her bedroom wall. She watched Eric study the composition and knew instantly when he saw it. His mouth dropped open.

"You see it, right?"

Eric nodded and raked his hands through his hair. "Unbelievable."

Beth turned her attention to the painting and traced her finger along the gray outline of a woman, almost hidden in one of the vibrant red flames near the top left corner. But she was there all right, with a river of gold hair that blended into the rest of the piece and a featureless face tilted downward, as if looking at something below her. Beth let her gaze travel down the painting to the object of the woman's attention: a tiny gray oval in the lower right hand corner, nestled in a teardrop shape. Abstract and faded, the figure was comprised of soft, quick strokes, a bit like a Chinese character. A small dash for a mouth, two smudge for eyes. The figure lurked in the shadows. Barely discernible. But once Beth saw it, saw *him*, she couldn't see anything else, couldn't interpret the markings any other way.

"I saw her first," Beth said, looking again at the outline of the woman, "And I knew it was Amber. And then I saw him. It hit me, Eric. I knew instantly what the picture meant. I knew what Amber was trying to tell me."

"But how can you be sure?"

"Because I *know*. I can't explain it. I just know. Think about it. The last thing she said to me was 'tell Michael I'm sorry.' And that day I helped paint her room, the day she got sick, our last conversation was about Michael's adoption. Trust me. I just *know*."

Eric turned away from the painting, paced to the window, and looked out in the darkness. "This is crazy. What are we supposed to do?"

"I don't know."

He turned to her. "What are the legal ramifications? Are we legally required to report this now? Is there a statute of limitation on abandoning a newborn? I mean, we're talking about a crime here, possibly attempted infanticide. This is a lot to take on. Are we supposed to call our social worker? The police?" He was pacing the length of the room now.

"I don't know."

"You can't just drop this on me, Beth, without giving any thought to how it's going to affect us—"

"I can't just *drop* this on you? You think I was prepared for this? You think somehow I knew?"

He stopped and looked at her. "You didn't have any clue? All the time you spent with her? No inkling at all? No mother's intuition or anything?"

She gaped at him. Why didn't he just slap her across the face? Why didn't he just say she wasn't fit to be a mother? "Thanks. Thanks a lot."

She grabbed her pillow from the bed and stormed out. Michael was sleeping at Evan's tonight. It was a good thing his bed was open, because no way was she going to sleep next to *that* creature.

Eric came knocking a few minutes later and said he was sorry. Didn't she think she was overreacting? Beth pretended not to hear.

He was not in her corner tonight. And she wasn't about to let him attempt to crawl back in it now.

෯෴

The next morning Beth woke up stiff. Michael's room gave off a distinct, slightly musty odor, and she vowed to make sure he cleaned out whatever dirty laundry lurked under his bed. She rolled out of bed, exhausted from tossing and turning, and stumbled to the bathroom.

Already dressed for work, Eric handed her a cup of coffee as she entered the kitchen. "I'm sorry."

A part of her knew his remarks from last night were purely a knee-jerk reaction, like her driving through town like a madwoman and breaking the cake plate, but she wanted to cling to something right now, even if it was anger. She sniffed, took the coffee, and brushed past him.

"I'm just shocked," he said. "I don't know what to do about this."

She took in his baffled expression, her resolve fading. "I don't either."

"And I really don't want anything to happen to Amber. I'm sure she's suffered enough. But I don't want to commit a crime here, either." He stared off into space for a while. "How do you think we should tell him?"

Beth leaned against the counter and peered into her mug. "Maybe we shouldn't."

"Not tell him at all? We can't do that. We can't

keep this from him."

She cocked her head in challenge. "Why not?"

"Beth, we're not going to lie to our son."

"It wouldn't be *lying*…"

"Yes, it would be. Lying by omission. I'm not saying we should tell him today, but eventually he's going to need to know. He has a *right* to know."

She sipped her coffee. And she had a right to protect him. Wasn't that her job?

Eric filled his travel mug. "We'll talk about this later." He headed for the door, opened it, and turned to face her. "Are you all right?"

She offered him a weak smile. "Couldn't be better."

His eyes flickered in concern before he stepped into the garage. Moments later, she heard his car back out.

Somehow, she'd convince him. Keeping Amber's identity a secret was the best thing they could do; it'd give Michael the chance to head to college with his identity intact. Carry on with life as usual. The kid had enough changes coming his way.

She sipped her coffee, her determination growing. And when her mind drifted to Amber, to her friend who'd fled to heaven knows where, she busied herself by making a piece of toast.

She had her family to think about right now.

Later that night, Eric agreed to not say anything to Michael so they could wrap their minds around the truth before handing it to him. As the days passed, each time Eric insisted it was time to tell Michael, Beth convinced him otherwise. She pushed the matter to the furthest corner of her mind and acted as if nothing was wrong. Michael wasn't home enough anymore to become suspicious anyway.

Gretchen, however, was more perceptive.

"Why are you acting strange?" she asked one day on the phone.

Beth laughed. "I'm not acting strange."

"Yes, you are. Stranger than usual, I mean. What's going on?"

"Just gearing up for the school year I guess."

The following Monday, after Miranda and the study women came and left, Beth walked into her bedroom and noted the resolution in her husband's eyes.

"It's time to tell him."

"Not yet. A few more days."

"When, Beth? Don't you think it'd be better for us to tell him now, so he can work through this before leaving for Madison?"

"But that's the thing. There *isn't* time. He'll be gone in just over a week."

"You're as stubborn as a mule. We're telling him tomorrow." He clicked off his lamp and turned on his side, away from her.

Beth picked up her novel from her nightstand, turned to her marked page, and pretended to read. Yes, she was stubborn. She could handle stubborn. What she couldn't handle was watching her son fall apart.

She stared at the words on the page for a while, then turned out her light and burrowed under the covers, weary but restless. Michael hadn't come home yet. He worked late tonight, she knew, and was probably off with friends now. The minutes ticked by, and she strained to hear the telltale sounds of his arrival: his car pulling into the driveway, the door jangling open, his footsteps down the hall. Yet she only heard Eric's rhythmic snoring beside her.

The night deepened. Each time a vehicle approached the headlights cast a flicker of light on the bedroom wall, and Beth sat up and listened for sounds confirming his safety. But when the hall clock chimed one, and still no Michael, her mind began tumbling down the never-ending spiral of *what ifs*.

સ∞ઉ

After trying Michael's cell phone a half a dozen times throughout the night, Beth gave into anxiety and called Gretchen. "Is Michael there?"

Gretchen grunted, apparently attempting to rouse herself. "Beth?"

"Did Michael spend the night?"

"Michael? No. What's going on? It's four in the morning."

"Did Evan come home last night?"

"Yes."

"What time?"

Beth heard the rustling of blankets, imagined Gretchen sitting up, clicking on her lamp. "Around eleven. Eleven thirty maybe. Why? What's wrong?"

Maybe she was overreacting, as Eric accused, but something in her gut told her otherwise. "Michael didn't come home."

"Did you try his cell phone?"

"Of *course* I tried his cell phone. I'm not stupid."

"Easy. I'm just trying to help."

Beth took a breath. "I tried his cell phone. Either his battery is dead, or he's not picking up. Do you know where they went last night?"

"To the movies and then out for something to eat, I think. Maybe he just lost track of time." Gretchen paused. "Maybe he's with a girl."

Beth clicked her tongue. "Thanks. That's helpful."

"I'm sorry. Just brainstorming here."

Beth rubbed her forehead with her fingers, sleeplessness and anxiety joining forces and turning into nausea. "I think I should call the police."

Gretchen didn't speak for a moment. "I'll pray."

Eric said to give Michael another hour, but Beth ignored him and dialed the police. In one breath she described what Michael looked like, what he was wearing, where he was last seen, and who he was with.

"How old is he, ma'am?" the officer cut in.

"Eighteen. He just turned eighteen."

"I'm sure he'll show up soon, ma'am," the officer said. "He's probably lost track of time."

"*No*. I don't think so. I think something's wrong." She hadn't conjured up the notion of mother's intuition, so why didn't anyone believe her?

"Since he's eighteen, I can't report him as a missing child. Does he have any history of mental illness, or is he on any medications I should know about?"

"What? No."

"Has he ever been in trouble with the law?"

"No. He's a good kid. He's just…missing."

"After twenty-four hours I can write up a report for a missing adult."

Rage boiled inside of her. *He's not an adult. He's a child. My child.* "What good will that do?"

"We have your description of him, ma'am, so we'll keep a lookout, but like I said, I wouldn't worry too much. In most cases like this, they come home—"

Beth slammed down the phone without letting him finish his sentence.

❧

Dawn broke. Beth scribbled a note for Michael, just in case, and left it on the table. Then she and Eric hopped into the car and headed downtown to drive past any place that might produce Michael. It made no sense, she realized, but it felt like forward action. And she had to do *something*. Anything that mimicked productivity.

Eric slowed past one of Michael's favorite pizza joints that had been closed for hours, and Beth scanned the empty parking lot. No sign of Michael or anyone else.

"What if she told him?" she said, voicing the thought that had been circling in her mind for hours.

"You mean Amber?"

"Yes. What if she told Michael?"

"Do you think she'd do that? Why would she do that?" Eric asked.

"Who knows? Why would she..." Beth started to cry, the tears hot rivers traversing her cheeks.

"Did you try calling her? Just in case?"

"Yes. She won't answer." And what would she say if Amber had answered?

Horrific scenes played in Beth's mind. Michael lying in a ditch. Michael unconscious in a demolished car. Michael beat up in some dark alley.

Or maybe Gretchen was right. Maybe he was with a girl. Maybe he was just at a friend's house. But why wouldn't he have called...?

She closed her eyes, desperate to quell her

imagination. When she opened them, she caught her reflection in the window. *What are you doing?* she silently asked the haggard stranger with puffy, desperate eyes.

༒

It was Eric who decided to stop at Gretchen's before going home. He helped Beth out of the car as if she were an old woman. Dizzy with exhaustion, Beth let him, even clutched his forearm like her mother did.

Gretchen met them at the door in her terrycloth bathrobe. She didn't ask, she simply sought their faces and led them to the kitchen, poured them coffee and sat down with them at the table. Dave appeared and quietly joined them.

"Could we talk to Evan?" Eric asked.

Gretchen nodded, rose, and went to Evan's room. Minutes later Evan emerged in a rumpled t-shirt and boxer shorts, his red hair springing from his head like copper coils. He pulled out a chair and sat down.

"Evan," Eric said. "Can you tell us about last night? Did Michael say he was going anywhere, or did he seem strange to you?"

Evan stared up at the ceiling, his brows knit together in thought. "No. Not really. We went to the movie and then stopped at Tony's for cheese fries. Brenda was kind of driving us crazy, talking nonstop on the drive home. I mean, she's pretty enough, but she's as dim as a dying flashlight."

"Who was in the car?" Eric asked.

"Just me, Michael, Brenda, and Lauren. Michael dropped off Lauren and then me."

"And then Brenda?"

"Yeah, I guess so."

Gretchen's eyes flickered over Beth before she lowered her gaze into her coffee cup. It *was* a girl. The sleepless night, the anxiety, the frantic searching—all because he was off with some girl doing who knew what. The panic in Beth's stomach morphed into anger. "Evan, do you have Brenda's number?"

"Yeah, but I don't think he's with her, Aunt Beth. I mean, she's kinda hot and all, but Michael's not stupid—"

"Just get me her number. Please."

Evan disappeared and returned moments later with his cell phone. He punched a button and held it out to Beth.

Beth held the phone to her ear. A female voice uttered a sleepy hello, and Beth willed her voice to remain calm. "Hi Brenda, this is Beth Dilinger, Michael's mother. May I speak to him please?"

30

"Michael? Michael's not here," Brenda said.

Beth's anger shifted back into panic. "He's not? Look, I'm sorry to bother you, Brenda, but Michael never came home last night, and we're trying to track him down."

"I don't know where he is."

"What time did he drop you off last night?"

"I don't know. Eleven thirty maybe."

"Do you know if he was going straight home?"

"How should I know? I didn't care what he did," she said coolly.

She recalled Brenda's display of affection on the day of the party. Something was off. "Did something happen last night?"

Brenda sighed. "He was being a jerk, that's all. No offense or anything."

"None taken," Beth said instinctively, wanting to move the conversation along. "What happened?"

"Nothing, really. It's not even worth talking about…"

"I'm just trying to figure out where he is."

"Well, when I told him I could try and get him a job where I work in Madison during the school year, he got all mad."

"Where do you work?"

"On the House."

Her heart lurched. She locked eyes with Eric.

"Brenda, do you mind if I stop over? Just for a few minutes?"

"I'm not even dressed."

"That's OK. I just need to talk to you. Please?"

Silence. Then, "Yeah, I guess so."

અજ

After dropping Eric at home in case Michael returned, Beth followed Brenda's directions to her house—her parent's house—and rapped on the gleaming oak door. Brenda met her in a pair of teeny black shorts and an oversized sweatshirt. Her mop of hair was piled on top of her head with a clip. Barefoot, she stepped out onto the patio, radiating annoyance.

Beth smiled sheepishly. "You'll have to apologize to your parents for me for stopping by like this."

"My mom and Larry are on a cruise." She sighed, her expression softening a little, and plopped down into a wicker chair.

Beth lowered herself in its twin. "I was hoping you could tell me what happened last night. Michael's not answering his phone, and I'm pretty worried."

Brenda pulled her knees up to her chest and fingered her hot pink toenails. "We went to a movie that ended up being totally stupid."

Beth gripped the armrest of her chair. "Can you tell me what happened after the movie and after the restaurant?" she said as pleasantly as she could. "Michael dropped off Lauren and Evan, and then you said something about the two of you having an argument?"

"Yeah. Sort of. I mean, we didn't start off fighting. At first we were kind of making out..." Brenda stopped, glanced at Beth, and covered her mouth with the sleeve of her sweatshirt. "Sorry."

Beth squeezed her eyes shut, just for a moment, and forced a smile.

"So anyway, we were talking and…stuff, and at some point I told Michael that I could try to get him a job at the place where I work in Madison during the school year, you know, that it'd be cool if we could keep working together. So he said 'Where do you work?' and I said 'On the House.' He said, 'I'd never work there,' and I said, 'Why not' and he said 'I can't stand that place.' So I said 'That's so weird. You and Amber both.'" Brenda turned to her. "Amber is this waitress at work. You probably don't know her."

Beth nodded. "We've met."

"So anyway, he said something like 'What does Amber have against that place?' And I told him that she once lost something there."

Beth's heart took off. "She lost something?"

"Yeah, she told me about it at this party I had a few months ago. She said something about leaving something important there, or forgetting something…I don't remember exactly. Anyway, whatever it was, she never got it back."

Beth was going to be sick, right here on this girl's patio. "Did she tell you what she lost?"

"No, not that I remember. Maybe jewelry or something? Something valuable, I guess. Anyway, the weird thing is that she said she lost it on that exact day, the date of my party, I mean. Isn't that weird that she'd remember? It was years ago. I think she was my age or something. Anyway, when I told Michael about it he flipped out—"

"Wait. You told Michael about your conversation

with Amber? About her leaving something important at On the House a long time ago?"

"Yeah, and he completely freaked out. He said 'When was your party, Brenda?' and I said 'You were invited. Why didn't you come?' And he just kept asking me what day my party was on, so I finally yelled, 'June third, and why should you care? You didn't even show up.' He was totally rude."

Beth took a moment. She gazed at the wispy pinkish clouds overhead, stretched cotton brushing across a blue sky. A cardinal flew past and perched at a birdfeeder hanging from one of the trees in the front yard.

She let the truth sink in. Michael knew.

This girl had unwittingly destroyed her son's world with a few careless words, tossed his birth story at him like a pot of scalding water. Betrayed earth-shattering truth without knowing it, information she couldn't begin to understand.

Beth blinked and fought to maintain a neutral expression. Right now she had to fake her way through the moment, attend to this oblivious girl who'd made a mess of things and now sat pouting. Then she could fall apart. Find another cornfield. Break another plate.

She turned to Brenda, her game face secure, and forced out the words, "I'm sorry he was rude to you. He might have just been having a bad night."

Brenda pursued her lips and shrugged. She unclipped her hair, tossed her curls around, then twisted it on top of her head again. "What's this all about anyway? I don't get it. Did your family once own that restaurant or something? Was there some kind of lawsuit?"

Beth stared at Brenda, hoping to conceal her

disbelief. Heaven help her. "Thank you for talking to me."

☙❧

When Beth returned home, she found Eric on the phone, pacing the kitchen. She studied his face for clues, a smile, or a glimmer in his eye that might tell her they'd found him. She only saw anxiety. Eric hung up, raked his hands through his hair, and paced to the patio door.

She dropped her keys on the table. "Who was that?"

"Pastor Nate. I told him Michael's missing. He said he'd call some of the youth group parents to see if they know anything."

"You didn't tell him—"

"About Amber? No."

Beth peeled off her coat. She was still in the flannel lounge pants and oversized t-shirt she'd slept in. She hadn't even bothered with a bra. She looked at Eric and felt heavy with dread. More news to break. Another grenade to launch.

"Eric. Michael knows."

As she relayed her conversation with Brenda, she watched the vein in his neck ripple beneath his skin like a tiny snake. When she finished, she fell quiet and waited.

Eric fixed his gaze at something in the backyard. "We should have been the ones to tell him," he said quietly. "Not some silly girl." He opened the patio door, stepped out onto the deck, and clutched the railing. He dropped his head between his shoulders as if seasick.

Beth watched his back for a few moments and then tried Michael's phone again. Nothing. When she glanced at the deck again, Eric was gone.

A few hours later, around noon, Gretchen dropped by with a pot of soup. She set it on the stove, clicked the burner to low, then made a cup of tea for Beth and sat her down on the couch. "I feel like there's something more to this story," she said gently. "Is something else going on, something you're not telling me?"

Beth swallowed back a sob. "A curve ball. A big one."

Miraculously, Gretchen didn't question. She brushed back a clump of hair falling in Beth's eyes and took her hand as if she were a child. Memories from their girlhood, of moments just like this, when she rested in the comfort of her big sister, flooded Beth and she sat and cried. Gretchen sat with her for a long time without shushing her. Then Gretchen went to the kitchen, stirred the soup once more, and went home.

When Eric returned from wherever he was, Beth was teetering on the edge of full-blown panic. "What if this breaks him? What if he does something really stupid?"

"He's a levelheaded kid. He probably just needs some time by himself to figure this out."

"But where could he be? What if he—"

Eric threw his hands in the air. "Beth, what do you want me to say? I don't know! I don't have the answers. What do you want from me?"

Beth closed her mouth. Her stable rock stood quaking like a leaf. Hands on hips, his torso curved, his shoulders hunched, he looked utterly defeated. His demeanor pulled her back to a time twenty years ago, when their dream of having a baby lay shattered at their feet. When she'd shriveled into a shadow of the woman he had married. When she shut herself in her room for days, locking him out with non-responsiveness. And through it all, he had held it together. Kept his head above the rising flood of grief she had nearly drowned in, so he could pull her out. He'd let her fall apart so their marriage wouldn't.

She would not deteriorate into that woman again. God help her, she would not. She could be strong, too.

Gathering herself, her thoughts, her courage, she went to him and took his hands in her own. "Pray with me."

∾∾

An hour later, the phone rang. Beth sought Eric's eyes before answering.

"Mrs. Dilinger?"

It was a stranger's voice. "Yes?"

"Is this Beth Dilinger, Michael Dilinger's mother?"

"Yes. This is Beth Dilinger, Michael's mother." Eric was next to her in a second.

"This is Officer Jansen from the Madison Police department. I have Michael here at the Madison county jail."

The room began to sway. Beth gripped the back of a kitchen chair. "Is he OK? Is he hurt?"

"No, ma'am. He's unharmed. We picked him up for loitering and disturbing the peace outside a restaurant here, On the House."

Beth exhaled, her breath leaving her like a busted balloon. Of course. Of *course*. "Disturbing the peace?"

"He was throwing empty bottles in the back lot,

seeing how badly he could dent up a dumpster back there. Refused to leave when the manager ordered him off the premises."

"Can I talk to him?"

"He was free to call you himself, ma'am, but he declined."

A dagger stabbed her.

"However he didn't put up a fight when I offered to call you on his behalf. He seems more scared than anything, pretty broken up and sorry for his actions. Seems like a good kid. No previous record. I get the sense this might be an isolated incident."

Mercy was a beautiful thing, empathy a gift. "Yes," Beth managed. "Yes, he is a good kid. A good kid that's going through a difficult time. Thank you for calling."

"I have an eighteen-year-old daughter, ma'am. They're still kids in my eyes."

She began to cry. "We'll be there as soon as we can."

They left for Madison immediately. When Eric merged onto the interstate, Beth called Gretchen. "We've found Michael. Pray. Please pray."

Michael was sitting in an orange plastic chair in an empty room in the police station, a can of soda on the table in front of him. His eyes flickered over them briefly then back to the red aluminum can. When he stood up, Beth hugged him, and she felt his body stiffen.

"You knew, didn't you," he said after pulling away. "About Amber."

No more lies. "Yes. Not for long. But yes, I knew."

Eric thanked the officer, and they walked to the parking lot. Eric drove Michael home in Michael's car while Beth followed with the Toyota. Once home, Michael shut himself in his room and didn't come out for the rest of the night.

Beth collapsed into bed, pent-up tears drenching her pillow, and then fell into a dead, dreamless sleep.

31

Amber awoke early on Sunday morning, the loneliness as oppressive as fog. If she killed herself today, no one would know. No one would miss her.

Her mother might. Then again, maybe not.

She fingered the edge of the ivory sheet and surveyed the room's warm chocolate walls and felt a pang of guilt. This was Grandma's house, and she would not taint it with her blood. Could Grandma see her? Read her thoughts? She shuddered at the idea of Grandma peering down from heaven to witness her granddaughter gulp a bottle of pills. If heaven worked that way, she had no idea. Even in death, Grandma's hand of restraint remained steady on Amber's shoulder.

To make it up to Grandma, and to give herself a goal for the day, she vowed to go to church.

After showering and dressing and indulging in a quick cigarette on the way over, she crept into the last pew of First Methodist Church and pretended to read her bulletin. Other than the funeral, she typically frequented this church twice a year, when either poinsettias or Easter Lilies adorned the chancel. Whispered conversation buzzed around her. She was a stranger among a sea of friends. If anyone cast a smile in her direction she wouldn't know; she wasn't about to look around. One Christmas Eve, the pastor had the congregation stand and greet each other in the love of

Jesus. If that happened, she was out of here.

"Amber!" a voice called.

The sound of her name startled her. Amber turned and saw Jackie, the soloist from the funeral, sliding into her pew. The organ bleated and Jackie mouthed *it's nice to see you* as the congregation stood for the opening hymn. Throughout the service, Amber rehearsed what to say to Jackie. But on the heels of the benediction, a woman sitting directly in front of them turned around, grabbed Jackie's hand, and engaged her in conversation. Amber quickly gathered her things, slipped out on the other side of the pew, and out the front door.

∂∾√

The following day, Margaret's Chevy rolled into Ginny's driveway, and Amber felt an unexpected wave of relief. She descended the porch steps, wondering if her mother's visit might provide a remedy for the loneliness or, at the very least, an interruption.

The trunk popped open, and Amber lugged out her mother's big green suitcase. Margaret grabbed her tote bag and followed her up the walkway to the porch. She stopped and slapped one of the pillars. "Looks like this could use a good coat of paint."

Amber surveyed the cracking paint. "I've been thinking about it."

Margaret shifted her weight from foot to foot and the porch groaned. "A couple of these floorboards sound loose, too. Maybe we should just tear the whole thing off."

Amber stared at her. She'd just as soon cut off her arm. "It's nothing we can't fix."

"*We*?"

Jaw clenched, Amber hauled the suitcase through the house and set it next to the dresser in Ginny's room. Margaret plopped her tote on the bed, retrieved a comb, and plucked through her brassy curls. "I'm not even going to ask what happened to your great job in Elkin."

"Good. Don't."

"Well, you better find work soon—"

"Already did. At the Pick 'n Save just down the street."

Margaret looked at her in surprise. "Just remember, this isn't your little playhouse, Amber. It's more mine than yours. Or at least it should be."

Amber pinched the bridge of her nose and turned to leave.

"So what have you been doing?" Margaret called out.

"Sorting. Cleaning. I got through the hall closet. Lots of odds and ends I'll take to Goodwill. Coats. Mittens. Old magazines. Oh, and this." She picked up the shoebox sitting on the closet shelf and carried it to the bedroom. "You might want some of these." She gently dropped the box on the bed.

Margaret retrieved the box and began riffling through the collection of photographs. After a moment, she removed one and held it up to the light. She smiled. "I forgot about old Marmalade."

Amber squinted at the black and white picture of her mother as a child, holding an infuriated looking orange cat.

Margaret set the picture on the bed and continued riffling. She extracted another. "Oh boy. Look at this."

Amber sat down on the bed and studied the

photograph. A little girl, cocooned in a snowsuit, straddled a bicycle on a driveway flanked with snow. "That you?"

"Yep. My seventh birthday. I wanted a bike so bad that year. When Dad wheeled it into the living room, I wanted to ride it right then and there. Didn't matter that it was January. Mom told me it was too cold, but Dad said to bundle up. He shoveled off the driveway, and I rode up and down all day until I couldn't feel my toes anymore."

Amber studied the girl with the beaming smile in the photograph and held her breath, not wanting to break the spell of the moment, of sitting beside her mother and listening to her talk. Not yell or curse or complain, but simply give voice to a memory.

Margaret laid the picture on top of the one with the cat and returned to the box. "Oh, here we go. Look at this little stinker." She held out the picture for Amber.

It was a shot of the three of them, Grandma, Margaret, and herself, standing on the cement pathway in front of Grandma's house.

"You had the prettiest head of hair," Margaret said. "Look at those curls. After your bath I'd twist a section of your hair around my finger and presto—Goldilocks."

A sense of pleasure rushed over Amber. "I remember that."

"From the looks of it, this must be Easter morning. Only time Mom ever wore a hat. I can almost hear her now. 'Put on a smile. It's time for church.' We all had to measure up to her inspection. Somehow, Dad managed to wiggle his way out of going and went fishing instead. Lucky man. I used to beg him to take me with." She tossed the picture on the bed. "I hated that church."

Amber picked up the three-generation picture and studied it. Grandma's hair fashionably fanned out against her shoulders, and she clutched the hand of a small girl with the yellow ringlets. Margaret stood on the other side, slightly separated, her arms dangling at her sides, her mouth a grim line.

"Why?" Amber risked. "What was that church like?"

Margaret snorted. "Like all churches. Stuffy. Hypocritical. They didn't want anything to do with me. That's for sure. The rebellious daughter of Virginia and Jack Swansen."

Amber zeroed in on her mother's young, worn face in the photograph. "Grandma knows they didn't treat you right. She wished she could have changed that."

Margaret let out something like a grunt. "Oh, that's rich. Wished she could have changed it? She was the ringleader."

"She was sorry, Mom. She told you."

"You don't know the half of it. You never knew her like I did. You, her precious granddaughter who could do no wrong, you have no idea how mean she could be."

"She changed over the years."

"Well hooray for her and hooray for you. I got the wicked witch. You got the holier-than-thou hypocrite. Not sure which version is worse. But I knew her, the *real* her, in a way you never did."

"But she was *sorry*."

"What good is 'I'm sorry'? Sorry doesn't change anything. It doesn't erase *this*." Margaret rolled up her sleeve and presented the scar again, the scar Amber could trace in her sleep.

"I see it. I've seen it a hundred times. You said something nasty, and Grandma got mad and threw a dish at you. It hit the counter and broke and a piece of it cut your arm. I know. I know, I know, I *know*. She was *sorry*."

"That wasn't the worst of what she did. If you only knew."

"Grandma never denied any of it. She knew she'd done you wrong. She only wanted to start over with you."

For a second, Margaret sat motionless. Then she shoved the box of photographs across the bed. "Well it's too late now, isn't it?" She shuffled out the door.

Amber flopped backward on the bed. Was that triumph or regret in her mother's voice? Did her mother think if she let go of her bitterness for one second she'd disintegrate? If they could get through this afternoon without ripping each other's hair out it'd be a miracle. She watched the ceiling fan blades give chase until she grew dizzy, then sat up, took a breath, and joined her mother in the living room.

Hands on hips, Margaret stood scanning the room. "What are we going to do with all this junk?"

"We could do a yard sale with whatever we don't want."

"That's a lot of work. And for what? A few bucks?"

Amber sighed. "OK, let's sort out what we want first, and then we'll figure out what to do with the rest."

Margaret strolled over to the curio cabinet housing Grandma's teacup collection and stroked the cherry wood. "This is pretty nice."

"I thought you said it was junk?"

Margaret huffed in disgust. "Amber, don't start."

"Fine. Take it. It's yours.

"Oh, *thank* you for your *permission*."

"Could I have a few of the teacups, or is that too much to ask?"

"That depends. I want the china."

Amber felt her mouth drop open. "*All* of it?" She'd hand washed the silver-lined dishes countless times, after birthdays or Christmas, or anytime Grandma wanted to celebrate.

"What would I do with an incomplete set?"

Amber howled with laugher. "Give me a break! As if you don't live off of paper plates every day of your life. There's enough china to split between us."

"If we're splitting up the china then I get the teacups," Margaret said and crossed her arms over her chest.

This was wrong. All this inspecting and bickering over Grandma's things as if they were bartering at a flea market. So many of the items whispered a story. Could her mother hear the echoes at all?

Amber went to the curio. "Grandma already gave the prettiest one away."

"What are you talking about?"

Amber twisted open the door and picked up a turquoise cup. "She used to have this real dainty one, with hand-painted Monarchs all around it, even one on the inside of the cup and on the bottom of the saucer. One day I noticed it was missing and asked about it. Grandma said she'd given it to a friend of hers. Jackie, actually. The lady who sang for the funeral."

Margaret shook her head. "Nice. That thing could

have been worth something."

"That's what I thought at first." Amber traced her finger along the gold rim of the cup. "But Grandma was all excited when she told me about it, said it was fun to make Jackie so happy." Amber put the turquoise cup back on the glass shelf and turned to her mother. "You can have first pick."

Margaret's face brightened in surprise. "OK. But how about you tell me what you've already taken."

"What do you mean what I've already taken?"

"I just figured that with all the time you've been spending here you've probably claimed *something*."

"Fine. I've claimed her Bible, a lemonade pitcher, and a framed cross-stitch. Is that OK with you, or do you want those, too?"

Margaret looked amused. "Nope. They're yours. If you want her Bible, have at it. Don't let me stop you." She examined a mother of pearl cup and set it back on the glass shelf. "I figured she'd get to you eventually."

Amber studied her mother for a moment. "What is that supposed to mean?"

"I knew she'd shove her religious garbage down your throat. I just didn't know you'd swallow."

"She didn't shove anything down my throat."

Margaret raised her eyebrows. "Oh? Then why do you want her Bible?"

"Because it *belonged* to her…because I *want* it. Why should you care?"

Margaret crossed to her. "Because if my daughter has turned into a holy roller I'd like to know. I'd like to be prepared for another fanatic in the family."

"I'm not a fanatic…"

She cocked her head. "Are you sure about that?"

Amber inhaled, ready to fire off a comeback but

closed her mouth. Of course her mother would be shocked to discover she'd become the very person they'd mocked all of their lives. She was shocked herself. She chuckled. "I don't know, Mom. Maybe I am. For the longest time I thought Grandma was a little loony, but when I started reading the Bible—"

"Hold on. You started reading it?"

"I started going to this study and something clicked. I don't know how to explain it, but the more I read, the more I wanted to read, and the more I wanted to find out about this Jesus guy who...who..." She searched for words, scanning the room until her gaze fell on the blond-haired, docile looking Jesus confined to a frame on Grandma's wall. "Who didn't seem anything like *that* guy," she said, pointing.

Margaret slumped down into one end of the sofa and rubbed her eyes. "Shoot me now. You're a Jesus freak."

Amber sat down on the other end. "Mom, just listen to me. For years Grandma tried telling me about how God had forgiven her, how she'd been given a second chance at life, but I always blew her off. And then, after she died, I realized she might be right. And if she was, I wanted a second chance, too. I've done things I'm not proud of, things that would shock even you. I just got sick of my life, of all this guilt. I figured that if it's true, if Jesus died to...to...pay for my mess, to make things right, then I'd be crazy not to grab on to that." Amber fell quiet.

Margaret pushed herself off the couch, walked to the front window, and peeled back a drape. For a minute, she stood motionless, one hand on her hip, one hand clutching the floral fabric, staring at the front yard, at the maple tree Amber knew she and Grandma had planted together years ago. Margaret released the drape and turned around.

Hope stirred within Amber. Maybe they could start over, start from scratch. Maybe somehow Grandma's death could be the catalyst to mend them together.

"Mom. Say something."

Margaret sighed. "What do you want me to say?"

"Whatever you want. Whatever you're thinking."

"Fine. I'll tell you what I'm thinking." She locked eyes with Amber. "I think you've lost your mind. I think you've bought into Mom's religious garbage because you feel guilty, because you're weak, because you can't stand on your own two feet."

Amber sank lower into the couch, suddenly a child again, cornered by her mother's words.

"I thought I had at least raised you with half a brain in your head. I thought you were smarter than this—"

Stupid little girl. Stupid little girl who believed God actually loved her. Stupid little girl who thought saying sorry could make up for all the bad.

Margaret continued ranting, her words stinging like hail. Amber longed to put her hands over her ears like she had done as a child when her mother screamed at her or Grandma or a boyfriend. A heavy hopelessness thudded inside of her stomach, and the bleakness of her life pressed into her like a lead blanket. Grandma was gone. Beth and Gretchen and Michael were lost to her, and she was shackled to her past. As hard as she tried, she couldn't get away from it. There was no escape. Not for her. She was nothing but a used up, worn-out woman. Just like her mother.

Amber hung her head and shut her eyes. *God, help*

me.

"Grandma was a self-righteous hypocrite who only wanted to turn you against me. This whole Jesus thing is a way for people to act like they're better than everyone else, a crutch for the weak. Is that want you want? To be weak?"

Yes. She was weak. Desperate. And she couldn't pretend otherwise anymore. Amber cradled her head in her hands, drowning under the words.

Yet through the clamor of her mother's tirade, a quiet voice strove to break through. Words washed over her; words that, without her knowing it, had quietly taken residence in her heart. They surfaced from their hidden place and whispered over the roar of her mother like a soft wind.

In Him was life, and that life was the light of all mankind. The light shines in the darkness, and the darkness has not overcome it.

"Don't be stupid, Amber. Grandma tried to get me to buy into that trash, but I know better and I thought you did too—"

He came to that which was His own, but His own did not receive Him. Yet to all who received Him, to those who believed in His name, He gave the right to become children of God.

"You of all people should know better. Of all the brainless things you've done, Amber, this takes the cake—"

The right to become children of God.

Margaret fell silent as something settled itself in Amber's heart.

Children of God.

Amber lifted her head and studied the resentment etched in the lines of her mother's face, the glistening fury in her empty blue eyes. Suddenly, she only saw a hollow vagrant of a woman, a woman with no parents and no home. The truth draped over Amber like a warm shawl: she did not belong to her mother anymore. She belonged to her Father.

She straightened and stood. "You can have the teacups, Mom. Grandma's given me enough already."

Then she picked up a box of books she'd been meaning to sort, went to her room, and gently closed the door.

32

Beth flipped through the stack of photographs until she found what she was looking for: a shot of Michael on graduation day in front of the lilacs. A blond tuft of hair poked out from underneath his navy cap, and his pride spilled into his eyes.

She placed the picture on the table and riffled some more, searching for the group shot she'd snapped at Bible study a few weeks ago and planned on making copies for everyone. She found it and laid it beside the first photo, overlapping them until Amber and Michael's faces sat side by side. Why hadn't she noticed before?

"It's the eyes," she said to Eric when he entered the kitchen. "How could I have missed it?"

"You see it now because you know it now."

Yet she couldn't shake the accusation of his initial response; as Michael's mother, she should have picked up on *something*.

Eric kissed her cheek and headed to work.

Beth tucked the photos into an envelope and glanced down the hall, wondering how long Michael would keep to his cave. She wanted to know everything, absorb every detail, experience every emotion he'd felt when Brenda flung the truth at him. How had he managed to drive the three hours to Madison, and what had transpired at that insidious dumpster? She wanted to join him in that dark, terrible place, help him sort out the jagged pieces, tend to his gaping wounds. But he was eighteen, pulling further away from her day by day.

To distract herself, Beth preheated the oven to 350 degrees and paged through a cookbook. Every good and gooey thing required an oven set at 350. An hour later, she pulled out a pan of monster bars and filled the dough-encrusted mixing bowl with hot water and dish soap.

Michael entered, his hair still damp from his shower, his backpack slung over a shoulder. "I'll be at Evan's."

She dried her hands on a towel. "Don't you work today?"

"Tonight. I'll leave from Evan's."

"Will you be home later?"

He grabbed a banana without a further glance. "I'll be at Evan's." He closed the door firmly behind him.

∂∞∾

That evening, when Miranda showed up on her doorstep, Beth felt a rush of foolishness. She lightly smacked her forehand. "Monday. I completely forgot."

Miranda eyed her. "Are you OK?"

"No, but come in." She led Miranda to the cluttered living room and began gathering newspapers and magazine strewn across the coffee table. She picked up the laundry basket of clean towels she'd yet to fold and started for the hall.

"What can I do to help?" Miranda asked.

Beth stopped, grateful Miranda recognized the immediate need, and didn't probe. "Do you mind running the vacuum?"

While Miranda vacuumed, Beth tackled the bathroom with a roll of paper-towels and a bottle of Windex. At least she had plenty of treats to serve. Not only this morning's concoction, but also a half dozen apple scones from yesterday morning. In these last two days, she'd done little more than whirl around the kitchen, tossing things like butter and sugar and chocolate into a bowl, combinations she knew would give her exactly what she wanted. Last evening's sourdough loaf had been particularly cathartic, with all the beatings it required. Even after all of her pounding, after she'd transferred her pent-up frustration into its suppleness, the thing swelled and rose and came out a lovely golden brown, crusty on the outside, soft and sponge-like on the inside. Yes, food was magic.

Eric said she was making him fat. And she had noticed her thighs did seem to jiggle more these days. Oh well.

Miranda wrapped up the cord on the vacuum and wheeled it back into the hall closet. Then she turned to Beth, her eyes displaying concern.

"I can't go into it right now," Beth said. "I'm sorry. Probably shouldn't expect much from me tonight." She headed to the kitchen to start the coffee.

If Miranda felt rattled, she hid it like a pro. Beth hid behind her role of hostess. She served drinks. Smiled. Made small talk. Made sure to look at whomever was speaking. Periodically nodded in agreement. Laughed when others laughed. It was only when Janis shared about the betrayal and hurt she felt after her recent divorce that Beth momentarily jolted to attention and tuned in for real. She wasn't the only one with problems.

"I guess I just came to a point when I realized I needed to let go and let God," Janis said, concluding her narrative.

Beth strapped on a smile but inwardly bristled. Really? Was that it? She'd read that phrase on bookmarks too many times to count. Yet life wasn't always that simple or didactic. Life couldn't always be reduced to closed doors, opened windows, the Serenity Prayer, and God knows best, could it? The curly-cued words splashed across her coffee cups and ribboned along the top of stationary didn't always cut it. Certainly a nugget of truth lay buried behind such clichés, but what about the mess of life? What about loose ends that never tied up? And yet here she sat, pretending everything was fine, while a tempest raged in her soul. She glanced at the faces in her living room. Were they all masking a tempest of some kind?

The truth was, you couldn't bleed over everyone all the time, couldn't spill your heartache to anyone with a pair of ears. Even Miranda, who Beth had grown to love and admire, couldn't be privy to the full story of Michael and Amber. For all of their sakes. As of last night, Gretchen knew everything, and that was enough.

Beth had shared every last detail with her sister as they circled the block under a smattering of stars. Occasionally, Gretchen stopped short and gaped at her. When Beth ran out of words and felt the threat of tears, Gretchen pulled her to herself and cried as well. Then they marveled at the inconceivability of it all—surely God's hand was in this—and then Gretchen promised to pray. A look of realization crossed her sister's face, and Beth couldn't help but chuckle. Prayer. That's how she'd gotten into this mess, wasn't it? Gretchen had prayed her into it.

Dangerous thing, praying.

Beth sipped her coffee, thankful for the faithful confidant of her sister.

And what about Amber? Who would walk beside Amber and listen to her pour out her heart? She recalled the staggering woman from the pub and felt a rush of alarm.

Don't let her do anything stupid, Lord.

Michael's birth mother had haunted Beth's thoughts since day one, and her emotions toward the girl—as she'd always imagined her—changed as swiftly as the wind. Shock and horror initially, and compassion, too. And pity. And ultimately gratitude because his birth mother had accomplished something Beth could not: carry Michael in that most hidden place and give him life, even if she'd disregarded that life. The irony never failed to smack hard. Michael was hers because his mother had abandoned him.

No doubt, Michael grappled with this fact, too. Over the years, Beth had seen the struggle behind his eyes, witnessed his bouts of rage, helped him grapple with his unanswerable questions. As wonderful as it was, adoption came with loss, and Michael's seemed to include a double shot. If her own feelings toward his birth mother were complex and shifted on the tides of emotion, Michael was riding a tsunami.

And now the faceless birth mother had a name. The phantom mother was Amber. Her friend.

The squeak of the kitchen door jarred Beth to the present, and she glanced over her shoulder in hopes of spying her son. She caught Eric's profile instead. He'd told her earlier that he was running out to buy something, a tool or a part. Something important and not important, for the washer or the dryer or some other machine in the house that didn't seem to matter right now.

To Beth's relief, Miranda ended with a quick prayer, and on the heels of the *amen*, she darted to the kitchen to dish up monster bars and secure her smile. She could pretend for a few more minutes. Conceal the tempest for a little while longer.

Later that evening, Gretchen called to report that Michael was spending the night. He didn't stop home the following day and after supper, Beth succumbed to her anxiety and dropped by for a visit and to unload some of her baked goods.

"I think I've gained five pounds this week," Beth said, setting the Tupperware container on her sister's table. She heard Michael's voice in the family room.

Gretchen grabbed two grocery sacks from underneath her sink, and they headed outdoors.

"Do you mind?" Beth asked while they made their way to Gretchen's garden. "Having him here?"

"Of course not. Do you?"

"I want him home."

Gretchen loosened the wire fence to keep out the rabbits and waded into the tomatoes plants. "He'll come home. Just give him time."

"We don't have time. It's been days, and he hasn't said a word to Eric or me. He hardly looks at me. It's not good to keep all of his emotions bottled up."

Gretchen titled her head in that proverbial look of challenge. "I don't think he is."

"What do you mean? Evan?"

Gretchen nodded. "Evan has his shortcomings. Believe me, I know. But I gotta hand it to him. That kid has loyalty in spades."

Beth plucked a Better Boy and grinned. "I know. I remember that fistfight in junior high." She sniffed the fruit then set it in the paper bag. "I just feel like I'm losing him."

"You are losing him to some extent. Not just because of this whole Amber thing, but because that's normal. But, Beth, Michael knows who his family is. He *knows*. He has to wrestle through this, though. This is a defining moment for him. He has to deal with the loss and rejection all over again as if his birth mother—as if Amber—abandoned him yesterday. That's a massive undertaking. Don't rush him."

"But he's off to school soon. What if he heads to college without talking to us at all, without figuring out what to do? If he wants to get in contact with Amber then we need to—"

"Stop trying to control everything!" Gretchen rubbed her forehead and sighed. "Look. It's only natural for you to want to orchestrate all of this for him, and I'm sure, as his mother, you're feeling the brunt of his anger, but I really think you need to back off."

"Spare me your psychobabble."

Gretchen froze, nodded, and bent over her tomatoes.

A basketball thumped on the driveway, and Beth turned to see Michael attempt a layup. Evan tried to block him, but the ball swished through the net anyway. Michael laughed. Actually *laughed*.

She turned back to Gretchen. "Michael's lucky to have him."

"Peanut butter and jelly."

She plucked another tomato. "And I'm lucky to have you."

Gretchen smiled and like every summer of their adult lives, handed her a sack of bright red tomatoes.

❧❧

Michael came home the following evening. He wordlessly consumed his dinner then sat for hours on the sofa in front of the TV. After a while, Eric joined him, and as Beth cleaned up the kitchen, she could hear them occasionally rattle off a statistic about one of the players or randomly comment about the commercials that cut into the pre-season game. She wanted to scream. She wanted to shake them both and clunk their heads together.

"Don't you think you should talk to him?" she prodded Eric later that night while she undressed for bed.

"I am talking to him."

She huffed. "About something that matters."

"Beth. Give it up. Let us deal with this in our own time."

She climbed into bed and yanked the blankets tightly under her chin.

Eric climbed in beside her. "Trust me on this. You can't force the issue. He'll talk when he's ready." He managed to finagle his arm underneath her and pulled her close. "Beth. I'm in your corner."

She let her head fall on his chest, in that niche just below his collarbone that perfectly fit her head. "And I'm in yours," she responded with some effort.

❧❧

The following afternoon, as she was sliding out a

sheet of peanut butter cookies from the oven, Michael shuffled through the door and clanked his keys to the counter.

"How was work?" she asked.

"Fine." He kicked his shoes off by the door.

"A manila envelope came for you. It's on the table." Spatula in hand, she began transferring the sand colored circles to a cooling rack. Michael started for the hall.

"It might be something about orientation or your dorm assignment."

"I'll look at it later."

"Michael, you might want to look at it now because some of these things are time sensitive —"

"I said later!"

She switched tactics. "Want some cookies? Peanut butter."

He paused, turned, and slouched back into the kitchen, as if he were doing her a favor. He swiped a cookie, tore it in two, and popped half of it into his mouth. She poured two glasses of milk. He took a drink, grabbed another cookie, then turned to leave. Her insides boiled. Time to address the elephant dancing across the room.

"Michael. I'm worried about you."

He chewed and shrugged. "Don't be."

"I just want to know how you're doing, how you're dealing with all of this. Talking about it could help, you know."

He let out a small, chilling laugh.

"Sometimes you need to say things out loud to figure out what you want, to sort through your feelings." She took a cookie for herself, broke off a portion and ate it.

"OK, Mom. Let's share. Let's have a heart to heart. Oh, wait. Why didn't we do this last week? When you *knew*."

"I was blindsided, still trying to wrap my mind around it myself before telling you." Shame niggled. She also had decided not to tell him. "You're right. Dad and I should have been the ones to tell you. I'm sorry. How are you doing?"

"What do you want me to say?"

"Anything! Say anything."

Michael gulped down the rest of his milk and thudded the glass to the counter. He turned and looked out the kitchen window, offering her his profile. He braced himself against the counter with his palms, his jaw rigid, his eyes unblinking. "I hate her."

Beth cringed. She took a breath, determined to simply absorb the truth of his emotions, the truth of the moment, and not talk him out of it. She studied his blond curls at the base of his neck. He'd let his hair grow out this summer, allowing the soft curls from his boyhood to make a reappearance. She longed to twist a lock of gold around her finger like she'd done when he was four.

"I don't know how she ever was allowed to step foot in this house. *My* house," he said.

The truth began to dawn. He felt violated. It didn't matter that he was the one to work with Amber, that he was the one to accept a ride home from her one night, that Gretchen, not her, had invited her into the backyard. For some reason, in spite of all of that, *she* was to blame. Maybe there was something to be said for Gretchen's psychobabble. She, his mother, had befriended the enemy. It was her fault.

Beth dropped the spatula, suddenly feeling so

tired she needed to sit down. She went to the table. "I'm sorry. Michael, I'm sorry about all of this. If I had known that Amber..." But she stopped. If she had known...what?

She supposed she could have told Miranda no. Find somebody else to host. She could have told Gretchen not to pray for her. She could have bid Amber *welcome to Elkin* and left it at that, never invited her to study, never deepened the friendship. Her obedience had resulted in her child's pain. Anger welled up.

Right in this moment the events of the summer didn't seem to be wonderfully orchestrated; they felt cruel. Like trickery. What was God doing? Where in Scripture did it say trust God, and He'll rip your heart in two. Obey Him and it'll cost you the happiness of your son.

Wait...wait.

Beth closed her eyes, reeling to keep up with the rushing currents of her thoughts. Would she have blatantly disobeyed God if it meant shielding Michael from pain? Everything in her yearned to restore this child, to go back in time and undo the steps that had led them here. Yet she couldn't deny glimpsing a beautiful picture emerging from the mess, a flaming phoenix fighting to rise above the ashes.

She waited for him to say something more. He only wiped his mouth with his hand and resumed his trek to the hall.

They were done talking for now. It was a start. A good start.

As he walked past her, Beth held out the manila envelope. "At least take this to your room."

"Don't know why I should listen to you," he said

quietly, coolly. "You've only been playing mom all these years anyway."

Her breath left her. She pushed back her chair, stormed over to him, and grabbed his arm, aware of the pain her nails might be inflicting on his skin. She forced his six-foot frame to face her.

"Playing mom? I've been *playing* mom? Who sat up with you all night when you were sick? Who paid to put braces on your teeth? Who went to all your swim meets? Me. Your *mother*." She locked eyes with him. "Don't you ever, *ever*, say anything like that to me again."

He blinked, and his eyes clouded in regret.

Maybe he would have apologized. Maybe the angry façade would have fallen away and they could have truly conversed. But she didn't give him the chance. She was drowning in a sea of emotion, sputtering and flaying and likely to make everything worse if she didn't leave. She willed her eyes to remain dry and headed for her bedroom and closed the door.

She wept as noiselessly as she could, so quietly that after a minute she heard Michael exit through the kitchen door and back his car out of the driveway.

33

Working at the Pick 'n Save proved to be far more monotonous and paid half as much as Amber had earned at Winston Hill, but it provided a paycheck. She scanned a loaf of rye bread and touted the grand total to a woman with ghastly colored pink lips who demanded the bread go on top. Last time it was squished. Barely fit in the toaster, she grumbled.

Amber only smiled and while Ms. Lipstick swiped her credit card, she gave the heel of the loaf a furtive squeeze before placing it on top of the eggs. "Have a good day," she chirped as a can of black olives from the next customer rolled down the conveyer belt.

"Amber!"

Startled, Amber looked up at the next customer. Jackie.

"I didn't know you worked here!"

"As of two days ago," she said and grabbed the olives.

"So you're staying in town?"

Amber scanned a gallon of two percent. "I'm at my grandma's trying to sort and clean and get the house ready to put on the market."

"Do you plan to stay until it sells?"

Plan? What plan? "Probably."

Jackie sighed and shook her head. "I love that little house. So many good memories. I'll have you know I've shared many glasses of lemonade and heart-to-hearts with your Grandma on that front porch. I'm sure you have, too. I'd love to come over and help," Jackie offered. "I'm sure getting the place ready to sell is a big undertaking."

Amber peered at Jackie, disarmed by the cloudburst of kindness. "OK."

"I'm free this evening. I could drop by after supper if you want. Say, seven?"

Amber scanned an Italian loaf and set it on the top of a full bag. "Sounds great."

❧

Before walking the six blocks home, Amber bought two frozen pizzas, a bunch of bananas, and six lemons. She ate half the pizza for supper and after cleaning the kitchen, carried the ingredients for lemonade to the porch. She settled the lemons in the sturdy wooden bowl that forever sat on the small table next to Grandma's rocking chair, the yellow ovals as bright and eager as front row students, simultaneously annoying and admirable.

Amber parked herself in the rocking chair and cradled a lemon in her palm, its optimism taunting her, a punch of color showing off in a dismal world. She felt gray, and longed for color, longed to paint. Longed for Grandma, longed for Beth. Longed for Michael.

Minutes later, a brown sedan pulled up, and Jackie climbed out, her purple blouse another pop of color. Amber waved and Jackie made her way up the porch steps, wordlessly reached for a lemon, sniffed it and smiled. She took a seat in the swing. "She was a wonderful woman," she finally said and pressed the lemon to her heart. "I miss her already."

Amber set her lemon on the cutting board and cut it lengthwise.

"My girls will miss her, too."

"How old are your girls?" Amber asked.

"Sixteen and fourteen. Not the easiest ages. I've called my mother more than once to apologize for what I put her through. Jessica, my fourteen-year-old, is so much like me it's terrifying. I'd do anything to spare her from making the same mistakes I made, but you know teenagers. I'm the last person she wants to listen to. She'd listen to Miss Virginia though, and Ginny listened to me. And faithfully prayed for all three of us."

With the fluidity born from years of practice, Amber squeezed the last bit of juice from her lemon and discarded the carcass in a bag under the table. "That was Grandma. Always praying."

"I think she sensed we needed it. For a while there, I think I radiated desperation. I love my girls to pieces, but the last few years have been rough."

Amber looked up. "Since they became teenagers, you mean?"

Jackie sighed. "Since their father split for San Diego."

Diving into someone else's problems felt like diving into a cool lake on a sweltering day. Amber waited for elaboration.

"I'm sorry," Jackie sighed. "You don't want to hear this. I didn't come here to burden you with my baggage."

"No, I don't mind. When did he leave?"

Jackie seemed to survey her for a moment. "It'll be four years this October. We're all still—" Her voice broke. She shifted in her seat and smiled sadly at the lemon in her hands. "Before the divorce the girls looked up to him like he was Superman. He could do no wrong. And then suddenly, it was like someone threw a bowling ball through our front window. *Bam.* Everything changed. Shattered. Seventeen years of marriage, gone. He packed up and left us for some woman he met on the Internet. The *Internet* for crying out loud." She leaned forward and picked up the knife. For a moment, Amber wondered if she might stab the table. But Jackie set the lemon on the cutting board and sliced it in two.

"The one good thing that came out of this whole mess is that it drove me to my knees and back into church," Jackie said as she placed half the lemon on the juicer. "There's nothing like pain for God to get a hold of you. I don't know where we'd be without our church. I really don't. Your Grandma played a huge role in that."

Amber recalled the butterfly teacup Ginny had given Jackie with such joy. "Grandma mentioned you a few times. She didn't tell me anything about your divorce, though."

Jackie shook her head. "Oh no, she wouldn't. Our group has shared a lot over the years, but we're pretty tight. What's shared with the group, stays with the group." She tossed the used lemon in the garbage bag under the table. "Enough about me. Your turn. How are you doing?"

"I'm doing OK."

Jackie leaned back and studied her. "Are you?"

Amber slashed another lemon. What else could she say? She pressed the fruit on the squeezer, and the juice trickled down the inside of the glass like tears. "Hanging in there."

"It's been good seeing you in church."

"I've been wanting to thank you for singing at her funeral. It really meant a lot."

Jackie smiled. "It was my honor."

Amber took up another lemon and rolled it along the top of the table, readying the juices. "That song you did, 'To God be the Glory,' really meant something to me. It's hard to explain, but something clicked. A lot of what Grandma had been trying to tell me finally made sense. About starting over. About God's forgiveness."

Jackie went still. "Really?"

"Later that day I became a Christian."

Jackie looked shocked at first. Then she smiled, her hazel eyes glistening. "Amber, that's wonderful! Thank you for sharing that with me." Still beaming, she looked away, toward the treetops across the street, and then turned back to Amber. "You must know how much your Grandma loved you, how faithfully she prayed for you.'

"I know."

Jackie's smile grew impish. "I have to tell you something. I've been praying for you, too. All four of us have, in fact, in our little prayer group."

Amber's checks burned.

"Don't worry. Ginny never shared any details. Only that she loved you, and she longed for you to understand how much God loved you, too."

Amber looked away, needing a moment to process this. It was no secret that Grandma prayed for her, but a group of women she'd never met before? She felt small but significant. A single bead in a long necklace.

Jackie's grin broadened. "Oh, Amber, your grandma would be overjoyed. What a roller coaster you've been on! I guess you've certainly had your share of ups and downs this month, haven't you?"

She shrugged. Jackie had no idea.

"So, like I said, Ginny didn't share much about you so fill me in. I gather you're single?"

Amber nodded.

"And do you have any children?"

Just like always, the question hit like a wrecking ball. *Whack, whack, whack*, striking her down, down, down until she was nothing but the girl from eighteen years ago, a girl running in darkness on that horrific June night. A girl who *had* a child but had abandoned him. A monster who'd killed her own baby.

Yet, miracle of miracles, he lived. Today, for the first time, a different answer rose above the guilt.

I have a son, she thought, and then heard the words, and realized she'd spoken them out loud. Somehow, the syllables passed her lips and now floated around like dandelion puffs.

Jackie looked at her in surprise. "You have a son? Ginny never mentioned that."

"She never knew." Again, words tumbled out against her control.

"She didn't?" Jackie's brow wrinkled. She closed her mouth, stared at Amber, then at the street, then back at Amber. "How old is he?"

"Eighteen." How could she turn this ship around now?

"Does he live with you?"

"No."

"So, he lives with his father?"

Amber dug her fingernails into the dimpled flesh of the yellow sphere in her hand, the bright ball that had suddenly gone bleary. She cleared her throat. "Tell me more about your girls. I'd love to hear more about…" Her voice rang with bright falseness. She gripped the lemon tighter, the juices oozing through the piercings left by her fingernails, leaving her palm sticky and tight.

Jackie touched her arm. "Amber. What is it? What's really going on?"

The world shifted at the question. Something about Jackie's tone cut her to the core. She couldn't play the game anymore, couldn't pretend anymore. Couldn't choke out a *Nothing, I'm fine.* Wounded, bleeding people were *not* fine. Girls who left their babies to die were *not* fine. They needed help. She needed help.

And here sat Jackie, holding out the pearl of friendship, even as a fragment of the hideous truth dangled between them. Stuffing it back into that deep, dark place seemed impossible. She had to speak it. Release it. Bleed it dry.

She looked at Jackie, contemplated the depths of her gold-flecked eyes, weighing their loyalty.

"If you need to talk, I'm here to listen," Jackie said. "And I know how to keep a confidence."

For some reason—Grandma's own trust in her maybe—Amber believed her. She squeezed the lemon harder and let out a small, soft laugh that ended up sounding more like a moan. "How much time do you have?"

"As much time as it takes."

Amber clutched the lemon between her hands and set her gaze on the weathered floorboards at her feet. After a moment, the buried words rumbled to life, unearthing themselves from the deep corners of her memory. At first, they emerged slowly, quietly, but within a matter of minutes, they poured forth like rushing water. She talked until the sun kissed the tops of the trees, until she was spent, until there was nothing left to tell. And then, when she was finished, as depleted and wrung out as the lemon carcasses crumpled in the bag at her feet, she sat back in her chair and waited.

Jackie sat silently, her eyes peering into the empty, darkening street.

A sudden burst of horror filled Amber. What had she done? Destroyed another friendship before it had begun? Irreversibly repulsed a kind woman who loved Grandma, who'd only stopped by to help her clean the house?

After a full minute, Jackie turned to her. She gazed at her without flinching. Then she leaned forward and grabbed her sticky, soiled hand. "God's grace is sufficient, Amber. Even for this."

34

In the days following the kitchen confrontation with Michael, tension ran thick. Beth sensed his penitence, but so far he'd said nothing to her. Nothing beyond statements that started with *please pass the*...or *where's my*...Sometimes she felt his eyes flicker over her, vulnerable and expectant, but she wasn't about to broach the subject. That was his task. When you did something hurtful, you recognized the wound you caused and then made amends. You apologized. Wasn't that how she'd raised him?

The kitchen incident wasn't the first time Michael had used his birth mom as a weapon. She recalled him playing the adoption card a few times while in the throes of puberty. Once when she forbade him to see a particular movie with a group of friends, and he snarled that his real mom would let him; and another time when she and Eric insisted he accompany them to church, and he argued that his birth mother would never force him to go. His assumptions were probably right in both cases. Not that it mattered.

The words stung even though it was clear these were outbursts resulting from him not getting his way and adolescent anger and moods that turned on a dime. In the past, she and Eric absorbed the words without much commentary, Michael calmed down, and they all moved on. His remark two days ago, however, left a bruise.

The words hadn't tumbled out in rage or teenage challenge. He'd spoken them indifferently, callously. As if he meant to wound her deeply. She had no desire to shut him out, especially now, but at the same time, he was old enough to take responsibility for his actions. To take the initiative and set things right. For the most part, he ignored her.

Thankfully, he talked to Eric. And not only about stupid TV commercials and pre-season games, but about things that mattered. Amber. College. Dare she hope it? His feelings?

"I don't want him to hate her for the rest of his life," Beth said one night to Eric over a dinner for two of perfectly ripened corn on the cob and garden tomatoes. "For his sake. That could destroy him."

"I don't think he wants to hate her."

"So how does he get through this? How does he move beyond this hatred and bitterness?"

Eric looked at her quizzically, as if she should know the answer. "Forgiveness. How else?" He doused a fresh cob with salt and dug in.

Forgiveness. Well, she'd just snap her fingers and make that happen.

Later that night she reached for her Bible and turned to the account of Joseph. She skimmed the story until she came to what she deemed the climax, the twist of fate: the reunion scene of Joseph and his brothers. The brothers who threw him in a pit. Who sold him as a slave. She always loved this scene and savored Joseph's summation of his brother's deeds: *You intended to harm me, but God intended it for good to accomplish what is now being done...*She read the scene over again, letting it settle into her soul.

She set the Bible on her nightstand, clicked off her

lamp, and allowed her mind to drift to that very first night home with Michael, when she rocked him to sleep, encased in the soft yellow nursery. The rush of mother-love shocked her. She cradled him to her breast, knowing her body lacked the ability to sustain him with physical nourishment, but vowing to provide for him in every other way. Here he was. Lifted from the rubble of a fallen world and placed in the shelter of her arms. Her love for him swept through the empty alcove of her heart and ignited a fierceness she'd never known before. This child was hers, no matter what any blood test would say. Fully, irrevocably *hers*.

That night she thanked God for her closed womb because in her arms lay the most beautiful baby in the world, and what if she had missed him? Tears flowed, first in utter joy, then in thankfulness, and then in sorrow because Michael had been abandoned and out there was a girl who had done such a thing, a terrible thing, that resulted in Beth's good and, she believed, Michael's good.

A new thought seized her: what about his birth mother? What about Amber's good? Was it Amber's throbbing guilt from her crime that had thrust her to her knees and brought her to repentance? When God had denied Beth her biggest desire years ago, said no to having a baby, was He preparing the way for the path they were on today? The path that not only brought them to Michael but had also led them to Amber? For Amber's ultimate good?

God intended it for good to accomplish what is now being done. She felt her body yield to sleep while a part of her mind kept vigil, praying that Michael might soften, heal, and grasp this elusive thing called forgiveness.

❧❧

The next morning, shrouded in her bathrobe, Beth stood glowering at the calendar. Only four more days, and she'd be back teaching kindergarten. Only six more days and Michael would be gone. She examined the little car Michael had sketched in the calendar square, a UW-Madison pendant flapping from the window. In six days, they'd pack up the car, drive him to the university, put sheets on his bed, take him out to lunch, and say good-bye. End the season, a season as sweet and fleeting as her lilacs.

She sighed and ground four scoops of Kenyan beans, shook the coffee dust into the filter, and pressed the button to start it brewing. She needed it strong. She was in a mood.

Tightening the sash on her bathrobe, she studied the decorative mugs lining the shelf above her kitchen sink. She hardly ever used them. A bright red one splattered with yellow sunflowers wooed her. She'd have to wash it first, but sometimes even the smallest indulgence boosted the spirit.

Standing on tiptoe, Beth reached for the mug. Suddenly, the right side of the shelf tipped, sending the mugs sliding along the bottom of the shelf until they smacked into the side of the cupboard. Her arms shot over her head to brace the shelf as the counter dug into her stomach. If she let go, or even shifted her grip slightly, the mugs would crash.

"Michael!"

She strained to hear sounds of stirring from the hall. Eric had already left for work.

"Michael! Help!"

She heard shuffling. Michael stumbled into the kitchen, shirtless and rumpled, rubbing his eyes. He squinted at her.

"Hurry! Grab the mugs."

Comprehension seeming to dawn, he darted over, snatched three mugs and set them on the counter, then rescued the remaining trio. He lifted the shelf from her fingers. "Looks like the nail broke off."

Beth let out her breath and shook her hands. "I'm glad you were home."

He sniffed and ambled out. She watched him go and felt herself tense. Sighing, she filled the sink and began washing the mugs. Moments later, he reappeared, pulling a hooded sweatshirt over his head. "Did you make a lot of coffee?"

"A whole pot."

The mugs clean, she filled the red floral one to the top and a navy one halfway. She set the blue mug and the sugar bowl before Michael who asked if they had any half and half.

Beth scanned the contents of the fridge, amused by his recent interest in coffee. A self-induced rite of passage, she supposed, a pursuit that somehow stamped him college ready in his mind. She found the creamer and set it on the table.

He drizzled in at least a quarter of a cup. "That thing was about freshman orientation by the way."

"What thing?"

"That packet. The one you wanted me to open the other day."

"Oh. OK." She joined him at the table. "You feeling ready?"

He shrugged. "I guess so." He sipped his coffee, his eyes darting restlessly. He licked his lips a few times, sat forward, sat back. "I didn't mean it," he finally said softly. "About what I said. You're my mom. I know that. I don't know why I said that. I'm sorry."

Beth covered his hand with her own. "I know. And I know this is a stressful time for you."

His features relaxed as he sat back in his chair. She thought she heard him sigh.

"So," she said and retracted her hand. "Is there anything in particular you want to do these last few days?"

Michael smirked. "You make it sound like I'm dying. I don't know. You could make enchiladas with homemade salsa. I'd be up for that."

"Okay. I'll make it for your last meal."

He gave her a look. "Mom. Stop."

"Your last meal before the dorm, I mean." They fell quiet and Beth sipped her coffee, keenly aware of the fragility of the moment. It was as if they were caught up in a dance, weaving around the question that hung between them. If she stepped on his toes would the conversation stop? Would one slip on her part destroy the moment? Like her hand holding up those coffee mugs? She went to the refrigerator, found a package of bagels, and popped one into the toaster. "Chicken enchiladas. Got it. Anything else?" she prompted. "Anything else you want to do?"

"You're trying to ask me about Amber, aren't you?"

"Maybe. Yes."

"You're not too subtle about it." He stirred another dose of sugar into his coffee. "The thing is, she never said anything to me. She knew, when I saw her in the parking lot, she knew and she never let on."

"She wanted to protect you. She didn't want to burden you with having to figure out what to do with her."

"Little good that did." He took another sip then slouched in his chair, slouched so far his right leg extended the full length of the table. "Or maybe she doesn't want anything to do with me."

"No," Beth said. "That's not true, and I'm sure of it."

His eyes flashed to her. "How can you be sure of anything? She *left* me, Mom. To *die*. What makes you think she'd want anything to do with me now? All these years you've told me about how mixed up she must be, how she must regret what she did, how horrible she must feel. Well maybe she doesn't regret a thing."

How she wanted to swoop in and embrace him. He was but a vulnerable little boy clutching a coffee mug. She crossed the room and sat down. "Michael, I *know* she regrets it. I know if she could undo the past she would. She left Elkin because she feels she doesn't deserve to be in your life. She didn't want to complicate things. She left without telling you because she didn't want to hurt you."

He laughed bitterly. "That was nice of her."

The bagel popped. Beth sat motionless. In her closet, leaned up against the wall hidden underneath her dresses, sat a symbol of Amber's regret and—she believed—love. But would Michael see it? Or would such a thing only unleash his anger? Would he want to destroy the piece because Amber had created it, the one who created and tried to destroy him?

As a little boy, Michael clung to a stuffed monkey someone gave him as a shower gift, and one day he asked her if his birth mother had given it to him. Beth gently told him no. He asked if she'd given him his fuzzy green blanket. No, Beth answered, she hadn't. His face contorted, and he glanced around his bedroom with something like panic. What *had* his birth mother given him, he'd wanted to know. *What*? Beth set him in her lap and twisted a lock of his hair around her finger and told him she had given him many things. His hair. His smile. His strong body. His smart mind.

But these answers felt wanting, even to her.

She gazed at her son. Today she could hand him something tangible, something to hold on to. He had a right to see the painting, to absorb and interpret it for himself. To discover Amber on his own.

Wordlessly she stood and went to her room and brought back the canvas. She clutched it to her chest, as if somehow her love might seep into the colors.

Michael looked at her curiously.

Beth took a step toward him and held out the painting. "This is for you. From your birth mother."

kk

An hour later, they were backing out of the garage. "What if we're wrong?" Michael asked. "What if she's not there?"

"Then we'll go out for pizza." But she knew they'd find Amber. She knew it in her bones. They made their way through downtown, past the shops and a few residual summer tourists, and crested a hill.

"She almost hit a deer. Right on this road," Michael said.

"What?"

"That night she drove me home from work, when we had burgers on the deck? She almost hit a deer. It came out of nowhere, and she came this close." He chuckled and held up his thumb and index finger, separated by an inch. "Missed by a hair. It was something. We both kind of freaked out."

Beth glanced at her son. She recalled that evening when Gretchen rounded the corner of her house with Amber by her side, how her anger melted as they chatted around the patio table. Funny that neither Michael nor Amber had mentioned the deer. "You never told me that."

What other memories had they shared? Or would they make in the future?

A piece of Michael had always remained inaccessible to her, a hole neither she nor Eric could ever completely fill. Having a child through adoption required a certain brand of sharing, a realization that a portion of your child's heart will always belong to someone else. Up until now, sharing Michael with his birth parents, his past, played out in a purely abstract, emotional way. She shared him in theory. All of that was about to change.

She felt a dull throb in the pit of her stomach.

Would a time ever come for her to share the keepsakes of Michael's childhood with Amber? Pull out the plastic bin full of treasures? A wisp of blond hair from his first haircut. Lopsided drawings on faded construction paper. Plaster-of-paris handprints. Homemade cards written with crayon and misspelled words. *I luv mi mom. I luv mi hows.* And the stories, the funny things Michael used to say—all the unseen gems tucked away in her heart—would she share those? She thought of the cross-stitch Amber had held out to her at Ginny's house, the tiny x's that represented far more than the picture they constructed. A whole world resided in that fabric if you looked close enough, if you chose to see it. A tribute of love woven with bits of thread.

Amber would understand.

Michael took a swig from his soda and nestled it back into the cup holder. "I still don't know what I want. You know that, right? Us going to see her today doesn't mean I want her in my life."

"This visit will be whatever you want it to be."

"I mean, after today, I might not want to see her ever again."

"And that's OK." It seemed like a miracle that he wanted to see her at all, that Amber's painting had prompted him to find her.

They rounded a cornfield, and Beth remembered the sharp, pointy stalks, the coldness she'd felt huddled in the dirt. "Maybe I should go in first. Give her a moment to prepare."

"No."

She glanced at him. "Honey, she has no idea we're coming."

"I need to go on my own," he said quietly, firmly, and Beth resisted the urge to protest, to argue how much they both needed her in this moment while he opened Pandora's Box and freed his past, most of which wasn't pretty. She loosened her grip on the steering wheel, loosened her grip on him. Let go. Let go. Let God. Maybe she'd underestimated the saying.

"OK," she said. "I'll wait in the car. Come and get me when you want."

She stopped at an intersection and felt Michael looking at her. She turned to him.

His eyes held a kind of affection she hadn't seen in years. He placed a hand on her arm. "Mom," he said. "Thank you."

If she could shift into park and stop time she would. But he squeezed her arm and turned to look out the front window again. Her foot lifted off the brake pedal, and she focused on the road before her, a long, dark ribbon that didn't seem long enough.

35

Amber mounted the porch steps, armed with the folder from the bank containing spreadsheets of interest rates and glossy brochures with smiling families in front of Cape Cod houses. Jackie had been right. She could hardly believe it, but the impossible seemed to be veering into the achievable.

When she and Jackie met for breakfast last Saturday, Amber happily basked in the warmth of the moment, the café with its dated gingham curtains, the steaming blueberry pancakes in front of her, Jackie's lively eyes. She felt light and warm and—somewhat shockingly—content.

Jackie prattled on about her girls, about how one of them was pining over a pair of eighty-dollar boots she claimed she *had* to have with school lurking around the corner, to which Jackie said she'd better save up her babysitting money.

After a while, Amber told her she planned to stay in Spring Valley. Jackie beamed. "I was hoping you'd stay," she said. "I was also hoping you'd join our little prayer group, you know, take your Grandma's place."

Amber let out a quick laugh. "Like I could take her place." She told Jackie she'd think about it, but first things first. She needed to find an apartment.

And then, somehow, Jackie pinned down her secret wish. "Why not stay in the house?"

Because the house didn't belong solely to her,

312

Amber had explained. Half of it was her mother's and, if it were up to Margaret, the thing would be sold already. Jackie listened, nodded, and then mentioned she was friends with the president of Community Bank. Amber said she was happy for her.

"You're not tracking with me," Jackie said, chuckling. "Why not look into buying the house?"

It seemed like an impossible dream. For starters, Amber said, she didn't have that kind of money. And secondly...well, Jackie had met her lamb of a mother.

When Jackie asked if a realtor had appraised the house yet, Amber said yes, and the place was worth less than they'd hoped.

Jackie lit up. She rummaged through her purse, pulled out a crumbled scrap of paper, and jotted out a name. "Call him," she ordered. "Set up an appointment. He'll let you know if it's feasible. This market might work to your advantage."

It turned out that Jackie was right. According to Jackie's banker friend, buying Grandma's house was feasible. Now it all came down to the whims of her mother.

Amber set the folder on the porch table and before she lost her nerve, speed-dialed Margaret. After a couple of rings, Margaret answered. Amber assessed her mood after only a few words: distant but not hostile. Pacing the length of the porch, she eased into the subject, relaying how the realtor said not to expect an easy sell in the current market, how it was, after all, an old, outdated, two bedroom house in a small town.

"Great. Just great," Margaret huffed. "The thing is going to be more trouble than what it's worth. I don't have time for this. I just want it sold."

Amber recognized the wide open door. "I agree.

Everyone I've talked to thinks it'd be best to sell right away."

Margaret snorted. "Just point me to a buyer."

Amber forced herself to take a breath and said, "That's why I'm calling, actually. I think I've found one."

"You're kidding? Already? Who?"

"Me."

"You?" Margaret spat the word like an accusation.

"Just hear me out. If I buy out your half of the house we wouldn't have to pay any realtor fees and watch it depreciate, sitting on the market for months or years on end. I'll take care of all the repairs, maintenance, everything. You wouldn't have to do a thing. I've talked to someone at the bank, and he didn't think it'd be difficult for me to be approved for a loan. You'd get your asking price."

Margaret was silent. "And what exactly are you going to do with the house?" she finally asked.

"Live in it."

"You want to *live* there?"

Amber ran her hand across a porch pillar. More than anything. "Yes. I do."

"I should have seen this coming. You always did seem to think that house belonged to you for some reason."

Deflated, Amber sank down into the swing and closed her eyes, readying herself for the twist of the knife.

"But under the circumstances," Margaret said, "I don't think I'm going to get a whole lot of offers."

Had she heard right? "You mean, I can buy the house?"

"I just want the place sold. As long as your loan

goes through and I get my money. It's pure robbery that you're entitled to half of it in the first place, but I can't change her will, I guess. I'd rather sell it now than wait forever."

Amber thanked her mother. She told her she'd call just as soon as she heard from the bank and they could get the ball rolling. She hung up and leaned back in the swing, her heart galloping as the invisible roots of the house hugged her ankles, securing her to the place she loved, the place she belonged.

She was home.

She rocked, the breeze sweeping through her hair. Then she jumped up and padded through the house, surveying each room with new eyes—homeowner eyes—imagining what she'd fix and change and what she'd leave alone. She lingered in the hall, envisioning it painted a bright blue or green, with black and white photos strewn across, photos of Grandma and Grandpa, her mother and herself. She'd include some of the interesting black and white photographs she'd uncovered, pictures from generations past of people she'd never met but made up her family history.

She suddenly longed for a picture of Michael. Just one.

She stepped into Grandma's bedroom, smiled at the wedding ring quilt, the antique dresser, the vase of tacky plastic flowers, and decided to leave it as it was and meandered back to the living room. For months, Grandma had talked about painting this room a mossy green. This is where she'd start. By giving this room a fresh coat of green, a color of new life.

She went to the kitchen, poured herself a glass of lemonade to celebrate, and returned to the porch, barefoot and happy to have the day off. Later she'd call

Jackie, who'd most likely whoop in delight, and maybe they could all go for ice cream, the girls, too.

She sipped her drink and examined the porch. It did need a lot of work. Scraping and repainting was one thing, but her mother was right. The structure itself seemed comprised. Grandma had alluded to needing to get it fixed but they never got around to it. How much would foundational repairs cost? Right now, she hardly cared. Somehow, she'd manage. Maybe Jackie had another friend, someone who could give her an estimate or at least point her in the right direction. She thought of Grandma's friends at church who asked her at the funeral, almost in a pleading way, to please let them know if she needed help with anything. Maybe together they could save the porch. Even if it meant tearing it down to build it back up.

She heard a car pull up and glanced at the street, expecting to see Jackie's brown sedan, but spied a blue Toyota instead.

Her heart stopped. She knew that car.

Behind the driver's side window, she saw Beth. Beth glanced her way, and then turned to whoever sat beside her.

The truth slammed into her. Someone sat beside Beth.

She felt the wind tousle her hair but couldn't move, couldn't manage to unglue herself from the swing. Her heart thumped out a staccato prayer: *Could it be? Could it be?* The car door opened, not Beth's, the passenger side, and all of a sudden, there stood Michael.

He looked at her for a moment, shoved his hands in his pockets. Like a dream, he began walking toward her, up the cracked cement path, past the maple tree, until he stood at the bottom of the porch steps.

Amber forced herself to rise to her feet, her eyes never leaving him. Finally, his eyes flashed over her, revealing a hundred emotions. Anger. Sadness. But also curiosity. Also longing. And hope.

She felt pierced with remorse, with her inability to fix the past. What could she do for him? What could she offer? Only the truth, hold it out like a smooth stone washed up from the tide, hold out the truth of what she had done and who she once was, and who she was now.

The porch steps creaked as Michael climbed up. He reached the last one and stood before her.

Amber peered into the blue pools of his eyes and saw reflections of Grandma and her mother and herself, and an ocean of questions. She ached to embrace this boy, to cling to this dream and feel that he was real, this miracle before her. But she would not flood him with blathering emotion. She had no right. That he was here, on her porch, was more than she could hope for. She clutched her hands together in front of her and intertwined her fingers so as not to reflexively reach out and hug him and ruin everything. Maybe later. It was all up to him, but maybe later.

She could not, however, restrain her smile. "I'm so happy you're here."

His shoulders seemed to relax a fraction.

She freed her hands and motioned toward the rocking chair. "Would you like to sit down?" Her words sounded formal, but why shouldn't they? She was meeting her son.

He crossed over to the chair and sat. His gaze flickered over the yard, over the wooden bowl of lemons, then rested on her. He spoke one small word, one little question, and as honestly and lovingly as she could, she let the story unfold.

When she finished, she leaned forward. "I know I don't have the right, but I hope that someday you'll be able to forgive me."

Michael's gaze shifted from her face to the floorboards, his eyes stormy and frenetic. Abruptly, he stood. He took a lemon from the bowl and walked to the edge of the porch, his back to her. One hand clutched a pillar, the other the lemon.

Amber traced the wooden bowl with a shaky finger and waited.

He turned around and her hand went still then dropped to the table. He slid into Grandma's chair again and stared at the lemon in his hand for a long time. Finally, he looked at her and smiled in a shaky, almost shy way, his eyes glinting with moisture.

Amber sat spellbound, silently rejoicing in the softness of his eyes, how they lacked steely accusation or hatred but held hints of sadness mixed with hope, and a glimpse of a something yet to come. Something so beautiful, so fragile, it took her breath away: the first faint traces of forgiveness.

He rested his arm on the table and covered her hand with his own. "I want that, too."

It was enough. So much more than enough.

Publisher's Note

When Rachel Allord came to us with *Mother of My Son*, I was moved by this story of forgiveness and redemption. Each year a number of young women find themselves dealing with unwanted pregnancies. Unfortunately, some of these women, like Amber in the story, make desperate decisions that oftentimes lead to paying legal consequences.

I hope the message in *Mother of My Son* helps to illustrate how one devastating decision can affect an entire life—in truth, several lives. Although in this work of fiction, Amber was not charged with a crime, she suffered greatly for her choice to abandon her baby at a dumpster. If you are, or someone you know is, faced with an unplanned pregnancy, please do not despair. There is help and hope—even if you are not able to raise the child yourself. I urge you to seek a safe haven location (if your jurisdiction has a Safe Haven Law) or other adoption outlet. You may not be able or ready to raise your child, but he or she can be the fulfillment of a prayer for another family, just as Michael was a blessing to Beth in *Mother of My Son*.

If you are one who is suffering with the guilt or shame of a past decision, know that God offers forgiveness and salvation to all those who seek Him. No matter who you are or what you have done, you are never alone.

About the Author

For more information about the author, Rachel Allord, visit her website at www.rachelallord.com.

Thank you for purchasing this Harbourlight title. For other inspirational stories, please visit our on-line bookstore at www.pelicanbookgroup.com.

For questions or more information, contact us at customer@pelicanbookgroup.com.

Harbourlight Books
The Beacon in Christian Fiction™
an imprint of Pelican Ventures Book Group
www.pelicanbookgroup.com

May God's glory shine through
this inspirational work of fiction.

AMDG

CPSIA information can be obtained at www.ICGtesting.com
Printed in the USA
LVOW10s0137031113

359764LV00004B/690/P